# A SMALL-TOWN WESTERN MM ROMANCE

I0714791

# COPYRIGHT

Storms Inside Us: A Small-town Western MM Romance
Original Copyright © December 2022 by Punk Rose Press
Storms cover by Sarah Kil of Sarah Kil Creative Studio
Release date: December 2022
All Rights Reserved



Ebook ISBN 978-1-955633-12-3
Print ISBN 978-1-955633-13-0

# PUNK
# ROSE

PRESS

# ALSO BY GRETA ROSE WEST

Wild Heart: Welcome to Wisper

A Short Story

Join the newsletter for this short introduction into the Cade Ranch world and for extra goodies and scenes. Sign up on my website.

gretarosewest.com


## THE CADE RANCH SERIES

Book 1 - BURNED: A Cade Ranch Novel

Book 2 - BROKEN: A Cade Ranch Novel

Book 3 - BUSTED: A Cade Ranch Novel

Book 4 - BRAVED: A Cade Ranch Novel

Book 5 - BLINDED: A Cade Ranch Novel


## THE WISPER DREAMS SERIES

RIVERS BETWEEN US

STORMS INSIDE US

MOUNTAINS DIVIDE US

# ACKNOWLEDGMENTS

There are many people behind the scenes, without whom, I wouldn't have a book to publish.

Peter, my editor is numero uno. Thank you again, this time for helping me find some fun in a sea of sad.

To Joanne, my copyeditor, who sends me margin comments that look like this: "Why English grammar, why?!" when she discovered that saltshaker is one word but pepper shaker is two. Seriously, why???

Tracy, thank you for finding missing words and thank you for always showing me my own poetry. It feels good when you see it too. Your new tattoo is the most bad-ass thing I've ever seen, and I'm honored. Love you, Sistah!

Mijn vriend, Cece, bedankt for sending me get-well care packages all the way from the Netherlands and for all the email knuffles after my surgery. They made me smile, and working on my Dutch kept me occupied when it hurt too much to write. You just sent me another email, and I know I've translated it incorrectly because I think it says that my cat has a hangover. Lol.

Sarah, thanks again for finding ways to make my characters so sexy on their covers. This one was no exception!

Thanks to my BETA readers, M, Geri, Barb, and Tracy, and to my ARC team. I was so scared when I published my first book that I'd never find people who wanted to read for me, and now, we're forming a tribe. I love you all!

To The Avett Brothers, who will never see this, but just in

case… I watched your documentary, and I know y'all feel some kinda way about your song "No Hard Feelings", but you should know that that song is one I hold tight to my heart. It helped—is still helping—me process my dad's passing. It helped me write this book too. Thank you.

And lastly, to my family. The whole sordid bunch, related and not. My sisters have become a part of my team. Stephie, you're really good at helping me fill plot holes, and Liz, you're just a bad influence at signings! ;) Thanks for being there for me, and thanks for forgiving me when all I can talk about is books! I'm so supported and loved, and I never would've written a word if that wasn't true. Thank you. Love you.

*This book is dedicated to the children of alcoholics.*
*If only it was this easy.*
*God, grant me the Serenity to accept the things I cannot change, Courage to change the things I can, and Wisdom to know the difference.*

*And to the Cade brothers:*
*Thanks for giving me Breo.*

TRIGGER WARNING:

There are themes of sickness due to ALS (a progressive neurodegenerative disease that affects nerve cells in the brain and spinal cord causing loss of muscle control, also known as Lou Gehrig's disease), parental loss, and a little PTSD in this story. The hero struggles with waking up to life after three years of drinking himself to sleep. It's a romance novel, so there aren't a lot of details within, but it's there, like a stinky beer-can ashtray in the morning that no twelve-year-old should have to throw away, but they do because their parent is lost. IYKYK.

If you're triggered by substance abuse issues, please read with caution, and know that I'm right there with you.

Visit https://www.aa.org to find a meeting if you need one.

# PROLOGUE
## BRADY

HE WAS DRUNK, but still, he was beautiful.

Theo Burroughs was some kind of enigma to me, a sad, tortured rich guy, but there was something behind all that. I was certain he wished people wouldn't see him that way. I imagined it was a hit to his pride, but then again, his pride had kind of disappeared lately.

It was true, he'd been through a lot, though that didn't exempt him from behaving like every other responsible adult. But something about this man spoke to me.

No, that wasn't right.

He unnerved me. Knocked me off balance somehow. And I was known for being balanced. Brady Douglas, the lawyer, always the calmest person in the room.

I dreamt about him at night, but I barely knew him even though I'd been his lawyer for a hot minute. I'd never met someone so closed off.

So when he suddenly appeared outside my office door one summer morning, I was more than a little surprised.

"Mr. Burroughs?"

He spoke slowly. "I, uh… Well, I'm sorry. You're busy. I

—shit." His shirt was rumpled, and he was wearing sweat-pants. I'd *never* seen Theodore Burroughs Jr. in sweatpants.

"It's okay," I said, trying to hide my confusion, but my face was doing its own thing. I couldn't help that. He looked like a bum. Billionaire to vagrant in 5.6 seconds? Except three years was probably a better estimate of the time it had taken the guy to fall from grace. "If you wanna wait, I can see you in a bit."

"I can go," my client, Fran Morris, said.

"No. Please, excuse me for just a minute." Standing from my creaky office chair, I tried not to knock over the fifty potted plants my mom kept leaving in my office because she thought they'd help me better connect to the universe or something. She was convinced I hadn't found my purpose yet in life. "Come with me, Mr. Burroughs," I said, trying to steer him back down the hallway.

"I'm sorry," he said to Fran, and I could smell the alcohol on his breath. Had he started drinking already, or was he still drunk from the night before?

"Excuse us, Fran. I'll be right back."

Leaving her in my office, I closed the door and ushered him toward the empty waiting room in the little law firm I shared with my mom.

"I need to talk to you," he said.

"Okay, that's fine, but I'm with a client right now. If you wanna wait, I can see you after I'm done." I winced. "Or maybe you'd like to come back when you're a little more… prepared?"

"Pr-prepared?" He blinked and swayed a little.

"Um, yeah, you know, maybe if you got a little rest? Drank some water?" *Dried out?* But I didn't say that. I was trying to be subtle, but it didn't seem to be working, so I took the direct route because Fran was waiting, and she had real problems, things that could impact her and her daughter's lives. "You need to sober up, Theo. G'on home. Get some sleep, and we can meet tomorrow mornin', okay?"

"Of course," he said. "I'm sorry. I've been waiting to talk to you. I mean, I didn't have an appointment. I just meant, I've been *wanting* to talk to you, but every time I try, I lose my nerve." He hung his head. "I'm sorry. This isn't me. I-I… I don't know who this is, but it isn't me."

Reaching for his hand at his side, I touched my fingers there, and he looked into my eyes. "It's okay. Is what you wanna talk to me about urgent?"

"No. I need to tell you—no." He shook his head.

"Alright then. Get some rest, and we can speak tomorrow. Can you be here at nine?"

"Yes, of course. Thank you."

"Would you like me to pick you up on my way to work in the mornin'? I mean, will you need a ride?"

"No," he said. "Don't be absurd. I'm a grown man."

"I didn't mean anything by it. It's just that you live in Jackson, and I haven't noticed you drivin' a car. Do you have one?"

"No. Wait. You've noticed me?"

Smiling, I said, "You're hard to miss." Wasn't that the truth.

He hung his head again. "Because I'm a wreck, right?"

*Because you're a beautiful wreck.*

"No," I said, "just 'cause you aren't from Wisper, and because of your work with the Cade family. I think everyone around here notices you because of your generosity. That's all I meant." I touched his hand again to gain his attention when it looked like he was having a hard time with what I'd said. "I'll see you tomorrow, okay? Nine o'clock."

"Okay." He gripped my hand and held it, inhaling deeply, his eyes filled with so much… regret? "I'm sorry."

Unfortunately, tomorrow morning rolled around, and Theo Burroughs was nowhere to be found. In fact, I didn't see him again for three months, unless catching glimpses of him entering and leaving the old newspaper building he'd bought across from the local coffee shop could be considered "seeing him." I called twice, but obviously he didn't need my help anymore, or he would've reached out again, and I didn't want to go chasing after more of his business.

Something was bugging me about that morning outside my office though. It was the look in his eyes, the palpable feeling of sadness and despair coming off of his body—the same feeling I recognized in myself when I thought about my dad.

Which was confirmation to me that I should stay out of Theo Burroughs's life. I had my own problems. I couldn't help him other than legally, and if he didn't ask for even that, there was nothing I could do.

# CHAPTER ONE

## BRADY

THIS TOWN WAS an old friend and my worst enemy. It had always been that way, even when I lived hundreds of miles from here. It had been my enemy as a young gay man, when I wanted so desperately to tell my family and friends who I was inside, but the people in my hometown weren't ready for it.

Eventually, I came out, and now, as I walked the streets of downtown Wisper, Wyoming, surrounded by ripe fall vegetables and jams and honey for sale at the farmers market behind the courthouse, I was reminded how much I'd missed my old friend when I was away.

Coming back home when my dad got sick wasn't a choice. I needed to be here. His ALS was robbing more of his life every day, and I couldn't miss one second of the time he had left. That was three years ago, give or take, and it hadn't taken long for his disease to strip him of every moment we hoped we'd get. One day he could walk and talk and feed himself, and the next, he couldn't. Maybe it was more gradual than that, but that was how it'd felt when I realized he'd never hug me or speak my name again. He communicated in other ways though. He was still there. His mind was sharp, but he was stuck.

I wanted him to have some way to escape the prison his body had become, drug him somehow so he wouldn't feel so trapped, but my mom wouldn't allow it. She refused to believe he'd want that. And maybe she was right, but that was how Wisper had become my enemy again. No matter how hard I tried, I couldn't get what my dad was going through out of my mind.

Most days, I wanted to scream. Who I would scream at, I had no idea. Whose fault was it that my dad had lost every necessary ability to be my dad? Whose fault was it that he couldn't laugh anymore or get pissed off and holler at my sister and me when we bickered at the dinner table, the way we had when we were kids? We were both adults now, but we still fought and argued like teenagers sometimes.

Now, he couldn't yell at us and say, "If I have to tell you one more time to be kind to each other, you're gonna regret it!" He never punished us. I'd never even been grounded. My dad was the kindest, most loving man I'd ever known, but he promised it enough times. After so long, since he never followed through, Bonnie and I turned it into a joke, and anytime he was mad about something, complaining about some jerk he'd run into at the grocery store or a customer of his who'd stiffed him, Bonnie and I would recite, "If you can't learn to be kind, Dad, we're gonna make you regret it!" It always lightened his mood, made him laugh, and he could move on from his bad day.

He couldn't do that now. Every day was a bad day for him. They were bad for my mom, Bonnie, and me too. Everyone was always telling me I needed to find the joy in life even though my dad was dying a slow death right in front of me—but how? No one ever clued me in as to how the fuck I was supposed to do that.

I'd given up my impressive corporate law job in Boise. Now, I spent every day at my mom's local law office and every night in my childhood home with her, Bonnie, and Dad, telling family stories, reliving the great life we'd had filled with laughter and love. The one we were about to lose forever.

It was heaven and hell at the same time.

What would life look like when he died? What would it sound like? Smell like? I was so tired of the smell of death in slow motion.

It was a beautiful, sunny autumn day as I walked down Main Street, but I couldn't smell the crisp fall air or the Douglas fir trees I'd loved so much as a kid 'cause my dad had convinced me they were named after our family. As I found my way through the bustling farmers market, I couldn't smell anything but antiseptic and bleached bedsheets.

"Brady Douglas? That you?"

"Hi, Mrs. Melton. How're you?"

Sissy Melton swatted my ass as I passed her booth. She was Wisper's oldest and feistiest farmer at eighty-four years old. "Sonny boy, don't you dare call me Mrs. Melton. You know my husband died twenty years ago, and I don't need a dead man's name to identify by. I'm Sissy to you. Here." She pushed a wooden basket full of her famous homemade jars of jams into my arms. "That's for your mama and sister. How's Bonnie doin'? She gonna have that baby anytime soon?"

"Yes, ma'am. Another month or two, I think. Thank you for this. She'll love it." I held the basket up and smiled, thinking, *Bonnie will probably spread the jam all over a tuna sandwich. Freakin' weirdo with her disgusting pregnancy cravings.*

"And how's your daddy doin'? He hangin' in there?"

"He… uh." What was I supposed to say to that? No, he's not hanging in there? He eats through a tube in his gut and stays stuck in a bed because he can't move? "Yes, ma'am. We're takin' it day by day." Sissy didn't mean any harm by asking the question, but it still hurt to answer. "I'll tell 'em all you say hello." Giving her the best smile I could fix on my face, I tried to wiggle out of the conversation. "Gotta get goin'. I have a meetin'."

"Bye now," she said, waving me off and focusing on Myrna Bettison and Callie DuBois, who were picking through Sissy's wares, asking questions about her canning process that they'd known the answer to for years. Sissy rolled her eyes at the women, and I made my escape, but she called after me, "Get a haircut, young man. You look like a hippy-dippy!"

*Right, 'cause having long hair is a crime.* I waved and walked faster.

Gene Owens had called last week and asked to meet. I'd known him my whole life, but never really had the occasion to talk much to him. His son and daughter had been a few years behind me through school.

But since I'd been retained by Theodore Burroughs, the former CEO of a huge international company and Wisper's only resident gazillionaire, business was making its way to me slowly. If I could handle a client like the reclusive Theo, surely I could handle a rancher's needs.

The thing was, I barely spoke to Theo Burroughs. The legal work I'd handled for him was a few years ago, and since then, I spoke to him maybe twice a year about the Cade Ranch trust he'd made me manager of.

When I met him, Theo Burroughs had been a mess. He

still was, but he'd gone through something really bad back then, and I remembered feeling sorry for him.

I'd just moved home and quit my job. I put out a shingle, basically, which really just meant that I made a website and posted my services in the local papers, and he was the first client to hire me without a firm to back me. Eventually, I incorporated my practice with my mom's, but back then I was still a lone wolf...

*"Hello, Mr. Burroughs," I said when I knocked and entered his hospital room in Jackson, Wyoming.*

*The guy had been beaten black and blue by someone, and I winced internally, wondering what the other guy looked like, when my eyes landed on his battered face.*

*"Uh, I'm Brady Douglas."*

*I'd done my research and was a bit intimidated. This guy had inherited a multi-national corporation from his father, and Burroughs International Finance was a Fortune 500 company. Theodore Burroughs Jr. himself was on the Forbes list. What he could possibly want or need from me was baffling. Didn't he have legal teams to handle his affairs? As in more than one?*

*When he turned his head to greet me, the gaunt-looking man in the hospital bed with shaved black hair and bruised brown skin was less than impressive, but beautiful, and I gasped. Like, out loud. Even covered head to toe in cuts and welts, with a seriously swollen eye, a cast on one arm, and bandages everywhere, he was gorgeous, so beautiful and handsome that he took my breath away, but the look in his eyes was... haunted. Something very grim had happened to this man, and I felt a little sick to my stomach when I thought about what that could possibly be.*

*He'd had no visitors that I could see. There were no get-well cards or bouquets of flowers decorating his room. The*

*TV wasn't even on. The guy had just been lying on his bed in the hospital alone and in silence, staring at nothing.*

*"You asked to meet?" I prompted. Didn't he remember he'd called me?*

*"Yes." His voice was gravelly, maybe from disuse, but he didn't clear his throat. He wasn't smiling. Honestly, he looked a little dead inside.*

*Stepping forward, I set my briefcase on a small table against the wall and pulled out a notepad. Yeah, we had phones now that could record everything, but I liked the feel of pen and paper. "What can I help you with?"*

*"I need a trust set up for Cade Ranch. Do you know Jay Cade? He said you were friends with his brother."*

*"Yeah, I know the Cade family. You're workin' with 'em?"*

*His eyebrow twitched a little. "I didn't expect you to have an accent."*

*"Uh, I grew up here. I sound like everybody else who lives in Wisper, I s'pose."*

*"But you only recently moved back."*

*"I did—wait. How do you know that?"*

*He didn't sound pretentious, more like it didn't matter at all, when he said, "I'm a very rich man, Mr. Douglas. I don't hire anyone unless I've had them seriously vetted. I know you went to the University of Wyoming for undergrad and law school. I also know you recently left your job at a nationally successful corporate law firm to move home and work with your mother in her small-town practice."*

*There was no judgment in his tone. I guess I'd expected there to be, and maybe that was because I was judging myself. I never imagined I would move back home. By now I thought I'd be making well over six figures a year, living in some overpriced high-rise condo in a big city. I hadn't thought much past that, so I had no clue what life I was giving up when I moved home, but it didn't really matter anymore. I was here. My dad's recent diagnosis meant that I needed to make the best of the situation so I could stay close to him and so I could help my mom.*

*Mr. Burroughs looked at me, really looked, his eyes roaming all over my face, to the top of my head and back down to my loafers. "The only thing I don't know about you is why you moved back to Wisper."*

*I fidgeted a little. It wasn't a secret, but something in this man's expression told me I didn't want him to know my vulnerabilities. "That's private, if you don't mind. But I'm a qualified trust attorney. It was what I was beginning to specialize in when I worked at Thompson and Mavery in Boise. So, what kind of—"*

*Mr. Burroughs moved, twisting to the side, trying to sit up and swing his legs over the edge of his bed, but he gasped in pain, grunted loudly, and held his ribs.*

*I stepped forward, dropping my pen and paper to the floor. My arms went out in front of me, reaching for him, though I had no clue what I could do to help. But seeing him in pain like that tore at my heart. I was so damn tired of seeing strong men hurting.*

*When he heard me moving closer, he opened his eyes and looked up.*

*"Who did this to you?" I asked before I could stop myself. "Why? Why would anyone do this to you?"*

*He blinked once, and there was something in his green eyes. Green like sage, which was disarming because it was almost like I could see through them, like the color of his eyes made him vulnerable somehow.*

*Abruptly, he closed them again, hung his head, and the moment was gone. "That's private."*

Touché.

*"I already have legal representation for my personal legal matters, Mr. Douglas. You're here because you have trust experience and you're local. So, let's get to work, shall we?"*

*"Of course. I apologize. And please, call me Brady. We don't have to be so formal." Bending to retrieve my pen and pad from the floor, I shook my head. I had no clue why I'd asked. It just came out, but he shut me down with skillful ease.*

*From the way he'd looked me over, I thought there was a possibility he might be gay, but this was a professional situation, and he was, hopefully, a client, so it didn't matter. And clearly, he was in no place to flirt or connect with anyone, and neither was I.*

*I'd just keep the fact to myself that I was more attracted to him than I'd ever been to anyone, even as bruised and broken as he was. I'd do this job for him and probably never see him again, my dad would die, and I'd get the fuck out of Wisper.*

*And this time, I'd stay gone.*

Right. Three years later, and I was still here. Still miserable, still pretending not to be for my mom and dad's sakes. But this was my home, and this was where I was needed. Never mind what I needed. Never mind that I hadn't been touched in more than three years. I hadn't been kissed. I hadn't been able to look in someone's eyes and see something other than pain reflected back at me. God, how I wished for that.

When I spotted Mr. Owens by the Teton County Co-Op booth, I waved to him, shutting my mind and my pathetic dreams down. New business kept food on the table, and it was keeping my mom's dying law practice afloat, which was how we were paying for the part of my dad's care that wasn't covered by insurance. No time for love now, or even sex.

"Well, if it ain't a young Brady Douglas, Esquire," Mr. Owens boomed. Wiping his dirt-covered hands on his overalls, he held one out for me to shake. "Thanks for meetin' me here. Farm life means no downtime. Not even time for love, my mama used to say." He laughed.

Wasn't that the story of my life?

"This is fine, Mr. Owens. It's nice to get outta the office for a bit. What can I do for you?"

# CHAPTER TWO

### THEO

"NAME'S DEVO. SHE/HER/HERS."

I stared, a little dumbfounded, as a short young woman approached me, the sun shining on her back through the open door before it shut with a *thud* behind her. When she was two feet in front of me, she stuck her hand out. "Technically, my name's Devona, but everybody calls me Devo. You must be Theo."

"Yeah. I mean, yes. I'm Theo Burroughs. He, uh, him." What had I been doing before she walked in? I couldn't remember. I was in some kind of fog, and I kept losing my train of thought. "What are you doing here?" I shook my head. "I mean, can I help you with something?" I hoped not. I was so tired. I just wanted to sit in a corner and sleep.

"Nope. It's me who can help you. José over at the diner said you were startin' a community center here."

Devo looked around the dark and run-down former newspaper building with its exposed brick walls and splintering wood window frames covered in chipped white paint. Old, bent metal blinds covered the big Main Street–facing windows, but sunlight peeked through, illuminating millions of dust motes floating in the air. There were a few metal folding chairs leaned against the front wall, a card table that looked like it would flop over at any second, and a coffee pot plugged into an outlet near the door, but it sat unused on top of a pile of old phone books. *Did they even make phone books anymore?*

The silence in the empty building was deafening. It had been ever since I'd bought it.

There was no "community" here. This woman, Devo, was the first sign of life in the place, even though I'd been here almost every day for months. I was practically living here.

It was a far cry from the swanky offices of my investment company headquarters back in Boston. The company I'd sold. The one I felt lost without because, if I wasn't Theodore Burroughs Jr., King of Burroughs International Finance, who was I? I'd been that guy for more than a decade. Now, I had no clue who I was.

I wasn't my sister's protector anymore. I'd been that guy for a long time too. She didn't need me like she had after our parents died. She lost her sight in the accident that killed them, and we'd been forcefully propelled into adulthood, me especially because she had so many medical issues and there was no one else to take care of her. But she was moving on without me now, living a life of her own with her boyfriend, Finn Cade. She had a whole new family, a job, and a purpose.

Unlike me, which was why I'd found myself in this deserted and dilapidated building, staring at a young woman dressed in baggy jeans slung low on her hips and a tight white T-shirt. She was short, maybe five-foot-two, with dark brown eyes, broad cheekbones, and chin-length black hair that flipped out in odd directions when she tucked it behind her ear.

She reminded me of Brady Douglas, and I pictured him in

my mind, his hair growing longer every time I saw him. When we'd first met, it was an inch long. Now, it was sweeping his collar, and he was always tucking it behind his ear like Devo had just done.

She looked at me expectantly, like she was waiting for me to say something and like she thought I might be a little peculiar as I stared at her, open-mouthed and not speaking, but I didn't know what to say.

Yes, I did want to open a community center with the building I'd bought in the middle of downtown Wisper, Wyoming, but I was at a loss as to how to start. It was a foreign feeling since I had always been the one in charge. I was usually the guy with all the answers, and now, I had none.

"Okeydokey then," Devo said, eyebrows rising in uncertainty. "So, you want some help or what?"

"With what?" Exhaustion was making it hard to stand up straight. I leaned against the dirty wall.

She looked around again. "With whippin' this place into shape. You can't have community meetin's here, not with the place in shambles like it is. You need to paint, and we should probably do some repairs." She kicked her black-and-white striped tennis shoe against a crumbling baseboard, then smiled up at me. "So, what's first on the list?"

"But, um, who are you?"

"Told ya, name's Devo."

"Right, but why are you here?" I shook my head again. She'd already said. "I mean, why do you want to help me?"

"Like, obviously 'cause this town—no, the whole state—needs more support for workin'-class peeps and for the LGBTQ+ community, and I'm all about it. I was lookin' for a job, but this'll do."

"But I mean, this is all volunteer stuff. I haven't offered a job."

"That's cool. It's worth my time." She eyed me, doubt turning her smile into a frown. Her features almost looked elfin. She was cute, but the aura she was putting off was anything but. "You do want help, don'tcha? Or are you one of those macho guys, thinks he can do it all alone? 'I'm an island' and all that bull?"

"An island? No. I-I need help. Yes. But I don't really know what I need help *with* yet."

She tossed her arms up in the air. "Oh, well, see, I can assist already. I know where we can start. I used to help my uncle flip houses. So first, we need to decide what you wanna do with the space. Which rooms are gonna be used for what, you know? That will tell us if we need to tear down any walls or not."

"Tear down walls?"

"Yeah, like, are you gonna offer a rec space, a place for teens to hang? We gotta have a room for twelve-step meetin's. You know that, right? Folks around here have drug and alcohol problems just like everybody else."

"Yes. I know that." *I might be one of those people.*

"Okay, so what else we gonna offer?"

I'd actually thought a lot about it. It kept me up at night, dreaming about creating a place for people to find common ground. Maybe we could even do outreach, offer the people and businesses in the area inclusivity workshops. It had been a dream of mine since college. I'd been so scared to come out to my parents. I'd hoped it wouldn't be a big deal to them, but my father was always on me to look the part of the rich, successful businessman, and I was worried being gay wouldn't fit on top of being half-Black. I never got the chance to find out for sure, though, because they died before I'd worked up the courage to tell them.

But when I would lie in bed at night, worrying about their reaction, I thought about a place like the community center I wanted to build. A place for people to come if they felt alone or scared or bullied by intolerance or if they were just being beat up by the world.

But one of the main reasons I wanted to do it was because Wyoming had a pretty negative history when it came to LGBTQ issues, and I realized when I'd first come to Wisper for an investment opportunity at Cade Ranch that the exact place I'd dreamed about so long ago was sorely needed here. I'd known it when I saw the look of panic on Kevin Cade's face the day we met, when he realized that I had known he was gay. His brothers hadn't known back then, and he was terrified they would find out. He'd never had any support, and he hadn't known how to be himself because of it. Now, he was out and happy, in love with a man, but I realized there were probably a lot more people in the area like him, and this town was such a friendly place, the people good and kind. I thought a community center could thrive here. Wyoming might look to an outsider to be an unusual choice for me, but this was where my sister had settled, and maybe I wasn't quite ready to be without her. She was the only family I had left.

My dream was to provide services for the community at large, LGBTQ or not—employment services like interview training and computers for people to be able to find and apply for jobs. People could volunteer at the center, learn how to give back and to live outside themselves, find a bigger purpose by helping others. They could support each other in all kinds of ways.

And lately, I was the one who needed that support. I

needed to find my place in the world again, and I needed help. I was utterly lost and alone, fighting my own demons, trying to hold them at bay.

The biggest demon? The time I tried to kill someone. It was as far off the rails as I'd ever gone, and I couldn't seem to find my way back from it. My sister and I were in London when I was notified, but I still remembered every detail from the phone call I'd received when the police told me my boyfriend and employee was shot dead in my house in Boston: the static on the line when I couldn't respond, the way my heart felt like it'd stopped and fell thirty stories into the dirt, the loss of the love I hadn't had the chance to feel. And two days later, the panic I'd felt when my sister's life was threatened if I didn't pony up hundreds of thousands of dollars. I'd tried to deal with the man making the threats myself, and it was something I'd regretted every day of my life since.

I'd tried to tell Brady Douglas about it once. He was my lawyer here in Wisper, and I tried to admit to my intent to take another person's life, but it was too hard, and all I could remember was drinking until it didn't scare me anymore, and then I'd wandered into his office. I doubt he remembered, but I thought about it every day. I'd wanted to tell him to ease the guilt I felt, but there was something else compelling me to talk to him. I had no idea what that was, though, so I continued keeping my distance.

So, Devo was right. I did need help. Just maybe not the kind she was offering.

But something told me I could trust her.

Plus, there wasn't anyone else. Maybe that wasn't exactly true, but there wasn't anyone I could imagine asking for help. I didn't want anyone to know how far down I'd fallen.

"Well, I guess, do you want to see the rest of the building? Maybe you could help me figure out what else to offer." I held my arm out in front of us, indicating that she should walk ahead of me, and I realized it was the first time in a long time I'd had the energy to show any interest in my own idea. If she'd shown up yesterday, she would've met a very different man. Maybe "met" was the wrong word, because if the brain fog was any indication, I was probably passed out on the floor at this time yesterday. How pathetic that I couldn't even remember.

"What did this place used to be? I'm not from here. I'm from Barton, just down the highway a bit. It's a little smaller than Wisper."

"It was the local newspaper. Really, smaller? Wisper's the smallest town I've ever been to. I can't imagine smaller."

She laughed. "A one-stoplight town. They exist. So," she said, grabbing the old wooden banister leading to the second floor. I was a little worried the stairs might cave in when we put our weight on them. "I heard you're gay? That true?"

"Uh, yes. Yep. But where did you hear that?"

"I'm not sure, just around. But I'm gay, too, much to my father's dismay. My mom's been pretty accepting though. We're part Apache. My family comes from New Mexico. She doesn't care so much who I love, just that I do. The Apache believe that some LGBTQ and non-binary people are Two Spirits, and many have been leaders in our tribe throughout history."

"Really? That's amazing."

"Yeah. My mom believes our path has been pre-deter-mined, that we have a purpose to fulfill—a destiny. And it's not about who that destiny leads you to, but more that you follow it and do the good deeds you were meant to do. There's a lot more to it, but that's the gist. I've known I was into chicks since I was young, and my mom has always been supportive. What about your parents?"

"Oh," I mumbled, following her up the stairs, stepping gingerly on each plank of wood in case I was right so I didn't land on my ass in the basement when the whole thing caved. I'd had the building assessed and had been assured it had good bones, but still, it looked like a haunted, old, crumbling dump. "They probably would have been supportive, but they died before I told them."

"I'm sorry, man. That's rough."

It took what felt like way too much energy to respond, but I finally did. "Thank you. Yes, it was, but my sister's supportive." Or she would be, if I'd let her be.

Devo walked down the hallway, sticking her head into each room for a few seconds, and I stood at the top of the stairs, thinking about the first time I'd seen the building. I'd had so much excitement back then, but lately, it was all I could do to remember why I'd gone through all the trouble to buy the damn place.

"This room here would make a good business center." Devo turned in the doorway of the third room in the second-floor hallway, leaning against the doorframe. "You could provide computers and printers for people to use. We could hang some bulletin boards for businesses to post job opportunities, trainin' programs, that kinda stuff." Huh. Hadn't I just been thinking about that? It was like she was reading my mind.

She moved to the next door ten feet down the hall. "And in here, maybe like a little thrift shop, you know? So the people lookin' for jobs can find proper clothes to wear to interviews." She thought for a moment. "Where would we get the clothes from though? Oh! I know. We could have donation drives around Wisper and nearby areas. And we could set up a donation drop, like Goodwill." When I didn't answer, she turned to face me fully. "You don't like that idea?"

"What? Oh, sorry. It's a good idea. Apologies. I'm just a little… tired today." When I said it, I felt it, and I staggered back against the wall.

"Whoa, man!" She ran toward me, reaching out to grab my arm. "You almost fell down the stairs." She yanked me forward a little, and I slid down the wall at my back. Devo sat next to me. "I know we just met, but what the hell's goin' on with you? Are you okay?"

"I… No. No, Devo. I don't think I am."

She was quiet for a few minutes, and we sat in silence. It was a real silence. I wasn't thinking about what to say, and I didn't think she was either. She seemed at peace in the silence, but then she spoke, and from that point on, I couldn't remember a time she'd ever stopped talking.

"I asked around about you, and I looked you up. I'm gonna be honest. I knew this'd be a volunteer thing, but you're rich, so I hoped I could prove myself to you, and maybe later, you'd offer me a real job. There isn't much work for someone like me around here 'cause I know nothin' about horses or cows. I finished high school, but that was as far as I went. I had my first real relationship right after graduation, and I put everything I had into that woman. We were together for three years, and they were the happiest years of my short life so far, but when she left, I wanted to die. I couldn't figure out how to live without her, you know?" She swung her head to the side, inspecting the lack of expression on my face. "I heard you lost your boyfriend a couple years ago. He was murdered?"

My sharp intake of breath was so loud between us, and I looked into her brown eyes. I couldn't speak. The words wouldn't come, so I nodded.

Devo turned away from me, focusing on the wall across from us, and she grabbed my hand and squeezed. She asked, "What was his name?"

I stared at the side of her face, remembering him. Remembering Tim. It had been new—we hadn't been dating more than a few months—but I'd thought that I'd loved him. I remembered the nights we'd spent in my office talking about everything from our families to our dreams and desires.

Tim was a Bostonian down to his bones, Red Sox ball caps and all. He had been my driver for a year before we'd acknowledged our attraction to one another, but the day he told me he was gay, everything changed between us. Now, I knew that it was love, yes, but I didn't think he was *in* love with me. And maybe I hadn't been in love with him either. I was in love with the idea of being in love. It was a short relationship, but he was my first real boyfriend since college. I'd had sex before him, but never with someone I could picture settling down with. I had loved him, though, and the sex was good and frequent, and I had quickly become addicted to it.

"Tim," I finally whispered. "His name was Tim."

I was sad he was gone, but I didn't miss him the way I missed my parents. I didn't long to see him again. And just like everything else in my life, I felt guilt and regret about Tim. Now, knowing that it hadn't been the real thing, that we hadn't been soul mates or destined for each other or whatever people called it, I felt even worse when I thought about him because it had all been for nothing. And maybe if he hadn't been with me, screwing me six ways to Sunday in my ridiculously overpriced town car or in my office, he could've found someone he would've fallen in love with.

And he wouldn't be dead.

Devo smiled, squeezed my hand again, then dropped it. "I know what you need. C'mon. Let's go for a drive."

"GOTTA BE HONEST, man. I thought you'd drive a Jaguar or a Bentley or somethin'. Do you even own a car?"

"No. I guess I just haven't gotten around to it yet."

"How do you get to the center every day? You live close by?"

"No. I rent a house in Jackson. I usually take an Uber or a cab, and I sleep there sometimes."

"Sleep there? I didn't see a mattress or anything."

"No, on the floor."

"You sleep on the cold, dirty, hardwood floor?"

"Sometimes."

Devo shook her head and focused back on the road.

"Where are you taking me?" How had I ended up in her truck? What was wrong with me that I would climb into a stranger's car and let them drive me to wherever?

She peeked at me, then said, "I think you need a connection. You need somethin' to ground you. I know just the place."

"Why are you doing this? You don't even know me."

"Well, like I said, I'm hopin' you'll give me a job. And I think a community center is just what we need around here. Times have been hard for a lotta folks. It's a good idea, and I wanna be a part of that. And…" She sighed and peeked back at me again. "I-I get it, man. I can see you're hurtin'. Maybe you're a little lost. I've been there. I understand. Tell me I'm wrong?"

"No. You're not wrong."

"Okay. Then I've got just the thing."

Fifteen minutes later, she parked her old, rusted Chevy truck in a pull-off on the side of the highway. She stepped out, and slowly, I followed. We made our way down a rocky hill, Devo sure-footed and steady, and I was a stumbling, panting mess by the time she stopped. I hadn't had this much exercise in months. I used to run five to ten miles on a treadmill at the gym every day. Now, I wasn't even sure where the closest gym was.

"Here. Have a look. If that view don't make you wanna live, I don't know what will."

Following her outstretched arm to the horizon, I took a deep breath and prepared to be unimpressed. Wisper was surrounded by mountains. I saw them every day, but honestly, I had no interest in—

When my eyes focused on the world in front of me, my heart stopped. It was a little cold in early October, but I couldn't feel it as I looked out at the Teton Mountains. We were standing on a bluff, and it felt like the edge of the world, the dizzying heights of the peaks in front of me, layered with the whitest snow, down what felt like miles to the canyon below. The day was overcast, pitching us in a monotone world, like a black-and-white movie, except for the deep pine and emerald greens of the trees. They were so green, they were almost blue, and they did ground me. They felt like a direct connection to the earth.

Funny, I hadn't ever thought I would want or need one.

Exhaling, I watched my breath turn to steam in front of me, and that was when it happened.

That was when I came alive again.

The mountainscape in front of me turned from black and white to colors everywhere. Those famous craggy peaks were blue and black and brown and gold, with bits of sunlight highlighting the gleaming snow in a few lucky places. The heavy clouds swirled around them, moving out of their way as if commanded by the rock so the world could witness their beauty.

So I could.

I could've sworn birds started singing, and if the clouds had cleared and the sun had come fully out, there would've been a double rainbow. Cheesy as it sounded, hope bloomed in my chest. My heart fluttered, and I was hungry and thirsty, and I wanted to hug someone. Devo was close, so I turned and reached for her, trapping her small body between my arms, pressing her against my chest like she was my sister. I missed my actual sister in that moment more than I ever had.

Devo patted my back. "Remember what I said about my purpose and destiny?"

I nodded once, still looking out at the awesome beauty over her shoulder.

"That look on your face right now? It might just be mine."

# CHAPTER THREE

### BRADY

THERE WAS a text blinking on my phone, waiting for me to open it, when I got out of the shower. It was from Theodore Burroughs, which was weird. If he needed to contact me, he always called, or a few times, he emailed. But he never texted.

*"Good morning. Do you have time to meet today to go over the amendments we talked about for the Cade Ranch trust?"*

*"Sure,"* I replied. *"I'm stopping at Coffee Shot before I head to the office. Can you meet me there in a half hour? Or we can meet at my office later today if you have other business?"*

*"Coffee Shot sounds good."*

"Sounds good"? I couldn't remember one time Theodore Burroughs Jr. was so informal, so… normal. His emails always sounded more like, "Hello, Mr. Douglas. I would like to extend an invitation to you to kiss my ass whenever you please…"

I was thinking about that, wondering what was different

about his text, as I carried my mess of case files into my dad's room. Ah, whatever. I needed to go through them all later anyway. Who cared if they were organized or not?

My dad grunted from his bed when I said his name while I tried to uncrumple the files and shoved them into my bag. Living at my parents' was convenient so I could be close to help, but I didn't have an office, or even a desk of my own, and it was starting to become a problem. The bedroom I'd grown up in was eight-by-nine feet, so there was no fitting more furniture in there. The bed and dresser already took up too much space.

"Bonnie's gonna stay with you while I go to work today."

His lip twitched, trying to smile. He was happy my sister had come home. She lived in Texas with her husband and was pregnant with their first kid, but she knew she needed to be here now. Our dad would never get the chance to meet his grandchildren, and that was hard on all of us, so Bonnie being around, watching old John Wayne movies with him, with her big belly and her weird spicy cheese cravings, was like Christmas morning every day to Dad because he was well aware of how little time he had left. She'd wanted to be here since we learned about his ALS, but her and Gerry's finances wouldn't allow it. Now, there really was no choice. We were close to the end.

Leaning down and kissing his forehead, I breathed in the scent of his skin, which somehow still smelled like summer— wood shavings, warm mountain breezes, and lemonade. From three years old until I left for college at eighteen, I'd spent almost every evening with my dad behind our house, watching him build furniture. Sometimes he'd even let me help him when he had a big order or was really inspired. He made hand-carved pieces and sold them to local shops, but over the years, his reputation had grown, and he started selling his chairs and tables online. There were never two the same. Each piece was dreamed, designed, and crafted by him, and each piece was beautiful.

"Love you, Dad," I whispered, pulling back to smile at him. Holding his hands gently, I squeezed, remembering how big and warm they used to be. Now, they were cold and stiff.

His eyes crinkled around the edges, and I saw unconditional love on his face. He couldn't say it anymore, but it was there, and I felt it. I hoped I always would.

"What's on your agenda today?" Bonnie asked 'cause she knew Dad would want to know. She thought my "stuffy lawyer life" was boring. She was an artist like our dad, selling handcrafted purses and bags she knitted in her spare time online. Her day job was a receptionist at a dentist's office, but she'd given that up. She was planning to stay at home after she had the baby anyway, so it worked out.

"I have a meetin' with a client, and then it's precedent research for the rest of the day."

"Who's the client?" Bonnie prodded, trying to get more out of me.

"Bonbon, you know I'm not s'posed to discuss my clients' business with the common folk," I said and winked. Dad's eyes twinkled a little. Secretly, he liked when Bonnie and I ribbed each other. He used to say it was the sign of a good tether between siblings.

"Oh my God, you're so boring," she said, twisting her long hair into a bun on top of her head. Like me, she had stick-straight black hair, so it stuck out of her bun in every direction, like little needles.

I rolled my eyes and gave her what she was looking for. "I'm meetin' Theo Burroughs. He texted this mornin'."

Bonnie perked up. "Ooo, Mom said he's rich and *extremely* good-lookin'."

"I wouldn't know. He's a client."

"Oly said he's to die for and that you think he's 'handsome.'"

"Yeah, well, my friend has a big mouth. You just reminded me to tell her to shut it."

Dad grunted again and raised his brows when I looked at him, wanting to know if it was true.

"Yes, guys, he's very handsome, very rich, and very much a *client*."

He wiggled his eyebrows. It was maybe the only command of his body he had left.

"Dad!"

Bonnie giggled. "We gotta have some kinda gossip around here. And by the way, you might wanna do somethin' about all that before your meetin'." She motioned with a flick of her hand toward my general appearance. "You're startin' to look like Grandpa."

"What's wrong with lookin' like Toko? He's an old fox." He had hair down to his ass, and I'd always admired that. He wasn't afraid to show the Shoshone in him. But I'd grown up in a different time, and besides, who would hire a trust attorney if they looked they couldn't even bother to get their hair cut? But getting a haircut, now that I'd let it grow, was a sensitive subject *because* I was part Shoshone. It was a sign of pride and strength in our tribe. So many had been forced to cut their hair to fit into the outside world. It had never meant that much to me, but now… maybe that was changing.

And I wasn't a trust lawyer anymore. I was just a small-town, do-everything kind of lawyer. So then, maybe I could embrace my roots. Who would complain? My mom wore traditional clothing sometimes, mixed in with business-casual clothes, and she was always wearing jewelry her sisters or cousins had made. No one ever judged her for it. In fact, she got a lot of compliments.

I felt like I was topping one obstacle on another though. Adding "Shoshone" on top of "gay" maybe wasn't the smartest business strategy in such a small, conservative town.

When I came out to my parents during my first year of college, it was the scariest thing I'd ever done, but they didn't say, "Maybe it's just a phase" or "Are you sure?" They supported me from the get-go. My dad had had a seriously Catholic upbringing, so I was proud of him and he was proud of me. I never doubted it.

And Bonnie's reaction had been classic Bonnie: "Duh. I've known that since you were born, the day you forced me to share *my* parents with you. Did you think I never noticed my missing copies of *Royalty Magazine*? Everyone in this house knew you had the hots for Prince Harry. Weirdo."

Rolling my eyes at her, I leaned down to kiss Dad again. "Thanks, Dad. Thanks for lovin' me and always supportin' me. A guy couldn't ask for a better papa."

When I turned to walk out of the room, slinging his old leather messenger bag over my shoulder, I could've sworn I saw a tear fall down his face, and I quickened my pace so he wouldn't see them falling down mine.

---

WALKING INTO COFFEE SHOT, Wisper's local watering hole, I realized just how right Oly and my mom were.

Even dressed in a threadbare T-shirt and too-faded jeans that didn't fit him properly, Theo Burroughs was gorgeous.

Every time I met with him, I was hit with a wave of attraction. The guy could burn the place down with the look in his eyes alone. There was an air about him. Strong, steady, confident. It had been hidden these last few years, but I felt it now, like a charge in the air, and if I got too close, it would zap me.

The last time we'd met, his hair was sexy. Not quite black, it was more a deep brown, lightening at the ends as it grew out. The longer it got, the curlier it got, but today, it was cut short like when we first met. It faded behind his ears and down the back of his neck, leading down to his shoulders, and *damn*, those shoulders. They were wide, and he looked *good*.

He'd been a little out of sorts lately, always tired-looking and distracted. He seemed a little depressed if I was honest. Maybe a lot. I hadn't known him before he moved to Wisper, but my friend Luuk had told me the guy was a lot different now than he used to be. He used to be commanding, charismatic, and full of flirt, but since I'd met him and he'd hired me to be his local lawyer, he'd been almost lifeless.

But the five-day beard and slightly hollowed cheeks somehow didn't lessen his appeal. I was hit with an image of my hands on the tight traps and delts hiding under his wrinkled white T-shirt while I pounded into him from behind, my fingers tangled in his curly black chest hair, sliding slowly over his soft brown skin—

"Good morning, Mr. Douglas." He approached with his hand extended, looking at me quizzically when I coughed and sputtered my hello.

I cleared my throat and tried to at least look professional, even though my thoughts never would be. I couldn't help it. There was just something about him. "Just call me Brady, please, Mr. Burroughs. We don't have to be so formal." *Why was I always saying that to him?*

He smiled, and my knees tried to buckle. I'd never seen him smile like *that*.

Something had changed with Theo Burroughs. He looked… lighter.

And damn, that smile. It was sexy, too, but there was a hint of innocence there, and I swore I could see his inner little boy peeking out.

"Okay, then you do the same. It's Theo, not Mr. Burroughs."

"Sure," I said. "So, uh, I brought the Cade Ranch trust paperwork. I made the amendments like you asked. I just need you to sign 'em, and then I'll drop the new copies off with Jay later today."

"Oh, thank you, but I can do that. I was planning to visit my sister anyway. They're having a big dinner out at the ranch later tonight."

Laughing nervously, I said, "Yeah, I know. I was invited."

"Oh?" he said, and his cheeks lifted when he smiled again.

"Here's your coffee." Walt Finkle's granddaughter, Leslie Ann, delivered two large coffees to the little café table where we sat, and I dropped my leather satchel onto the chair between Theo and me.

"Thank you," Theo called over his shoulder when she left the drinks on the table and walked away without a smile or even an acknowledgment. I swore, that teenager got more teenagery every time I saw her. "I ordered for you," he said a little sheepishly when he turned back to me. "I hope you don't mind."

"No, that's great. Thanks." I lifted the to-go cup to my lips for a tentative sip of steaming, bitter, black coffee since we barely knew each other and there was no way he'd remember how I liked my coffee. It was nice that he'd ordered for me, even if black coffee made me gag, but when I took a sip, I was surprised with a creamy caramel latte, and my eyebrows shot up a little.

"I heard you on the phone when we were going over the amendments," he said, smiling again. "You ordered one."

"Thank you." I hadn't meant for it to sound like a question, but I was a little taken aback. The guy had never seemed to notice anything before. In fact, a few times after our meetings in the past, I'd wondered if he'd remembered anything we'd talked about at all. I was pretty certain he didn't remember barging into my office a few months ago. He hadn't mentioned it when he called about the trust amendments, but it was the last time we'd spoken, so I'd been expecting him to bring it up or at least to bring up whatever it was he'd needed my help with back then. I still had no idea.

I'd been more than a little confused that he was *the* Theodore Burroughs, former CEO of Burroughs International Finance, 'cause since I'd met him, he seemed more like Ditzy Burroughs, CEO of nothing or nowhere.

I'd seen him at Manny's Bar a time or two, drunk, wallowing or making an ass of himself, and I wondered if he might enjoy alcohol a little more than most people.

Or maybe he enjoyed that it allowed him to forget.

But today, he looked bright—in control, in charge, and present.

"Your hair's longer," he said, smirking, and when I only nodded 'cause I had no clue how to respond to that—never in a million years did I expect him to comment on my appearance—he kept on. "So, are you going? To dinner." Sitting back in his chair, he crossed his legs, resting his foot over the other knee, and he sipped his coffee. "At the ranch?"

I pulled my hair back, slipping a rubber band around it. I'd been too preoccupied to deal with it, and it was almost past my shoulders now, but the look on his face as he admired it made me self-conscious. The hint of interest I heard in his voice had me pausing too. I'd never gotten that vibe from him before. "Uh, I—yeah, I guess. I'd like to see Oly. That's my friend, Carolyn."

"I've met her."

"Yeah, so I s'pose I'll go. I'd like to see the kids too. They're gettin' so big." I still couldn't believe my friends were parents. I was happy for Oly, but I still felt like a nineteen-year-old kid myself. Thirty was fast approaching, and I was in denial.

"The twins are cute," Theo said. "My sister actually helped to deliver them."

"I heard about that. Oly tells the story all the time." I needed to find a way to segue our conversation back into a more business-focused direction. This was feeling more like friends meeting for a cuppa joe, not a lawyer and his elusive client, which felt really weird. "So, was there anything else you needed to talk to me about or just the amendments?"

He took a deep breath. "Yes, actually, if you have a minute, I wanted to talk to you about the center."

"Ah, right. Your community center. How are renovations goin'?"

He laughed a little. "They're not. I mean, I've been a little… distracted lately, but I'm ready now."

"Okay. What can I help you with?" I asked, and I smoothed my hands on my thighs. My suit pants felt too tight, and I was uncomfortable, especially since this mogul millionaire was dressed like a ranch hand. Why on earth did I insist on wearing suits? Sure, I was a lawyer, but this was Wisper—ranch country—and most of the people I dealt with on a daily basis were friends of my parents or people I'd known my whole life. They probably couldn't have cared less what I wore, and I wasn't practicing the kind of law that had me in the courtroom very often. That decided it—I was going to try to loosen up.

"Well, besides the obvious permits and things like that, I was wondering if you'd help me with local contractors. You know everyone around here, so…"

"Oh. I mean, yeah, I could give you a few recs."

"That'd be great. I'm actually planning on doing a lot of the work myself, but I'll need help with some of the bigger changes. Devo tells me we need to knock down a few walls."

"Devo?"

"Yeah, she's my new, uh, I guess you'd call her an assistant? Or maybe sidekick is a better word."

He smiled, and I think I blushed, imagining him in a tight superhero's outfit with a red cape whipping behind him. The image was hot, and my pants felt even tighter.

"Oh, and I need a car."

"A car?"

"Yes," he said. "Vroom vroom?"

"Right." Okay, this was *really* getting weird. Now he was making toy car noises at me, in front of a coffee shop full of other people, which was so not how I'd been picturing the guy. "I don't really know much about cars, Theo."

"Do you know anyone who sells them? There are dealerships in Jackson, but I thought I'd keep it local if I can."

"Oh. Uh, sure. What kinda car? Walt's brother has a used lot at the edge of town." I nodded toward Walt behind the counter, where he was nudging Leslie Ann to ring up a customer while she stared at her fingernails, twisting and turning her hand to admire their glittery purple color. I was sure previously owned cars weren't Theo's cup of tea but—

"I don't really care. Used is fine. Just something to get me from point A to point B."

*Huh.* I nodded again and hollered across the room, "Hey, Walt?"

Walt rolled his eyes at his granddaughter and called back, "Yeah?"

"Mickey still over at the lot on Morningside?"

"Yep. He's got some beauties right now. You lookin' for a car, Brady?"

"Nope, Mr. Burroughs is though."

Theo glared at me, arching a brow.

"I meant *Theo's* lookin' for a car."

"I'll call Mickey," Walt said, "let him know you're comin'."

Theo smiled at Walt. "Thank you, Walt. That's perfect."

"Alright, well, anything else today?" I asked him, hoping he'd say no 'cause it would take me a little time to adjust to this new Theo, my client—my *professional* client, I had to keep reminding myself. I was all kinds of weirded out today, and no matter what ridiculous face I made, Theo just kept smiling. He looked plenty flirty and charismatic to me.

"No. That's it, I think."

"Okay, I have some things to do today," I said, pulling the Cade Ranch trust paperwork from my satchel for him to sign. He didn't even look them over. He scratched his signature onto them with my pen and slid them back to me. "But I can meet you over at the center tomorrow mornin' if you'll be free?"

"Great. That's perfect." The smile on his face was so big, showing a little more teeth than he probably intended. Something was clearly different about him today.

"Okay," I said, standing, and held out my hand. "See you then."

"No, I'll see you tonight. At the ranch. For dinner?" He

sounded hopeful as he gripped my hand in a firm shake, lingering a second or two too long before he dropped it.

"Right," I said. "Uh, yeah, see you tonight."

He kept smiling as I escaped, almost tripping over my own feet 'cause I couldn't get out of there fast enough.

What in the world?

# CHAPTER FOUR

## THEO

DRIVING MY GRAY, new to me but old to the rest of the world pickup truck back to Jackson, I found myself whistling. The truck was a little dinged and rusted on the outside, but the engine seemed strong and capable. When I'd walked to his used car lot, Mickey Finkle had shown me under the hood, and I acted like I knew what he was talking about when he'd said the transmission had another hundred-thousand miles in it and that all the hoses and the brakes had recently been replaced. Having a brand-new car used to be a priority in my life. Now it seemed like such waste of energy and money. I never really cared about cars. That was my dad's thing, but he was gone, so there wasn't anyone left to impress.

Brady drove an old Nissan Sentra, and he looked good in it. He looked good standing next to it, getting into it, and getting out. The man looked good in everything. I was fascinated with his hair. It was dark and shiny, and the color set off his light brown skin. The longer it grew, the sexier he got.

I wondered if he knew how attractive he was, but no, probably not. He seemed like a humble man. Always professional and kind, and definitely not someone who flaunted his good looks.

Not like I used to.

When I got there, I parked my new truck outside the Jackson Hole All Denomination Church, climbed out, and tucked my hands inside my pockets.

I'd never been to an AA meeting before. I had no idea what to expect, but I knew I needed to do this. And finally, I wanted to.

I must've looked lost. I definitely felt lost, and a skinny older man wearing a dusty brown cowboy hat and saggy, worn jeans noticed.

When he started toward me, standing away from the rest of the people waiting for the church doors to open, I lit a cigarette, just to have something to do with my hands. If I wasn't drinking, I didn't really want to smoke.

"First time?" the man asked. His face wasn't kind, and the lines there told the story of a long and difficult life.

I nodded. "Yes, sir. How could you tell?"

"You got that look."

What look? The "I have no fucking clue what I'm doing" look, or was it the "deer in headlights, scared shitless" look? Both applied.

"Don't much care to be called sir. Name's Charles Hutchins. Call me Charlie." He stuck his hand out for me to shake, and I exhaled the dirty air from my lungs and shook it. "My granddaughter calls me Chacha, but don't you do it, or I'll bust your lip."

"I apologize. I was only recognizing your—"

"My age? Well, that's fine. I don't mind bein' old, but 'sir' connotates that I've earned respect. I haven't. I'm an old drunk. Ain't sure there's anything less dignified than that."

Tipping his hat down just a touch, he looked me up and down. "How long you been at it?"

"Been at what? How long have I been an alcoholic, or how long have I been trying *not* to be one?"

"Either works."

"I quit drinking a couple of weeks ago."

"You come here 'cause some judge said you had to?"

"No, s—Charlie. I'm here because I can't stand the sight of myself in the mirror anymore."

"Good. That's a good place to start. C'mon." He motioned for me to follow with a wave of his hand, and I put my cigarette out on the sole of my shoe and tucked the butt in my pocket.

I had to disagree, but I kept that to myself. Waking up in the middle of Wyoming with no aim in life and a drinking problem at its peak was the worst place I'd ever been, but I followed him into the church, through a heavy wooden door, and up a flight of stairs to a balcony where fifteen chairs were arranged in a circle, and along the wall was a small folding table with a package of generic chocolate sandwich cookies and a well-used coffee pot on top. I could smell the cheap coffee brewing, and the sour aroma turned my stomach—or maybe that was my nerves.

Sitting next to Charlie in a metal folding chair, blinking at the too bright florescent lights above me, I planted my feet and clenched my hands into fists on top of my thighs. I was expecting some put-together, long-time sober leader to roll out a podium and start talking about how to stop drinking, maybe throw out a few inspirational quotes or five, but that wasn't what happened.

A woman who didn't look much older than me stepped out from behind a wooden door across the room, and she took a seat in a random chair. When she spoke, the low, gruff sound of her voice told me if I ever needed to bum a smoke, she'd be the one to ask. The red and white box in the pocket of the blue flannel shirt she was wearing was a dead give-away too. In fact, most of the people at the meeting were smokers, but I'd noticed Charlie was the only one who hadn't lit up outside.

The woman waited for people to sit while they filled paper cups with coffee, dumped in powdered French vanilla creamer, and stirred them with tiny wooden sticks, and when they were all seated in a circle around Charlie and me, all she said was, "Who wants to talk today?"

Charlie cleared his throat. "Reckon I oughta get it outta the way then." He stood and took a deep breath, and then spilled his feelings in a way I could only surmise made him feel like punching someone. But he didn't. He talked through it. "My granddaughter—aw, shit, I forgot. I'm Charlie and I'm an alcoholic."

Twelve mumbled "Hi, Charlies" echoed around the balcony, bouncing off the organ pipes behind us.

"Anyway, little Emmy came out to the house like she usually does on the weekends, and she stayed with me while her mama and daddy ran some errands in town. But this time, she got hurt. She tripped over a rock or her own two feet— who knows? She's a kid—and she banged up her knee. I cleaned it, put a Band-Aid on and all, but when my son and his wife came to pick her up, the look they gave me… Well, let's just say, it's a good thing I'm a *recoverin'* alcoholic, 'cause if I wasn't, the shame I was feelin' woulda made me drink." Charlie shook his head. "But you know, when they left and took my little Emmy with 'em, I got mad. I haven't had a drink in over fifteen years, and I haven't given my boy any reason not to trust me since then neither. When does it end? When are they gonna stop lookin' at me like I just murdered a field fulla puppies?" He crossed his arms, his face painted in deep tones of hurt and guilt, though I couldn't say which was deeper. "That's it then. That's all I got."

When Charlie sat, the woman looked at me. "You're new. You don't have to talk if you don't wanna, but we go clockwise, so you're next if you got somethin' to say."

"Oh. Um. O-okay." I stood. How to introduce myself? Should I go with Theodore? Mr. Burroughs? Loser with a capitol L? I went with, "I'm Theo. I… I'm an alcoholic, I think."

Looking around at the faces staring up me, I wasn't sure what to say. How much detail did they want? Was I supposed to talk about how I'd almost killed someone? Or maybe about losing the people in my life I'd loved? Or maybe how badly I wanted a drink, how much that disgusted me, and how I wished I could go back to the way things used to be, when I was on top of the world, not lying flat on my back in a dirty swamp, swimming in misery and desperately trying to reach the shore, but I couldn't. I couldn't move.

"Hi, Theo."

Blathered nonsense came out of my mouth, and it occurred to me that I'd never felt so disarmed. Even the first day of kindergarten, I was poised and confident, like I owned the whole school. I pretty much had, and I'd known it, but now I stuttered and stumbled over the words forming in my mouth. "I, um, my… my boyfriend was murdered three years ago, and I-I guess I didn't know how to handle that. A lot of stuff happened back then. Th-that's just one thing, but anyway, that's when I started drinking so I didn't have to feel. Before that, I'd never had a problem with alcohol."

Realizing too late that I'd set myself further apart than I'd meant to, that maybe I shouldn't have brought up the gay thing when I was the only black guy in a room full of white rural farmers and old men, my eyes flicked from one person to the next, looking for any sign that they were planning to harass me in the parking lot, but I didn't find that. There were only two women attending the meeting, and they were nodding, and of the men, there were maybe a couple of surprised looks, but most people looked sympathetic. Saying someone you'd known was murdered was a very powerful icebreaker no matter who you were.

"Anyway, uh, sorry if that's too much information, but that's the gist of my story."

I sat and felt Charlie's gaze on the side of my face for a few seconds, like a laser, but he didn't say anything, and the next person stood and began to talk.

That was it? Talking? How the hell was that supposed to help me? Wasn't there a workbook I could fill in or something? A few people mentioned the twelve steps alcoholics were supposed to work through, and I'd looked it up online, so I had a small understanding of what they were talking about. Other than that, people mostly shared the things in their lives that were hard or sad or frustrating, though the woman in charge shared that she'd finally passed her GED exam, and everyone clapped and whooped for her. She was really proud, and in that moment, I knew we needed to provide free tutoring at the center. If we could find some way to put the kind of smile on other people's faces like the one on Cora's, I knew it could help so many people.

After everyone was talked out, we stood and stretched, and people began to slowly introduce themselves to me. I was talking with Dimitri, a pig farmer only a few years older than me with sagging jowls and a belly to match, as we exited the church, and I lit another cigarette as soon as we hit the sidewalk. When he left, I stood there, looking up at the sun high in the big Wyoming sky, wondering where the hell I was supposed to go from here.

I hadn't heard him behind me, but Charlie cleared his throat. "So, you're one of—you're…?"

"Gay?" Somehow, I knew this was decidedly not a subject he and I would agree on, but he was still trying to make conversation with me. "Yes."

"Well, I s'pose alcoholism don't discriminate. It hits every kinda lifestyle."

"I guess it does," was all I said. I didn't bother saying that being gay wasn't a lifestyle. It was only one small part of who I was. It wasn't a decision I made.

"Sure, sure," he said. "Well, do y'all like to bowl?"

"Are you asking if every gay man likes to bowl?"

"'Course not. You. I mean you. You like bowlin'?"

"Um." I thought back to childhood. Had I ever been bowling? "I'm not sure I've ever been to a bowling alley. Why?"

"You ain't never been bowlin'? Well now. We gonna have to remedy that right quick."

I laughed, feeling relieved that he could find some common ground between us, even if my identity wasn't something he was comfortable with, though bowling wasn't something I knew anything about. But I was determined to do this—to stay sober—and I knew that this man was the start to that. It was funny to me that I still expected everyone to react to me being gay with negativity, and I was surprised more than I maybe should've been when people were accepting.

"No, I never have, but I'd love to learn. What do you need me to do?"

"You got a truck?"

"I do. I just bought it today," I said, feeling relieved that at least my new road beast would help me fit in. When I pictured it in my mind, I saw a roaring warrior bear when, in reality, my new truck was probably closer to an old barking dog. It sounded like a dog when the muffler coughed at high speeds.

"Alright then," Charlie said. "Follow me over to the Duck & Bowl. We're in a league, and we need another bowler on our team. Monica moved to Tuscaloosa a couple weeks ago, so you can take her place"—he narrowed his eyes, probably deciding if I was worth the effort—"if you're any good, that is. You can watch us first, and then maybe I can help you learn. I used to think it was boring, but it can get pretty competitive. Plus, it gives us all somethin' to focus on. Keeps us honest. You in?"

"I'm in," I said. "I can only stay for a little while. I have a dinner tonight."

He smacked me on the back a little too hard. "Well, alright then."

# CHAPTER FIVE

## THEO

I'D FINALLY FOUND something I knew absolutely nothing about: bowling.

Standing in my rental house in Jackson, I laughed at all my gutter balls, looking at myself in the bathroom mirror with *Bourne Identity* playing on the TV in the background.

I wanted to blend in at Cade Ranch tonight, but I had no idea what to wear. I could never look like a Cade, a cowboy —there was too much city in me—but I could at least look comfortable and approachable. I chose a navy blue small-knit sweater and a pair of jeans that probably cost as much as my monthly rent. I had no idea, because when I'd bought them, I'd had a personal shopper who dealt with all of that for me.

Making a mental note to order some Levi's, I turned to the side, evaluating the shape of my post-depression body. There was a bit of excess weight in the form of a pouch hiding my abs, but the rest of me looked the same. It was a far cry from the tightly packed muscles that had been the result of hours upon hours spent in the gym in my old life. And for what? That old body didn't have the ability to connect to my sister any better than the new one did. Muscles didn't stop people I loved from leaving. They didn't make a difference in my business or the lack thereof. But still, I missed the daily grind, and if I was focusing all my energy on being sober, being healthy would only help that, so maybe some kind of workout routine would be good.

My appearance hadn't even been a blip on my radar these last few years, but it was now. I wondered what people saw when they looked at me. Did they see my white father's eyes and my black mother's hair? Did they see the CEO Theo or the big brother Theo? Or did they see the falling-down drunk Theo?

The latter was probably the most likely, since that was who I'd been since moving to Wyoming after my stint in the hospital when everything in my life changed. Again. It changed once after the car accident that had cost me my parents and my little sister her sight, and it changed again when I decided to go all vigilante on the man who'd been blackmailing me for my parents' money. It had taken months for my old body—the one I'd thought was so strong—to heal from being nearly beaten to death.

Some wounds still hadn't healed, but they were the kind that couldn't be seen on the outside.

I'd made all kinds of questionable choices back then, like lying to my sister for years about her birth mother. Three years later, she'd finally forgiven me, but I hadn't forgiven myself yet. Our relationship had changed, but the secret I'd kept wasn't the only reason. Aislinn had changed too.

Her becoming blind at sixteen had altered both our lives. After the accident, she'd become completely dependent on me, but now she was changing right in front of me, transforming like a butterfly, and she was really living, not letting her disability hold her back. The pride I felt for her was intense, but it felt like when she began to live, I stopped.

Until a few weeks ago, I'd been trying hard to suppress that truth. But then I met Devo. I somehow figured out how to breathe again, and now, I wanted to *live* again. I was sick and tired of being sick and tired.

But I didn't want my old life back. I had no interest in being CEO Theodore Burroughs Jr. I just wanted to be Theo.

Unfortunately, I still had no idea who he was.

Whatever. If I didn't get out of my head, I was going to be late to dinner.

Driving to Cade Ranch, my stomach was in knots and my hands were sweating, which I realized was a little disgusting as I gripped the steering wheel in my used truck. It probably hadn't been cleaned in probably ten years. Before today, I'd never actually driven a truck, but I liked it. Driving down Highway 20 with my arm hanging out the open window, I felt like I belonged in Wyoming a little more than I had the day before as I passed the ranches and rural farm stores along the way. I passed a sign for a U-Pick pumpkin farm and wanted to stop, which was a surprise to me, but I didn't want to let Aislinn down by being late. I'd done enough of disappointing her lately.

Joining AA didn't stop me from wanting to pull off at the bar for a drink to calm my nerves, and I contemplated it as I passed Manny's on the outskirts of town, but I didn't do it. I wanted to be clearheaded tonight. I wanted to remember spending time with my sister. And I definitely wanted to remember talking to Brady.

How had I been so oblivious to him all this time?

He was the most handsome man I'd ever met, with his rich rust-colored skin and bright eyes. I'd never noticed before, but his straight, long nose and high cheekbones were captivating.

And those eyebrows? Dark and arched and sexy, like

behind his friendly guy-next-door persona was a man. Capital M.

Laughing at myself in the dark truck, I realized my attraction to him had nothing to do with all of those things. It was his voice. It was deep, but you could hear the smile in it. He always had a positive outlook, and he seemed so at ease in his skin. I envied him.

I hadn't felt real attraction to anyone since Tim. I'd been too drunk to notice anybody, even if they were standing right in front of me, which I supposed Brady had been. My sister had tried with the help of her friend Billie to get me living again. They'd taken me out, invited me different places, but I'd been barricaded so far inside myself, wallowing in guilt and fear, that it hadn't worked. After a while, they stopped calling.

Aislinn still checked in once a week, but when I didn't say a lot, she'd cut the call short, and I'd promise to call her back when I had more to talk about. Which I never did.

I felt awful about making my sister worry, and I promised myself I'd tell her I was sorry tonight. So when I pulled up and parked in the gravel drive in front of the Cade's white ranch house, I looked for her, but it was Brady I saw instead.

"Hi," he said as I joined him on the porch, and we waited together for someone to answer his knock, both facing forward, not looking at one another.

"Hi." I peeked at him out of the corner of my eye. The dim porch light was casting shadows across his face, making his lips look fuller and his eyes somehow even brighter. I couldn't help the smile on my face when he spoke. I really enjoyed the sound of his voice. Like the mountains Devo had shown me, Brady's voice was grounding.

"Uh, here," he said reaching in his back pocket. "I wrote down some recommendations for you for different contractors in the area. It'll save you some time so we don't have to meet tomorrow mornin'."

"Oh." The hope I had of getting to know him a little more dissipated quickly. He didn't feel the same toward me. Rightly. To him, I was just another client. I was awkward with just about every good-looking or charming man I'd ever met, and no matter who they were, I was convinced my sexual preference was the only thing on their minds. "Sure. Thank you." Taking the paper he held out, I tucked it in my pocket.

"Everything alright?" he asked, turning to look at me.

"Yes. Of course. I guess I was kind of looking forward to showing you around the center. Not that there's much to see yet. I don't know." Apparently, the new me said whatever was on his mind. *Awkward again.*

"Oh, um, okay," he hedged. "I figured you to be an efficient person. I thought savin' you time was a good idea." He laughed a little and dropped his eyes to his shoes, but he looked back up. He seemed confused about something, and it hit me: I was confusing him. I must've seemed like an entirely different person to him compared to the sorry excuse I'd been lately. And what was I thinking? He was my lawyer.

"No, you're right," I said. "It's fine. Thank you."

The door swung open, revealing a smiling Evvie Cade, and automatically, Brady returned the expression. I didn't. I was embarrassed, and all I wanted to do was run back to my truck and drive miles away to hide.

---

"THEO, what's going on with you? You seem different," Ace, my beautiful sister, asked, almost in accusation. I was amazed at the change in her, which grew every time I saw her. In the last three years, she'd become a different person. She was mature, responsible, and I couldn't remember her ever looking as happy as she did now.

"Nothing. I'm just happy to see you. You look good. How's Finn? How's the program going? Since I handed over management of the trust to Mr. Douglas, I don't get day-to-day information anymore."

Aislinn was the office manager of the equine therapy barn I donated money to every year. It was the last project I'd invested in before—well, before my world was knocked off its axis. Ace's boyfriend, Finn, owned it with his four brothers. She bossed them all around, and they feared her wrath if they veered off schedule. For years, I'd dreamed of this for her—a job and a life she could thrive in—and I'd hoped I could've helped her to find it, but she'd found it on her own, which just made me prouder. I knew our parents would've been proud of her too.

"Things are going well. We've had a bunch of new sign-ups for the winter program, and the guys are talking about building another house or, like, a barracks kind of building so we can help more veterans."

"That's great. I just amended the trust agreement to increase my donation, so maybe they can use it to build." What was I going to do with all my parents' money? Besides what I was using to renovate the center, I had no use for the excess.

We were standing in the living room Ace shared with Finn, and I offered her my arm when she reached for it and led her to sit at the long kitchen table where everyone was beginning to congregate because dinner was almost ready. She'd lived at the ranch for a few years, so she didn't need me to guide her—she would have memorized the house a long time ago—but it was nice that she reached for me anyway, and it made me realize I missed my little sister even more than I'd thought. We used to be together every day, but now, I was lucky to see her once a month. It was my own fault though.

Finn was cooking in the kitchen, but when he noticed Ace, he left his post at the stove to hug and kiss her. I thought he would've surprised her because of all the noise and conversation in the house, but like she was in total sync with him, when he touched her shoulders, she melted into his hands, and he wrapped her up against his body and kissed her neck and cheek.

"Did you tell him yet?" he asked her.

"Not yet," she whispered into his neck.

"Tell me what?"

"We're gettin' married!" he proclaimed. Aislinn smacked his arm, and that was when I finally noticed the small, simple diamond on her ring finger.

"Finn! You were supposed to wait! That's what this whole dinner is about. Billie even bought champagne. Now you've ruined it." She was scolding him, but she was smiling from ear to ear.

Tears pricked the corners of my eyes. I was losing my little sister, this time for good. I was happy for her, but the good news still stung.

And selfishly, I felt sad to be left behind.

"I'm sorry, baby, but I couldn't wait. You make me so happy, it's about to burst right outta my skin, like, like—"

"Like a dog with explosive diarrhea?" Finn's brother Kevin offered from the other end of the table.

His boyfriend, Luuk, smacked Kevin's arm and rolled his eyes. "What is the matter with you?" But then he laughed, and that right there was one of the main inspirations for the community center. To see Kevin, this red-blooded cowboy, openly loving his boyfriend and being comfortable as a gay man in a room full of people you'd never guess would be supportive—it made me proud and hopeful.

Kevin winked at me, and his brothers, Dean and Jack, pulled Finn away from Aislinn to shake his hand and hug him. They pushed him and messed up his long hair, and a little brotherly scuffle broke out. Brady and Oly laughed from the kitchen floor where they were playing with Oly's daughters, decorating a cardboard dollhouse with tiny plastic doll furniture.

Evvie came to hug Aislinn, and then Billie was pushing Evvie out of the way so she could hug Ace, so I stepped back, letting her have the moment.

My eyes stayed on Brady, like they had been most of the night. He looked like someone's young father, lifting one of the girls above him, tossing her up in the air and catching her as she squealed. She was laughing, but then her face turned red, and she wailed, "Put me down!" Brady lowered her back to the floor and winced when she ran away. That had to be Fiona. Aislinn had told me stories about the spirited little girl. Apparently, her sister, Mitch, was a perfect princess who never got mad and never screamed or threw a fit. I was certain she would be the one to cause trouble when they were older. Remembering my sister at their age, she'd always been quiet, too, and now, she was anything but.

I wondered then if being a father was in the cards for me. Would I sit on the floor with a man like Brady, playing with our children and laughing and then freaking out when they cried?

The thought was nice, but it terrified me at the same time.

And I wasn't sure if I deserved that kind of happiness.

Looking back at Ace, I realized she could have that, too, if she wanted it, and the love I felt for her was almost overwhelming. Realizing our parents wouldn't get to see her married put an ache in my chest. I had no idea about Heaven or Hell—we hadn't been raised in religion, unless you considered affluence a religion—but I hoped our parents could see Ace from wherever they were, and that they could see she'd found happiness.

"I am so happy for you both. Come here." I pulled my sister into a hug, whispering, "Thank you for including me in your celebration. I know I haven't been here for you lately, but that's going to change. I love you."

Ace's arms around my back hugged me tighter. "I love you too. Thank you for coming tonight. I've been so worried about you."

"I know, and I'm sorry. I didn't mean to make you worry."

"Are you better now?" she asked, still hugging me.

"I'm—I… I don't know, but maybe I'm getting there."

She pulled back, her eyes open but not seeing me, but she saw everything. "I'm here, Theo. Whatever you need. Don't you know that? I can be here for you the way you were for me all those years. Let me be part of your life?"

"I will. I'll try."

"Alright," Finn said, pushing Kevin into the refrigerator playfully after they hugged. "Enough of all this misty-eyed shit. Let's eat!"

AFTER DINNER, Ace fell asleep on the couch—living on a horse ranch had her alarm going off at four every morning—so I went outside for some air, trying to keep my distance from the alcohol everyone else was enjoying in the kitchen, and Finn followed.

When he caught me on his front porch smoking a cigarette, he blurted, "What the hell's wrong with you?" It was a filthy habit, but smoking helped with the not drinking somehow, though the taste of it wasn't nearly as appealing when I was sober. "Since when do you smoke? You know that shit will kill you, right?"

"Right," I said, and I took another drag.

"Seriously, man? Where'd you go? Where's the guy who waltzed onto my ranch all those years ago, confident as all get out? This guy here"—he pointed at my chest—"he looks like a sorry imitation of that guy." He shook his head, pity quite clear in his expression. "I don't mean to make light of your situation, whatever it is, but you remind me of my brother before he came out. You look lost."

"I am lost." The truth of that overshare stabbed at my stomach, but it wasn't the right time to mention AA. I didn't want to ruin Ace's celebration.

"Well, there's road maps all around you. Grab hold of one. Let it lead you back." He swiped the cigarette from my fingers and flicked it off the side of his porch. "Your sister needs you. She worries about you every day. This is supposed to be the happiest time of her life. You ain't gonna ruin that, now are you?"

"I hope not."

"Wrong answer."

"I'm trying, Finn," I said. "This is a pretty big surprise, and I'm feeling a little… rattled. Can you give me a minute to get used to the idea of my baby sister being married? She used to depend on me for everything, and now she's going to be a wife."

"Yeah, and thank the good Lord that's over with. She doesn't need you to decide for her anymore, but she wants you in her life." Cocking his head to the side, he said, "Is that what this is all about? Are you jealous she doesn't need you anymore?"

Before I was forced to answer, to admit that he was right, the kitchen door creaked open, and Brady and Luuk walked onto the porch. Brady looked between Finn and me, then continued whatever conversation he and Luuk were having, but Luuk's phone rang, and he excused himself to take his call.

"Well?" Finn asked, bringing my attention back to him and the lecture he was trying to give me. "Whatcha gotta say for yourself, Theo? You gonna keep puttin' your sister through the ringer, or are you gonna act like the mature adult you should be?"

I almost laughed—I'd forgotten how direct Finn could be. Men didn't usually talk so openly about feelings and problems, especially not straight macho cowboys, but Finn was different, which was probably part of the reason my sister loved him so much.

Sighing, I hung my head, completely exasperated with myself, but Brady interrupted.

"You ready?"

I looked up. He was talking to me. "Ready? For…?"

"Yeah, I thought we were goin' to the center. You wanted to show me that thing?"

"Thing?"

"Yeah, you know, the thing. You said that girl mentioned tearin' down walls. You wanted my opinion?"

"Oh. Right. Yes, I'm ready." *Oh, thank you.* Brady was rescuing me. I was a little embarrassed it had taken me so long to catch on. "Do you want to ride with me or just follow in your car?"

"I'll follow. I gotta get home soon. My family's waitin' on me."

"Of course," I said, like we had planned it. "I'll talk to you later, Finn."

Finn took a step back, accepting defeat. For now, at least.

"I really am happy for you and Aislinn. Congratulations."

"Thanks," he said, eyeing me warily, but Brady descended the stairs and I followed, thinking I'd never been more grateful to escape a conversation in my life.

# CHAPTER SIX

## THEO

I THOUGHT Brady would go a different direction when we turned off of Route 20, toward wherever he lived, but he didn't. He followed me downtown and parked behind my truck in front of the old newspaper building, then walked behind me up the porch steps and into pitch blackness.

"Devo turned out all the lights again. Hold on. Stay right there."

"When'd you get the truck?" he asked into the darkness of the foyer. "I thought you said you didn't have a car."

Feeling my way around with my hand on the wall, I found the light switch and flicked it on. Brady blinked in the harsh light, looking around the big open entryway.

"I walked to the used car lot after our meeting this morning."

"I could've given you a ride. That's over a mile," he said. "So who is this Devo? Where'd she come from?" He didn't say anything about the conversation he'd overheard between Finn and me, and I didn't either.

"Thanks, but walking's good for me. Uh, Devo said she's from Barton. Do you know it?"

"Barton? That's a small town."

I laughed. "Wisper's a small town. You know that, right?"

He smiled. "Yeah."

God, that smile. An urge to touch his lips was building inside me the longer he talked. They were full, and they looked so soft. "Anyway, she wants to help. She's just someone looking for…"

"Community?"

"Yes," I agreed. "Community."

"Ain't we all." He walked forward into the first room to our right. There were five large buckets of paint in his way, but he stepped around them. "So, what's this room gonna be used for? I remember comin' in here with my dad when I was a kid when he'd put his ads in the paper."

"Really? Ads for what?"

"He's a furniture maker, like a woodworker."

"Oh, that's cool. Where does he sell it? I could use some interesting furniture in my rental. What I have in there is pretty bland and boring. Not that I spend much time there."

Brady shuffled his feet, looking down at his shoes. "No, uh, he… doesn't do that anymore."

From the way he seemed to turn in on himself, his body language told me there was probably more to that story, but it wasn't something he wanted to talk about.

I stepped beside him, looking out at all the space in front of us. "So, I was thinking this could be a 'welcome to the center' room. Kind of a catchall. We could have information here about what else we'll have in the building. Bulletin boards for different opportunities around the community, meetings, groups, maybe even games. We could have a softball team or something. And maybe a little coffee and tea stand."

Brady looked around, pursing his lips and nodding.

"Devo thinks we should tear down that wall"—I pointed out in front of us—"to open things up. Then, I was thinking we'd build an office back there for me or whoever's running things at the time. The floor plan is identical on the other side of the hallway, so we've been talking about making it into a basketball court."

"Really? Wow."

"It wouldn't be regulation size, but just a cool place for kids to hang out, release some steam, you know?"

He nodded again. "That's a great idea."

"It wouldn't only be used for basketball. We could do all kinds of activities in there. Yoga, maybe, and um, job fairs. I don't know. I'm really not sure about the rest of the first floor, besides office space. I was thinking about opening a small daycare for people to use if they have an interview or a medical appointment. These are just ideas. Some probably not so great."

"No," Brady said. "I think you're on the right track. I mean, a community center is supposed to provide things the people who live in the community need. Daycare is a definite need."

"Would you like to see upstairs?"

"Sure," he said, and his eyes crinkled at the corners in another smile when I looked at him.

I was really nervous about showing him my project. My hands were sweating, and I couldn't stop biting the inside of my cheek. A few years ago, it wouldn't have bothered me. I would've walked into the space, decided on the spot exactly what I wanted, and then commanded someone to build it or make it or organize it. I would've announced my plans, expecting everyone to think I was a genius, which they used to do.

As if I was outside myself, looking down, I could see that

there had been something attractive and inspired about that old Theo, but now, I was terrified because this dream of mine was coming from the part of me I wasn't at all confident about. It was coming from Theo, the man. Not Theo the CEO, the business overachiever. It was coming from my heart, and it mattered because real people would come to my center, and they needed things. They needed ways to connect to their neighbors. Other parts of the state were growing and thriving, but the little town of Wisper was slow to catch up, probably because of how rural it was. A lot of people were struggling financially. They had fears and problems, and I was going to be offering to help them.

I had to get it right.

And it mattered because *I* needed it. I needed help and support. Even though I hadn't met them yet, those people were as important to me as the center would hopefully be to them.

In the moment, I wanted Brady to see all of that. I wanted him to see the beaten-down Theo. The business guy was a façade, and I didn't have the energy to keep it up anymore.

I wanted him to see me. The real me. I couldn't remember the last time I had wanted to show someone my true self. My soul. But now, I did.

That brought on all kinds of fears and insecurities of its own. Was I good enough? Special enough? Why would a beautiful man like Brady Douglas take a second look at me? He was smart and kind and generous, and I wasn't sure if I was any of those things. For the longest time, the only identity I had was an overentitled rich guy whose father had given him everything.

I wasn't unaware of how people saw me. They were partly right, but no one really knew the whole truth.

Brady followed me upstairs, and I showed him the rooms,

one by one, explaining the ideas Devo and I had about what to use them for. He was quiet while I explained, and I felt like I was talking too much, but I couldn't seem to make myself stop.

He looked in my eyes while I spoke, really looked, listening intently to everything I said, hanging on my every word, if his body language was anything to go by.

It made me even more nervous, but it also encouraged me to keep going, and it made me want him, so much that my hands twitched, needing to touch him. I didn't, of course. Instead, I shoved them into my back pockets to restrain them, and he watched me do it, his eyes following the movement, and they stayed down there for a moment before slowly traveling up my body, back up to my eyes.

Standing this close to him, I was struck by his handsomeness. Framed by long black eyelashes, his eyes were the richest shade of brown I'd ever seen, and I was a little obsessed with the black slash of his eyebrows. The character in the bend of their arches was like a smirk. His skin was smooth over his angular jaw and sharp cheekbones, and I wanted more than anything to know what touching him would feel like. A handshake for the sake of business was much different than a caress.

"So, that's it?" he finally asked when I hadn't spoken in more than a minute because I'd been too mesmerized by his face. I watched his lips when he spoke, and things stirred in me that hadn't felt a hint of life in the last three years. Things grew—*something* grew—and swelled and almost ached—and I needed to distract him so he wouldn't see.

"Ah, no," I said, walking around him and back out into the hallway, but I turned back toward him. I couldn't stop myself. "There's a third floor. It's not an attic, though the previous owner used it that way. He left some interesting stuff up there, but I was thinking I might clear it out and use it as an apartment." I motioned toward the third-floor staircase. "But you said you needed to get home. Do you have time?"

With his hand in a loose fist, he raised his forearm like he would check his watch, but he wasn't wearing one, and he didn't look away from my eyes.

"Yeah," he said quietly. "I can spare a few more minutes." It was almost a whisper, and the sound of his voice, gentle and arresting, made my body ache harder.

He followed me up the stairs, and when we got to the top, I switched on a tall lamp, the only light on the third floor, and turned to warn him of all the junk in our path so he wouldn't trip, but it seemed I'd caught him staring at my ass as we'd climbed the stairs, and his eyes darted up to mine.

He looked guilty and so damn adorable, his lips pursing in a tiny smile, though he was trying to hide it.

Something came over me, some invisible force, and I kissed him like our lips were magnets. It was only a fast peck, but when he didn't respond, I pulled back. Damn it. I'd done it again. I was a nervous, awkward idiot around him. I was mortified, and it felt like my skin would melt off my face, it was so hot. The pit of embarrassment in my stomach wasn't pleasant either.

Covering my mouth with my hand, I tried to apologize. "I-I'm sorry. I don't know what I—"

"You're my client," he whispered, looking in my eyes, searching them for any reason to explain why I'd kissed him.

"Yes. I apologize. I shouldn't have done that."

His eyes wouldn't stay in one place for more than a second. He was scanning my body up and down, but he stepped back until he bumped into the wall, and a pile of loose newspapers fell down around his feet. He didn't acknowledge the mess. "Theo, you're my client."

He didn't move, and I bent, crouching and reaching forward, piling the papers and sliding the precarious pile against the wall next to his leg. I stood, and he watched me rise. There was something in his expression, but I couldn't decipher what it was.

"You said that. Yes, please forgive me. That was inappropriate and unprofessional, and I'm—"

Taking one step toward me, he said, "Fuck it."

I must have looked ridiculous. I could actually feel my eyes grow to the size of lemons and my heart began to race, and then my face was between his hands, and his tongue was in my mouth.

He moaned softly, and I gripped his belt, tugging him closer. When I felt his hardness pressed against mine, I moaned, too, my fingers fumbling in their involuntarily attempt to rip through his jeans. It was hurried and clumsy, but I finally got them open, and I slid my hand inside.

Between pants of breath and the hot slide of his tongue between my lips, he said, "What're you doin'?"

"I want you. I think I've wanted you since the first time we met." I grabbed his dick, feeling his desire hard between my fingers as I rubbed him off.

"Fuck," he whispered, but his lips didn't leave mine.

"You want to do that too? You can. I want you to." Suddenly, I *needed* him to.

"Shit," he said, groaning, but he pushed his jeans down, and I squeezed. The warmth and familiar feeling of silky soft over bone hard was like a drug to me. He must've liked it, too, because he pumped his hips. "This is kinda fast."

"Not fast enough, in my opinion." When his jeans were low enough, I dropped to my knees, looking up at him and pulling his cock to my mouth. His fingers gripped both sides of my head, and I closed my eyes and opened my mouth.

Breath rushed from his mouth.

As soon as I tasted the cum beading out of his slit, it was like a switch had been flipped. I was crazed and so hungry for him. I sucked him so far down my throat, I choked, and his abdomen hardened and flexed when he pulled away from me, but I wasn't anywhere near satisfied, so my mouth chased his body, and I licked his belly, nuzzling my face against his obliques. He smelled amazing, like sex and man and need.

Slowly, he pushed me away, but he knelt in front of me, urging me to lie back. I hated to lose the connection we had, but, closing my eyes, I pulled my sweater over my head. The dust covering the floor stuck to my back and arms as I lowered myself because I was starting to sweat, but I would've bathed in the grit if it meant he wouldn't stop touching me.

With his eyes locked onto my chest, he popped open my fly and tugged, and just like that, my jeans were around my thighs.

Panic rose. "I don't have a condom. I'm sorry. I didn't think this would happen."

"It's okay." He leaned forward, his hands planted on either side of my head, and kissed me. "We don't need to go there right off the bat. This"—he hovered over me, rubbing his hard-on against my stomach, the warmth of his body making me shiver—"this is good. It feels good."

I couldn't look away as he descended my body, kissing and licking his way south. He stopped when he reached my chest, sucking my nipple into his mouth before trailing his tongue down the side of my body to my hips. When he got there, he kissed, opening his mouth like he wanted to devour me.

"I wasn't done with you," I said.

He bit down gently. "I know, but I haven't touched a man like this in a long time. I need to. Let me?"

I breathed, "Yes."

Laying his head on my hip, his nose was like an arrow pointed right where I wanted his mouth to be. His hair tickled my inner thigh, and he inhaled deeply, his hands sliding slowly down my legs, as far as my jeans would allow him, then back up. His fingers traced my muscles, dipping down between where abs used to be. Now, they were more like marshmallows, but he didn't seem to mind. His mouth followed his fingers, kissing as he moved over me.

Looking up at me, he slid down. He was trembling, and when he found his way between my legs, he stopped. He became still. I didn't even think he was breathing.

"Don't stop."

"I couldn't if you paid me to," he whispered, and he opened his mouth, taking me deep inside.

My body arched off the floor, and I felt like I was descending into madness because the feeling of falling didn't stop, even when he slid back, letting my cock fall from his mouth. It slapped against my stomach, and he raised to his knees, just watching me, his eyes tracing a path from my mouth to each shoulder and back down my chest and then lower.

He gripped me, rubbing his fingers up and down my shaft slowly, and I moaned.

"I wanna make you come." His eyes flicked up to mine. "I *need* to make you come."

Spreading my legs as far apart as I could since they were still trapped in my jeans, I nodded. Like I would argue with that?

I reached for his hair. I wanted to feel it, to run my fingers through it and pull it while his mouth was on me, but he grabbed my wrist and pushed it away, so I gripped the base of an old metal printing press behind my head. I was holding onto it so tightly with one hand that it ached.

"Both hands," he said, and I lifted my other arm. "I've missed this. I'm good at it." He looked down at my straining cock with a sly smirk. "But don't you come till I tell you." I nodded again, but he wouldn't take his eyes off my body. He said, "Say it. Tell me you won't."

"I won't come until you tell me to." Fire was burning through my veins, like a drug, but it was far better than alcohol had ever made me feel, and I couldn't help saying, "I never imagined you to be domineering."

"I don't know what this is," he said, and he released me. He kept starting and stopping. Touching me and pulling away. Was he afraid to feel good? Or was it me he was afraid of? "To be honest, I think it has somethin' to do with a billionaire CEO gettin' down on his knees for me."

Who was this man? What had gotten into him? Or had he always been this commanding and I'd just had no clue? And what was he doing to me? I'd never submitted to anyone. I'd always been the guy in charge, even in bed, even if I was the bottom.

But whatever this was, I needed it too.

His fingertips dug into my hips, holding me in place. "Hold that thing tight. What is it anyway?"

"Old printing press," I grunted. I could barely speak. The anticipation was heady.

"Is it sturdy?"

"Yes."

"Good. Don't let go, no matter what."

I gripped the cold metal harder and waited, and he licked his bottom lip and scraped his teeth over it, then firmly gripped my cock. I had hardened to the point of pain, and some kind of sound like a cry and a growl at the same time escaped my throat. The pain felt good.

It was a sign I was still alive. This was really happening, and I felt it. It had been a long time since I'd felt anything but apathy or sadness.

Slowly, he slid back on the floor, making himself comfortable between my thighs, and he blew on the wet cum already beading from the tip of my cock.

"Oh God," I moaned when I felt his hot breath wash over my skin.

He pumped slowly, and I surrendered because being with him like this felt amazing. I hadn't felt physical pleasure in a long time, and now, his every touch was pushing me higher and higher. The fact that we were doing this in the light, in the middle of downtown Wisper, made it even hotter.

"This is crazy," he said, but he opened his mouth and took the head of my cock inside, laving it with his tongue, lapping in slow strokes.

I was so hard, and I needed to come. "Please, Brady."

He moaned when I begged. My breath was coming faster and faster, and my heart felt like it would beat right out of my chest. Somehow, he worked my jeans lower while he sucked and licked, and I clamped my eyes closed, trying with every ounce of willpower I had not to come, but the euphoria was quickly making its way down my body, the warmth and the urgency pushing over me like the rush of a river after a storm.

I couldn't even be embarrassed about how little time it was taking me to get there. He was beautiful and strong, and it had been so long. Besides, I was already devising a plan to make him feel as good as he was making me feel.

When he reached up with one hand, pressing his middle finger to my lips, wanting me to open my mouth, I opened my eyes and parted my lips, sucking his finger inside. I tasted the salt on his skin, and I imagined it was his dick in my mouth. I sucked as hard as I could, and he groaned and pulled his finger out.

He touched it to the sensitive skin behind my balls, and my heart pounded. His heart was racing too. I felt it as he lay against my thigh, changing his angle. The heat from his chest seeped into me, sending a buzzing feeling through my whole body. Just to feel another human being touching my skin… I couldn't hold out much longer.

"Brady, I need to—"

With his mouth full of my cock, he said, "Not yet."

Cum and saliva flowed down my shaft, and he collected it in his hand, pumping up and down, flicking his tongue beneath my cockhead, flirting with it, teasing it, and my breath hitched in quick pants.

The smooth glide was too much, and my head fell back, smacking the hardwood floor. A cloud of dust rose in the air, and when I coughed, he spread my legs further with his shoulders between them, pressing harder with his finger, and every muscle in my body hardened and tensed. I was coming. Nothing could stop it.

"Now," he grunted.

Hearing the command in his voice was the final straw, and I moaned so loud, I thought it might bring the building down around us.

He sucked harder, and I let go. Nothing mattered in the moment but his body and mine, the look in his eyes and the way his skin felt against mine— I came in his mouth. It felt like I was orgasming for days, and when I opened my eyes, he was swallowing and licking his swollen lips, lust taking over his every feature. His eyes were so dark, they looked black.

"Fuck me." I couldn't believe I was saying it. No condom meant no sex. Period. But I wanted him inside me.

Pumping my cock again gently while I softened in his hand, he whispered, "Don't offer that to me. We can't. Not without a rubber."

He stayed between my legs, both of us trying to catch our breath while we stared at each other, both contemplating what I'd just offered, but then he pulled away, letting my cock fall from his hand. The heat from his body disappeared when he stood, leaving me freezing from the sweat cooling all over me.

His voice sounded a mile away. "I'm sorry." He ran his hand through his hair. "Shit. What've I done?"

He stumbled backward, and I sat up, my body still wanting to feel his, but I watched him plop down onto the stack of newspapers against the wall with his jeans still down around his ass.

I lifted up onto my elbows, ignoring the pain from my bones digging into the hard floor. "Brady, it's okay."

"Yeah, but you're my—damn." He dropped his head into his hand. "I'll find you a new lawyer. I shouldn't—it shouldn't be me anymore. I just broke every fuckin' ethical code there is."

I stood and walked toward him slowly, waiting for him to look up. When he did and I was a foot in front of him, I knelt and wrapped my hands around his hips, squeezing a little, loving the feel of his ass cheeks on my fingers.

"I don't want a new lawyer. I want you."

"Yeah but—"

He choked on his words when I lowered my head and swallowed his still-hard cock down my throat again.

"Oh fuck, your mouth feels good," he breathed, but he tried to pull out. "Theo, we can't."

"Mmhm." I opened my jaw, letting my mouth be the hole he wanted to fuck, and he thrusted his hips into my face. Faster and faster, he pumped, gripping my head, driving me lower and lower.

"Yeah. Oh God, that's so good," he moaned, and I heard his head fall back against the wall. Faster I sucked, hardening my tongue and flattening it to give him a better slide down my throat. He breathed my name and shoved me lower. I was trying to concentrate on making him orgasm, but at the same time, I was desperate to memorize the moment. I knew I'd want to relive it again and again. I wanted to remember how he smelled, the way his pubic hair was scratching my face and chin, and the sound of his voice when I made him come.

"Faster," he demanded, and I smiled around his dick, increasing my pace, my head bobbing between his thighs. "Yeah. God, yeah."

I was sucking so hard, my tongue was starting to cramp when he squeezed my head between his hands and his ass cheeks hardened beneath my fingers, and he became completely still while hot ribbons of cum coated my throat as he came in my mouth.

I swallowed and kissed his thigh, then straightened, still kneeling between his legs.

The lazy, satiated smile on his lips was beautiful. I could get addicted to it.

"This was amazing," I said, "but I can be professional with you. This doesn't have to change anything."

The smile disappeared when reality hit home, and I was instantly sorry I'd said it.

"This changes *everything*. I can't—" He shook his head quickly. "We can't..."

"I loved this. I don't mind if things change between us."

"Theo."

"What? Would that be so bad?" Leaning forward, I kissed his chest lightly over his T-shirt.

"Theo. No. You're a client, and we both have… issues."

"What issues? I'm single, you're single. Wait, you are single, aren't you?"

"Yeah, I am. I'm also goin' through hell right now with my family. I've got obligations. And you—you drink too much."

Dropping my hands, I sat back on my heels. Out of all the excuses he could give to deny what had just happened between us, that was the last one I had expected.

"I'm sorry." He reached forward, like he didn't want me to move away, but then he dropped his arms to his sides. "I didn't mean—I-I'm not tryin' to be an asshole. I just meant, we both have problems, and neither one of us needs the complication of a relationship. As good as this was—fuck, it was *so* good—it doesn't mean we should jump into somethin'. We barely know each other. It was just a hookup."

I hung my head, staring at nothing, embarrassed more than I'd ever been in my life. This wasn't the first time I'd found a quick blowjob that shouldn't have had any strings attached, but with Brady, it felt different, and that he regretted it made me feel shame. Another pit opened in my stomach.

In the heat of the moment, I'd forgotten about showing up at his office drunk off my ass. Obviously, he hadn't.

"Theo?"

Humiliation was roaring through me. I didn't want to, but I looked at him, and he cocked his head a little, the look on his face full of something… Was it pity? "I've seen you at the bar, and I saw you watchin' Jack Cade's glass of whiskey tonight, like it was your forbidden lover."

He'd noticed that? I hadn't even realized I'd done it.

"I ain't judgin' you," he said, his small-town country

accent coming out in this raw moment between us. "I'm just sayin' neither one of us is in a place to start somethin', that's all." He stood, and I did, too, slowly, then pulled my jeans up. "I'll make a list of other lawyers in the area. Maybe someone from Jackson would be better."

Picking my sweater up off the floor, I shook the dust out, then pulled it over my head.

"I'm…" He shook his head. "I'm sorry. I gotta go."

"Wait."

"This was a mistake."

"Brady—"

"No, Theo. I need to focus on work right now. Maybe you can't understand this, but for my family, it's literally life and death. And try as you might, you can't deny your issues. Do you even remember bargin' into my office a few months ago? I doubt it. You were lit at ten in the mornin'."

So I was right. When he looked at me, he saw someone spoiled and entitled. Oh, and I couldn't forget—Brady Douglas, my lawyer, or former lawyer, and the sexiest man I'd ever met, saw me as an alcoholic too.

# CHAPTER SEVEN

## BRADY

"SO, you left the ranch with Theo last night. What's up with that?" Wisper's self-appointed queen of gossip, Oly, asked me when we grabbed coffee the next morning before she had to be at All Animals Veterinary Clinic to start her day. She was one of three vets in Wisper, and with all the farms and ranches around, she was busy every day. I didn't know how she was managing a seriously stressful job and being a full-time mama to twins. I was impressed. I couldn't imagine taking care of one kid, let alone two. Her family helped, but still. I wondered if she'd slept at all last night as her mouth popped open into a huge yawn. She pulled her fingers through her mahogany hair absently, trying without much success to straighten the tangles she'd clearly forgotten to brush this morning.

"Nothin'. He wanted to show me the community center. You know, for business reasons."

Oly eyed me, doubt all over her face and suspicion ripe in her eyes. "Mmhm. Sure." She sipped her piping-hot black coffee, and I made a face. *How did anybody drink coffee like that?* "So, what lawyer-y things did you discuss?"

"Um…"

She didn't miss a beat. "Oh, I see. So things like, 'Do you like it hard?', or maybe 'How wide can you open your mouth?'"

I flushed red, and she screeched with the first sign of life she'd displayed since she met me on the sidewalk outside Coffee Shot. "I knew it! You're so bad."

Looking around the little shop, hoping no one had heard her and double checking that Theo wasn't there, I whispered, "Shh, Oly, stop. It was a mistake." He lived close enough, he'd probably heard her.

"What? Why?" she whispered. "Theo's gorgeous, and you deserve some hot lovin'."

"Yeah, but he's my client. Or he was. Obviously, that's over."

"Why? You can keep things professional."

"Seriously? It's unethical. I shouldn't have done it."

"Okay, so find him a different lawyer, and then ask him on a date."

"I-I—it's not the right time. You know, I've got my dad. My family. And he's, well, he's got issues too. It wouldn't work."

"Look, I don't know the details, but Aislinn says he's doin' a lot better than he was, and I didn't say you should marry him and have kids. I said ask him out. Have more sex. How can it be the wrong time for that? Sex releases endorphins, and that can only help with the stresses of life." She pitched an eyebrow, slurping more coffee. "Well, so how was it?"

"Oh my God, it was so good. I can't stop thinkin' about him." My face had to be purple by now, and when I remembered his hard cock in my mouth, I thought the whole coffee shop would catch fire. I fanned my face, but not as some kind of dramatic gesture. I felt like I was having a hot flash.

Oly giggled, and I glared at her. "Oh please. Since when are you embarrassed to talk about sex? When Dean and I got back together, it's all you wanted to talk about."

Covering my face with my hands and trying to rub the red away, I sighed. "Just never mind, okay? I gotta get to my cruddy office and do some work. I may be losin' the biggest client I'll ever be lucky enough to get, but I still have a bunch of small ones, and they need my services."

"Yeah," Oly said, swiping her finger down her phone's screen when it dinged. "Me too. Yola just texted. Man, that woman's a ball buster. You'd think an office manager should be sweet, but she's yellin' at me. I've already got a line of patients waitin' for me. But, hey, Brady?" she said while I busied myself, organizing my files inside my satchel instead of looking her in the eye.

Finally, I looked up. "What?"

"I'm here. If you need to talk about your dad, call me, okay? Any time."

"I know. Thanks."

She kissed my cheek, pulled on the ends of my hair like my sister was always doing, and disappeared through the door, the bell jingling behind her, and I sat back and looked around again. Coffee Shot was busy. The place was filled with at least seven people I knew, but I was so flustered from last night, and all of those neighbors and friends knew my parents, so I quickly gathered my things and got out of there. The last thing I needed was for one of them to ask about my dad. I didn't want to be reminded that he was dying. Like I could forget.

I MEANT to go to the hole-in-the-wall office I shared with my mom at the south end of Main Street, past the courthouse and located in the dingiest building known to man, but instead, I found myself outside the old *Wisper Gazette* building across the street from Coffee Shot, looking up at the sun glinting off the big windows on the third floor. I stood there staring for a long time, wondering if I should go in. I'd already made a list of lawyers for Theo to call, but I could've emailed him. I didn't have an actual need to see him.

But I wanted to see him. I'd felt like a heel last night when I walked away from him. The hurt and disappointment on his face was etched permanently into my memory, but I'd been so embarrassed by my actions and the way I'd spoken to him in the heat of the moment and how gross I felt about breaking every ethical law that had ever existed.

Moving back to Wisper was already corporate lawyer suicide, and getting involved with my client was just about as dirty as I could get. I was ashamed and pissed at myself, not to mention there were worlds between who he was and who I was. Getting into a relationship with him 'cause we'd screwed around was just about the worst idea in the world.

But I wanted him again, and that made me feel worse. What did that say about me? I knew what we'd done was wrong, but all I could think about was doing it again.

I'd never been so demanding with a hookup before. What the hell was that about? But I couldn't have stopped it for anything. Bombs could've rained down from the sky, blowing the world around us to smithereens, and still, I couldn't have stopped. And now, my face flushed again as I remembered his mouth on me, his tongue stroking cum out of me.

He was intoxicating. His mouth worked fucking wonders. *Damn it. No.*

It was wrong. I was wrong. Everything I'd been feeling—

the anger—had been building up inside me. It would find a way to work itself out of me in bad ways. I'd already found myself snapping at my mom and sister for no reason at all. Sex was one way I could try to control it, but not with him. Not with Theo.

"You gonna stand there all day, or you wanna come in?"

When I turned to the voice behind me, I had to look down to locate the person speaking, and I saw a short, skinny pixie of a thing with chin-length black hair and eyes that sparkled like obsidian, even with her hand shielding them from the sun.

"Uh, actually, I think I shouldn't—"

"C'mon. My boss is in there. Theo. Well, technically, he ain't my boss, but he's in charge. I'll introduce you. You lookin' to volunteer?" she asked, grabbing my hand and dragging me up two steps and through the door.

I didn't have to follow her, but I did. "What?"

Slowly, like she wasn't sure if I understood English, she said, "Are you here to sign up to help with the renovations?"

The nervousness I felt about seeing Theo was winding itself into a tight fist in the pit of my stomach, which reminded me of my fist wrapped around his dick. *Shit.* Looking behind her at the door, I was gauging my chances of escaping without being rude and without Theo seeing me.

"Sorry. No," I said.

She shrugged, and I heard Theo's voice.

"Brady?"

Turning toward the sound, I tried to hide the wince on my face. Theo stood at the end of the hallway, in the doorway to one of the rooms he'd said he'd probably use as an office, watching me. Confusion made him frown, probably because he hadn't expected to see me again so soon.

He looked good, better than he had last night, and definitely better than I'd seen him before that. He had more color in his cheeks, and even though he was unsure about me being there, when I looked at him, a hint of a smile played across his lips. It was in his eyes, too, and it was sexy as hell.

"Oh, there you are, boss," the rude mystery girl said. "This is—wait. You guys already know each other?"

"Yeah," Theo and I both said at the same time.

"So then, who are you? I'm Devo." She shoved her hand into mine.

"Oh right, the sidekick."

We shook, but then she said, "Sidekick?" She dropped my hand. "That's condescendin'."

Theo chuckled a little, his face lightening by the second. "Sorry, but you're a little difficult to describe, Devo. In a good way. This is Brady Douglas." He walked toward me, and when he was three feet away, he smiled genuinely, and the fist in my stomach dug its nails into my lungs, making it hard to breathe. Goddamn, the man was beautiful, his eyes like green sea glass on a dark-sand beach. "My lawyer."

And now, I couldn't speak. It took me a minute, but I finally said, "Former lawyer."

His eyes locked onto mine. "Right."

He wouldn't look away, so I did. I looked at my shoes and reached in my back pocket, pulling out the crumpled list I'd made for him of other trust lawyers and a couple of corporate lawyers in Jackson.

"Here, I wrote some names down for you." Holding the paper out to him, I peeked back up. Something about him intimidated me. Even though we'd messed around and I'd nearly finger fucked him on the dirty floor, I still felt small around the guy. I mean, he was this wealthy CEO badass from the big city, and I was a mediocre lawyer from Podunk, USA who had to check his bank account before taking a client to lunch to make sure there was enough in there to cover it. Maybe he wasn't at his best lately, but I was still light-years away from being the right guy for him.

"It seems you're always making lists for me." He took the paper, glanced at it, and shoved it in his own back pocket, and I tracked the movement with my eyes. Couldn't help myself. They landed on his hip, then fell to the curve of his junk under his jeans—the substantial junk that felt like heaven in my mouth. I could only imagine what it would feel like to fuck him, and I bit back a possessive growl that went so far past inappropriate, I couldn't see it in my rearview if I tried.

"This is awkward," Devo blurted. "I'm goin' across the street for coffee. Anybody want anything?"

I shook my head, but Theo said, "Yes, please. Here, take this." He pulled a credit card from his other pocket, and she snatched it from his hand with a smirk.

"You're predictable, man. I knew all I had to do was mention coffee and you'd whip out your wallet."

Theo rolled his eyes. "Get Brady a caramel latte, please, and get me, mm, you know, today I think I'll try a mocha. And get whatever you'd like, Devo."

She saluted him, then spun on her heel and marched toward the door.

"And see if they have any breakfast pastries left," Theo called after her. "Suddenly, I'm starving."

"10-4, boss."

The door creaked shut behind Devo, and Theo backed up against the wall, that hint of a smile growing quickly. He tucked his hands in his front pockets. "So," he said.

Nodding a little, I said, "So." All of a sudden, I didn't know what to do with myself, so I looked at my hands, then gripped them around my satchel's straps. "All the names on that list are good, tried attorneys. Any one of 'em can do what you need."

"Thank you, but I would rather have you."

"Right, but that's not an option anymore since… you know."

"Brady, are you under the impression that we did something wrong?"

"You didn't. I did."

"I instigated it," he said. "It's my fault."

"Maybe so, but that doesn't take the responsibility outta my hands. Besides, I was never the right lawyer for you. Sure, I've got a little bit of corporate experience, but for your needs, maybe a bigger firm with heftier resources would work better."

"Is there anything I can say to change your mind? I mean, you've been my lawyer for three years. I'm very happy with how you've handled the Cade Ranch project, and you know this town. You may not have a lot of resources, but you're the right man for the job."

Yeah, but which "job" was he referring to?

"Well," I said, "I s'pose if I did stay on, we'd have to agree that there can't be any more of… well, you know. We can't do what we did last night. There'd have to be boundaries."

His face fell a little, the smile slipping from his lips, but his eyes narrowed while he contemplated my offer.

"Okay. Deal." He was smiling again.

"I'm serious. If we do this, we cannot fuck. Ever."

The word elicited surprise. One eyebrow jumped. "Okay, but it's unfortunate. I enjoy talking to you, and last night was…"

Hearing that made me melt a little on the inside, but I shook my head. "Yeah, it was," I said, "but that's the deal.

Take it or leave it." Besides, he had enough problems. He didn't need me adding to them. And I had enough going on myself with my dad's illness and trying to help my mom keep up with his medical bills.

No, it wasn't a good idea.

He stepped forward slowly, and I backed up against the wall. He asked, "Are you sure? Last night really was amazing. I want to feel that again. I haven't felt so alive in months."

"I-it's just not the right time for me," I stuttered, inching away from him, stepping out of the magnetic hold his body had over mine. I wanted him so much, my dick felt like it might burst behind my department-store suit pants.

"Okay." He stepped back. "You're right. It's not the right time for me either. But I have a deal for *you*. Why don't we revisit this in a year? Isn't that what they say? When you start AA, you can't date for a year?"

"You're goin' to AA? Since when?"

"It hasn't been that long, but last night proved that it was the right decision. You were right about me craving a drink, and you were right that I have issues. I've been making everyone around me worry. And I..." He dropped his head, his eyes fixing on the floor between us, and he took a deep breath. "There's just a lot I need to deal with."

"That's good. I'm glad for you." I didn't mean for it to sound condescending, but it did.

He took another step backward and looked up. "Okay, so do we have a deal?"

"Yeah. It's a deal. No screwin' around for a year, and if we're still, well, you know, attracted to each other, then, and if you agree to hire a different lawyer, we can talk about it." That sounded reasonable. Who knew where either of us would be in a year. If he really was going to AA, after 365 days, he'd probably be a CEO again, and maybe I'd be gone. My dad would've—

"Okay, then if you're still my lawyer, I need you to go over the contract with the roofing company I hired. It's a big job, so I'd like you to make sure it looks right."

It was an excuse. He'd been in enough boardrooms, had read plenty of contracts over the years. A simple service contract wouldn't stop him up, but he was still paying me a monthly retainer, so I figured it best to do what he was asking, even if I knew he could've done it himself. This was the first step to honoring our deal.

"Sure thing."

# CHAPTER EIGHT

## BRADY

AFTER POWER WALKING the half mile back to my office with an overfull caramel latte spilling all over my hand 'cause the only thing I could concentrate on was the look on Theo's face when he came—the image would be burned into my brain for eternity—I found my auntie Lil digging through my desk drawers. She'd left my one measly file cabinet open with papers falling out the side, and Mrs. Stevenson in the waiting room was craning her neck, trying to peek in to see what all the fuss was about.

"What's goin' on?" I asked my mom's sister, our part-time receptionist and the woman who still pinched my cheeks every time I saw her unless I was quick enough to jump out of her line of fire.

"Oh, sorry, bunny, but your mama's already in court, and the lawyer for the Owens case keeps callin'. He wants the—"

"I know what he wants, auntie. It's okay. I'll take care of it." Colin Ames, opposing council in my client Gene Owens's case, had been calling, trying to get copies of Gene's land deed and his water rights permits, but I'd been stalling. Gene wasn't the most organized person. He hadn't gotten copies of his permits to me yet, so I wasn't sure if he had all his ducks in a row. Letting Colin know that was bad form.

The sounds of Theo's moans were still distracting me as I dug through the files that had been left in a heap on my desk, looking for the papers Lil hadn't been able to find. A man with Theo's kind of money, success, and reputation could snap his fingers and mountains would be moved if he wanted them to be. Why he would insist on staying with me as his lawyer was beyond me. There were probably a hundred more qualified in Jackson alone.

Was he only doing it for my benefit? Did he know about my dad? I didn't think so, but maybe he'd heard it through the grapevine. Or maybe it was because he was hoping to get some. I couldn't blame him there, and if I was being honest with myself, I wasn't sure I could hold to our new deal. I made a copy of the list of lawyers I'd given him and taped it to the inside of a desk drawer, just in case I needed it in an emergency. Like, you know, if his mouth just happened to fall on my dick accidentally, or something like that.

I wasn't trying to be so unprofessional in my thoughts, but Jesus. I couldn't even put a word to whatever it was that had happened between us last night. I mean, it'd been a while for me, so maybe it was just me being horny, but… it wasn't. I knew it wasn't.

An image kept flashing in my mind. My life was floating in front of me in pieces, like a cardboard jigsaw puzzle, and no matter how hard I tried to make it form into someone who *wasn't* Theodore Burroughs, Jr., gazillionaire extraordinaire, my most profitable client, the fuckers just kept fitting into place, and his sultry crystal-green eyes stared at me, trying to lure me back to the run-down three-story Main Street building.

*Shit.*

I spent the rest of the morning scanning files and making copies of the Owens case after trying to explain to Mrs. Stevenson why we couldn't sue Toys "R" Us for copyright infringement because that was the name she was trying to use for the small local toy store she wanted to open. I couldn't believe I had to explain that the only reason she'd had the idea in the first place was *because* of Toys "R" Us, and that they could sue *her* because they had been the ones to coin the name in the first damn place. She left angry, huffing that she'd tell my mama on me.

I'd planned on dropping paper copies of Gene's files off to Colin before lunch 'cause I couldn't stall forever, but my sister called, freaking out into the phone that she needed help with my dad. She was nearly hysterical, so I threw the files into the backseat of my car and raced home.

---

"BONNIE! WHERE ARE YOU?" I called out as soon as I walked in the door, but there was no answer. *Shit.* "Bon? What's wrong?"

When I got to my parents' bedroom, Bonnie was on the floor with my dad's head in her lap, her big belly bumping against it, and she was sobbing and apologizing to him. His body was sprawled across the hardwood floor, and I could see the pain in his eyes from the muscle spasms cramping his legs and neck.

"He jerked himself so hard, he fell out of bed," Bonnie cried. "I tried to get him back up, but I couldn't do it. I'm so sorry, Papa. I know you're in pain. I dunno what to do."

Dad closed his eyes, and one by one, tears leaked out in fast succession.

"Did you give him his meds this mornin'?" I asked, grabbing a pillow off the bed. "There's supposed to be a new muscle relaxant in the cocktail."

"Yeah, but I don't think they're doin' anything, bunny. Look at his face. He's in agony." Bonnie looked down, her tears dripping onto Dad's cheek, and she stroked his thinning gray hair and moved out from underneath him while I placed the pillow under his head.

"Call Britt. I'll get him back in bed."

"I did call her. She hasn't called back. That's why I'm here by myself. She had a family emergency, and the nurse on call isn't answering."

"Try again."

Bonnie left the room, and I tried to lift my dad, but the rigidity of his muscles made it impossible for me to do alone, so after only two attempts, I called Luuk to help me. Bonnie was too pregnant to risk lifting my dad, and my mom was still unreachable in court.

Luuk showed up five minutes after we hung up, and he brought Kevin with him.

"Thanks for comin' so fast," I said in the hallway outside my parents' bedroom.

"It's not a problem," Luuk said. "KC and I met in town for lunch today, so we weren't too far away when you called." Sympathy crossed his face. "We will do this, Brady. Please, let us. It shouldn't be you."

"He's my dad," I said, tears filling my eyes. I was trying hard as hell not to let them fall, but I felt like a waste of a son, and they fell down my face anyway.

Kevin clapped his hand on my shoulder. "We got him."

I nodded and stepped out from under his hand. I didn't want my dad to see me being weak. Swiping the tears away with the back of my hand, I followed them in. "Dad, you remember Kevin Cade? And this is Luuk. They're my friends. They're gonna help you, okay?"

"*Hallo*, Mr. Douglas. I am sorry *dat* you're having such a bad day. We will help you. Please try to relax as best as you are able."

My dad was beyond relaxation, but he opened his eyes, staring up at Luuk as they lifted him—Luuk's arms under my dad's arms while Kevin lifted his feet—and I knew he was probably wondering where Luuk was from. His accent was unique.

"Luuk's from the Netherlands, Dad. Pretty cool, huh?" I said, trying to distract him from the pain he must've been feeling.

When they laid him on the bed, he closed his eyes in relief but opened them again, looking up at Luuk. He blinked twice. That was his sign that he wanted us to keep talking.

"Tell my dad about the Netherlands, Luuk," I said, and Luuk looked at me. I nodded toward my dad, begging silently for Luuk to indulge him, anything to make him forget the last agonizing hour.

Luuk smiled and pulled the chair against the wall closer to the bed. He sat, and the kindness he always exuded calmed the frantic energy in the room. Bonnie excused herself, closing herself in the hallway bathroom, probably to cry in private, and I leaned against the door frame, listening to Luuk's voice and imagining that my dad still had the ability to speak. I imagined all the questions he would ask, and it occurred to me then that I hadn't heard his voice in months. I wondered if I'd saved any of his old voicemails so I could hear it again. My mom had already canceled his cell phone to save money.

"I was born in Oudewater, in *Nederland*. It is a small farming community."

Kevin snorted, interrupting. "Brady didn't say bore the guy with your whole life story, babe. He said tell him about the Netherlands."

Luuk rolled his eyes at Kevin, and a little smile sparkled in Dad's eyes. If he could've, he would've laughed at them.

"I apologize for my boyfriend's rudeness, Mr. Douglas, but do not worry because he was just about to go make Brady a cup of tea." Luuk said the last words while glaring over his shoulder at Kevin, and Kevin winked at my dad, then dragged me from the room.

We went out to the front porch instead, and when I sat on the hanging bench my dad had made when I was a boy, Kevin sat next to me. "You okay?"

I sighed so loudly that it hurt my chest. "Yeah. Thanks for helpin'."

"No problem. That's gotta be hard to see, man. I'm sorry."

"It's fuckin' torture. He's in so much pain, but there's not a damn thing I can do to help him. And he's all there, you know? His mind is strong, but he's trapped in his body. Sometimes, I think…" Inhaling, I looked out at the mountains behind the small development where my family had lived in my whole life, watching the clouds move over the tall, snow-dusted peaks. Even this early in fall, it was there, like a white shining beacon pointing toward home. Finally, I exhaled. "Sometimes, I think I can't take it for one more fuckin' second, and all I wanna do is run away."

I dropped my head into my hands, hating how the thought made me feel—like the shittiest son in the world. But everything inside me was screaming at me to run. To get as far away from the despair and death and indignity as I could. I wouldn't be able to handle it. I knew it. My dad wasting away every day in front of me was changing me.

And when he died? I couldn't even go there in my mind.

It hurt so fucking bad.

But no matter how much pain I was in, the pain my dad had to be feeling was so much worse. And I couldn't leave my mom or my sister.

I had no control over anything in my life. I felt helpless.

"You need to get laid," Kevin said. The look of surprise on my face must've knocked some sense into him. He winced. "That was the wrong thing to say. I have a bad habit of tryin' to lighten the mood at super inappropriate times. Sorry."

My shoulders dropped a little. "I… did. Kinda."

"You did what?"

"Got laid or… laid adjacent."

His eyebrows shot up, and he looked me up and down. "Who?" His eyes narrowed. "Shit. Theo? Was it with Theo? You left the ranch with him last night."

I didn't confirm his suspicion, but he knew anyway.

"Ha! Luuk owes me fifty bucks. Well, so how was it? Was he good? Tell me. Luuk's the only guy I get to talk to about sex. Teach me your ways, Obi-Wan."

I laughed a little at his joke. "It was intense."

"How was it intense? I'm gonna need a play-by-play. Where'd he put his mouth? His dick? Were you the bottom or was he? What position? Did you suck his cock?"

"Jesus!"

"What? Was there ever any doubt in your mind that my, ahem, certain brand of crassness wouldn't translate from hetero sex to gay sex? Seriously. Answer the damn questions."

"Since when are we friends who talk about our sex lives?"

"Since you're one of the three other gay guys in my town and you used to crush on my man. You owe me."

"I never crushed on Luuk."

"Yeah, you did, but I don't blame you. Everybody wants him. I mean, look at the man. He's to-fuckin'-die-for, but he's mine. Keep your mitts and your thoughts off and answer my questions."

"I'm not talkin' about this with you. Theo seems like a pretty private guy, and you don't need to know the details."

Kevin sighed. "Fine. Well, so you like the dude?"

Pursing my lips, I shrugged and shook my head. "I don't really know him."

"He seems like a decent guy to me. Down to earth even though he's, like, a gazillionaire, you know? When he first came out to the ranch to—wait a minute. Ain't you his lawyer?"

I winced. What an utter fucking mess I'd made.

"Shit, man. You're so bad, but that's kinda hot." He snickered and pushed his feet on the porch floor, swinging the bench like we were kids.

"Who is bad?" Luuk asked, pushing the screen door open and stepping onto the porch. "Your father is asleep, Brady. I think he was exhausted."

Kevin laughed, and oddly, I was happy someone could find humor in the situation. "Either that or your Dutch tales put him to sleep."

"I'm going to get 'You are so rude' tattooed across my forehead so you can see it every day. Maybe then you will be reminded to keep your mouth shut."

"Mm, yeah, or maybe across your upper lip so when I shove my—"

"Kevin!" Luuk and I scolded him simultaneously.

"What? What'd I say?"

"Come on, big mouth," Luuk said. "Let us leave Brady and his sister. I'm sure they'd like to have time with their father without us hanging around. I must get back to work anyway."

"Yeah, yeah, me too." Kevin stood, leaving the bench swaying. I lifted my legs, trying to remember what it had felt like when I was a boy and my dad would swing us back and forth. "My brother's gonna have my head if I don't get back soon." In a rare moment of sincerity, he turned back toward me. "But you call us, you hear? If you need help, or just to get away, drink a beer. Whatever. We're here for you, man. Okay?"

"Thanks."

# CHAPTER NINE

## THEO

"I CAN'T BELIEVE you're riding again, Aislinn. It was amazing to watch you today. You looked so natural up on that horse. Mom would've loved it."

Finn drove in silence while my sister and I talked. I'd followed through on my promise to be close to her again, and I'd spent the afternoon and evening at the ranch after she, Finn, and I had gone to lunch to talk about the wedding. Ace could ask for the moon, and I'd pay for it. Whatever she wanted for her wedding would be my pleasure to give her, and already, I was excited to walk her down the aisle. Technically, half of our parents' money was hers, but she'd never really had any interest in it, and even less now that she and Finn were together. They had everything they wanted in each other.

That hurt, which was why I was offering to pay for things for the wedding they hadn't even asked for.

Ace and I were texting more and talking on the phone a few times a week. She and Finn had come out to help me at the center, and every time I saw her, the happiness on her face made me proud and hopeful.

We didn't specifically talk about the darkness I'd fallen into. She didn't ask, and I didn't offer any details. Besides, things were changing. I was changing, and I didn't think weighing her down with my past misery would be helpful in any way. She was proud of me for going to AA, and for now, it was enough.

Not that I was cured. Not by a long shot, but I was trying. I hadn't had a drink in weeks.

"Thanks. I think about her all the time when I'm riding, though she would probably snub her nose at me in a western saddle."

"No, I don't think so. She'd just be happy you were doing it."

"Y'all are crazy." Finn scoffed and laced his fingers through Aislinn's on the seat between them. "Western ridin' is so much better than English."

Aislinn riding Western wouldn't be the only thing our mom would have a hard time believing. It would have blown her mind that Ace would date a cowboy, move in with him, or ride in his beat-up old truck. Or marry him.

"Oh shit," Finn said, squinting out his window. "Is that Brady Douglas?"

"Where?" I couldn't help the eagerness in my voice even though Brady had made it clear he would be sticking to our deal. I'd promised to stick to it, too, but it was hard to see him and not want him. Plus, it made me self-conscious. Had he agreed to our deal because he was hoping I'd forget about what we'd done? Did he really not want me? In a year, would he be with someone else? Someone less... complicated? It was only sex we were talking about, but if I was being honest with myself, I wanted more than that.

Three years ago, self-doubt would never have crossed my mind, but all I ever did anymore was beat myself down. My past was dragging me lower and lower. The day I'd tried to kill my blackmailer was like an oil stain in my mind. No matter how much scrubbing, it wouldn't come off. When Tim was murdered and my sister's life was threatened, I'd wanted to kill Blake Ormand, and I would have if he hadn't knocked me unconscious. He could've killed me. He almost did.

Could I have killed him? Part of me wanted to think I could have, but the rational part of me, the safe part, was desperate to believe I wouldn't have done it.

But all of me knew I would have. He was threatening my sister's life. He was threatening our way of life, and without it, without the money, who was I?

I had a rational reason to want him dead, but I could've called the FBI. He'd committed all kinds of crimes in different states, and I had enough status to get their attention. But instead, I took it upon myself to dish out the guy's punishment. Why had I done that? What kind of arrogance had I been plagued with to make me believe I could end another person's life?

And that fact was seriously fucking with me. How could I be the same person I'd always been if I was willing to end a life, no matter how awful the man? I wasn't God.

I had prided myself on being generous, always the first to help someone in need. I donated more money to various charities and causes in one year than my father ever had. I'd given up my own happiness to care for my sister. But when threatened, I'd become someone I couldn't recognize. Someone who could kill.

It was that thought and my inability to reconcile it within myself that had led me to drink myself into a stupor.

I didn't know who I was, and I was terrified of who I might turn out to be.

But the fog had lifted a little. Something had clicked

inside me the day Devo had taken me to the mountains, and I wasn't going to let those thoughts tear me up anymore—or I would try not to let them. I had the center to focus on, and that was a positive place to put my energy. I wanted to be worthy of my sister's love and my parents' pride.

I didn't want to despise myself anymore.

Bringing someone else into my mess was a bad idea, and I was constantly worrying that Brady knew all of this.

I couldn't stop thinking about him.

It was difficult now as he stumbled down the street, alone, looking like I probably had the last few years, clearly intoxicated. I wasn't sure exactly where he lived, but I didn't think it was near downtown since I'd seen him driving to work over the last two weeks. If he lived close, he would've walked to work. Stupidly, I looked for his car every morning when Devo and I went across the street for coffee.

"Stop the truck," I said.

"Theo? What's going on?" Ace asked, frustration clear in her voice since she couldn't see what was happening when Finn veered to the right side of the road.

"Everything's fine, but I'm going to help Brady." I squeezed my sister's fingers, then placed my hand on the door handle. "Finn, please stop the truck."

Finn slowed, then stopped next to the curb, and I hopped out into the crisp fall night. I didn't have a coat, just a thin sweater, but Brady was in a T-shirt, and I knew he probably wouldn't make it to wherever his inebriated mind was taking him. It was at least a mile to Manny's bar, if that was where he was coming from. It was a Wednesday night, so closing time at the bar had come and gone. I knew that for sure since I'd been asked to leave on many occasions when I parked my ass on one of Manny's stools to drink myself into a void.

As I walked in front of the truck, I heard my sister grilling

Finn. She'd become such an anxious person since the car accident, and now, all she ever did was worry about me.

"Where's he going?"

"Everything's fine, Ace. Looks like Brady's pretty drunk. Your brother wants to help."

Leaning across Finn, she called out the open window as I crossed the street, "Theo! What are you doing? Is this safe?"

I didn't look for oncoming cars, but this was Wisper, and I knew all too well from my own drunk wanderings that there wouldn't be any traffic. The only action downtown was the blinking of the red stoplight at the intersection where Main Street met Lincoln. The place was like a ghost town this time of night, and we were only two blocks from the center.

"Are you sure this is a good idea?" Ace asked. "Maybe you're not the best person to be dealing with a—"

Walking back to Finn's truck, I looked at my sister and her fiancé. Both of them seemed unsure about what I was about to do, Finn's eyes landing squarely on my face and Aislinn's searching everywhere, trying to understand.

"A drunk? Because I am one?"

Ace lowered her eyes, and the look of sadness crossing her face was like a punch to my gut. That look was the whole reason I drank in the first place. I'd let her down.

"Aislinn, it's the truth. I'm sorry I put you through that. I'm sorry I put us *both* through that. But right now, I'm sober, and Brady needs help. Besides, who better to deal with a drunk person than a drunk himself?"

"I ain't sure that's sound reasonin'," Finn said.

Aislinn's voice was a soft pleading. "Theo—"

"Baby, your brother's a grown man," Finn said. He raised his eyebrows, grilling me with the look in his eye. "If he wants help, he'll ask for it."

"I will."

Aislinn sat back, wrapping both of her arms around one of Finn's. "Okay, but will you call me in the morning?"

"Yes. I promise."

They drove away, and I felt relief that Finn loved my sister. He wasn't my biggest fan, and I couldn't blame him for that—we didn't have the friendliest history—but he was steady and strong, and when she was anxious, he calmed her down. He'd been the constant in her life these last few years. It was a role I had always intended to fill for her, but she didn't need me anymore. That reality was winding its way through me a little more every day.

*One day at a time.*

I snorted at the thought and jogged across the street.

"Brady?"

His head bobbed in my direction, but he didn't stop walking, so I kept pace with him.

He slurred, "Oh, great. Now it's you, and you sound like that guy. The guy. You know that guy?" His head was swimming. I could see it in his eyes, which were darting everywhere at once.

"What guy?"

"You know, the hot guy. The cute guy. That *sexy* fuckin' guy." He glanced at me, but his eyes were glazed over, his hair a mess and hiding his face, and I was sure he didn't realize who he was talking to.

"Are you talking about Manny Perez over at the bar?" I joked. "You look like you just came from there."

"Manny?" He giggled like a schoolgirl, and I tried really hard not to be charmed by the sound. "No way! I've known Manny my whole life. He doesn't have sex."

"Oh, no?"

"No! 'Sides, I'm talkin' 'bout Theo. Theodore. *The* guy. You know that guy?"

"I do know that guy. Or, well, I used to."

"I don't know if he even knows me, but we did fuck around."

"I think he knows you. I think he likes you."

He sighed really loudly and stumbled forward. I grabbed his arm, yanking him back so he wouldn't fall on his face, and when he straightened and turned to face me, he gasped. "Theo! Oh my God, we were just talkin' 'bout you. Wait." He blushed, though it was hard to tell since his face was already pretty flushed from the alcohol. "You didn't hear what I just said, did ya?"

I shook my head. "No. I didn't hear anything."

"Good." He hiccupped. "That's really good, 'cause I was telling you how you're sexy. You're that sexy guy, and we gave each other blow jobs. Remember?" He staggered forward a little, hiccupping again, and I steadied him with my hands on his arm. He was covered in goosebumps.

"I do remember. I think about it all the time. But don't worry about that right now. We need to get you inside. You're freezing. Come on. The center's just another block. I've got blankets, and we can even start a fire in the old fireplace. Sound good?"

"'Sound good?' Are you normal?" He laughed. "Ooo, a fire in a fireplace at your house and we can get naked? Oh yeah, that sounds really fuckin' good. I mean, I know we have a deal, but I'm hopin' we can… you know." He wiggled his eyebrows, but then his eyes darkened. "Goddamn, that was so good. Remember? You prolly don't."

"Actually, I was thinking you might like to sleep," I said as I steered him down the block with my hand on his low back. He stumbled again, and I wrapped his arm around my shoulders, carrying most of his weight the rest of the way. He tripped over his feet a few times, but I held him up, and I liked how that felt.

I could smell the alcohol on his breath. It was so strong, it probably could've caught fire, and it made me want a drink. *Badly*. There was a hollow pit in my stomach and a quiet buzzing in my head. My hands were shaking, but I tried my best to ignore them.

It was easier than I'd imagined it would be, but having someone else's problem to focus on helped. It made me realize that that was what I had always done. If I wasn't focused on Aislinn and her medical issues, I was focused on whatever project or investment I'd been working on, trying to help others realize their business dreams or even their personal ones.

I'd been so focused on other people that focusing on myself was foreign. Maybe that was partly the reason I hadn't been able to handle the trauma I'd gone through.

Maybe *that* was why I drank.

When we got to the center, I dragged Brady up the front steps and unlocked the door, and we landed on our asses in the entrance when he tried to push past me in the doorway.

"Whoop." He giggled again. "Uh oh."

I pushed the door with my foot, and it shut with a loud *thud*.

"Stay right here. Let me go get some water for you and a blanket." I tried to stand, but he pulled me back down.

"Theo. I'm drunk."

I kneeled in front of him. "I know. It's okay."

"I didn't mean to say what I said the other night. I didn't mean it."

"It's okay, Brady. Really."

"I'm so fucked up right now."

Brushing his hair away from his face, I couldn't help

myself. I tucked it behind his ear and kissed his lips softly, and he closed his eyes and sighed. It wasn't the way I'd pictured seeing him again, but he was clearly in pain, and I would've done anything to make it go away.

"Oh God. Don't do that. Don't be nice to me. I don't deserve it."

"You do deserve it."

"No. I'm a bad son. A bad brother. I'm bad at everything." Dropping his head into his hands, he cried, and I sat in front of him and pulled him into my lap, relishing the feeling of holding him and wishing that this was an entirely different circumstance. I wanted to be with him again, but not like this.

"My dad's dyin', Theo. He's dyin' a little more every day, and I can't fix it. And I wanna run away. I wanna get in my car and drive and never look back 'cause it hurts too much."

I didn't say anything. What could I say to that?

Leaning back against the wall behind me, I pulled him with me, feeling my own tears drip down in the space between his body and mine. His pain was palpable, and it reminded me of my own when my parents had died. There had been no one else, no other family to look after Ace and me, all of our parents' "friends" scattering to the winds when things got hard. I was alone and I was scared. Of course I focused on other people then. Who wants to live in the moment when the only thing there is loss?

"Can you make it go away? Please," he whispered. "Please make it go away."

"I wish I could."

He turned his head then, and his body followed, and he climbed over me, straddling me on the floor. The cold draft was seeping through underneath the poorly insulated front door, and I shivered.

"Why're you cryin'?" he said, watching a tear escape down my cheek.

"I don't want you to be in pain."

He hiccupped again, his deep brown eyes now clearer and staring into mine. "I'm sorry," he said, wrapping his arms around my shoulders and pressing his knees against my hips. He hugged me to his body. "I'm drunk. I dunno what I'm sayin'. I thought about it. What I'd say when I got here, but now I can't remember."

"You were coming here?"

"Yeah. I wanted that feelin' again. You know how it felt when we were together?"

"I do." *You have no idea how many times I've thought about it.*

"You said you wanted it again. Please, can we have it?"

His lips found my neck, and he kissed and licked a path to my mouth in a sloppy attempt to seduce me.

"No, Brady," I groaned. Even though it wasn't the sexiest come-on I'd ever received, it was Brady, and I wanted him more than I'd ever wanted anyone. I couldn't lie—the urge was there to get really drunk myself. Then it wouldn't matter. We could fuck until we passed out, and I wouldn't have to feel bad about taking advantage of him or of him taking advantage of me. But I couldn't do it. Not to him. "Not tonight. You won't remember this tomorrow, and I definitely want you to remember. Besides, we made a deal. I won't break it." The words were hard to say, but at least I could make a good decision where he was concerned.

He slumped against me, his muscles going lax, his breath rushing out against my neck. "You don't want me anymore, do you? I've ruined this. I'm sorry. You're like this perfect man. You're everything I've ever wanted, but when I look at you, I'm scared." Curling up in my lap, he brought his knees up to his chest, and I wrapped my body around his, holding him against me like a child.

"I want you. You don't know how much, but you were right. We both have things going on in our lives. And I'm far from perfect." I looked down at him in my arms. His eyes were closed, and this peaceful, childlike smile settled on his face. I knew admitting the truth to him now was cowardly. He wouldn't remember anything I said. He might've even been asleep already—but maybe if I practiced what I wanted to say, soon, I would find the courage to say it louder. I whispered, "Remember the day I came to your office?"

He nodded against my chest, his long hair tangling and sticking to his sweaty face.

"What I wanted to tell you that day was that I tried to kill someone. I *wanted* to kill him. You won't think I'm perfect if you wake up tomorrow and remember what I'm saying. I let my sister down, my parents. I let myself down. If you loved me, I'd let you down too. I don't know what to do with that. I don't know who I am."

"I know what you did, and I know who you are," he said quietly, falling asleep. "You're Theo. You're beautiful, and if you'd tried to kill someone to protect me, I'd love you even harder than before."

***

WHEN A NOISE WOKE me in the morning, I was freezing.

I'd managed to get Brady further inside the building, but we didn't make it very far. He tripped over my feet and landed in a heap on the floor in the front room, so I covered him with blankets and lay next to him after he passed out.

Thoughts about Blake Ormand kept me up all night, memories of chasing him through California and Nevada and the ensuing fight running circles in my mind. I hadn't eaten or slept in days. I had become obsessed. He almost beat me to death for my efforts, and I thought about what Aislinn would have done if that had happened. And I imagined if Brady had been there that night. If he'd seen me with a gun, ready to murder someone, what would he really think of me?

I knew the answer, and it made me sick to stomach.

"Boss?" I jerked my head to the sound of Devo's voice. She was standing above me, looking at me with pity spread across her small features. "Sleepin' on the floor again? I thought we talked about this. I told you, my mama said you could stay with us if you need a place."

"I have a place, Devo. You know that."

"So then why you on the floor? That can't be comfortable. And I meant a place to stay where you're not alone all the time."

"I wasn't alone." I sat up, a deep ache in my back and my bones creaking like I was a hundred years old. "I had a visitor."

"I don't see anybody."

"No. He must've left," I said, looking around for any sign of Brady. There was none.

"Okay, well, get up. My friends are comin' today to help us. Remember, I told you yesterday?"

"Shit." I rubbed my face with my hands. "No. I'm sorry. I forgot. Do you mind if I run home for a quick shower?"

Devo grabbed my hand, and I let her pull me off the floor. The scratchy wool blanket I'd used to keep Brady warm dropped and pooled around my feet.

"Do whatcha gotta do. I'll get coffee." She held out her hand, and I sighed and pulled my wallet from my pocket.

"Here." I handed her a credit card. "It might be easier if we just set up a credit account at Coffee Shot that I can pay monthly." In my head, I was making a mental note to order a card in her name.

Devo snorted, grabbed the card, and escaped out the front door, and I watched her go, remembering Brady on the floor there only hours ago. I wondered when he'd woken up. Was he still drunk? How had he gotten home?

I texted him. "*You okay?*"

Three dots appeared below my text, but just as quickly, they disappeared, and after staring at my phone for two minutes, I closed the app and went to retrieve my truck from the back alley. I climbed in, and the whole drive back to my rental house in Jackson was a blur. I thought about nothing but Brady. He'd slept in my arms, and I loved it—the feel of his body against mine. His warmth. His ass had a starring role in my dreams, and I could easily have had it in my hands, but I didn't make a move. I was sure he wouldn't remember if I had, and I hoped he'd barely remember coming to the center. He would only be embarrassed. He had enough on his mind. I didn't want to add to it.

He didn't text back, so after my shower and shave—yeah, some business mogul I was. Five o'clock shadow was a thing of eight days ago. I looked like a burly lumberjack—I called my sister. I'd promised to let her know I was okay this morning, and she was friends with Oly, Brady's friend. I wanted to know what was wrong with his father. Maybe Oly would know.

"Hey, sis."

"Oh, Theo. I'm so glad you called. I wasn't sure you would."

I winced. *Damn.* I felt bad about blowing my sister off for so long. "I'm sorry I made you worry. I'm okay."

"Good. How's Brady?"

"Oh, um, he's… I don't know. He slept at the center. He

was gone when I woke up, but I got him to drink a little water last night and he was out like a light, so I'm sure he's fine. Actually, I was wondering if you'd heard anything about his father. I know you're friends with Oly, and she's friends with Brady, so I thought you might know."

"Yes. Actually, I did hear about him. His dad has ALS. He's in the final stages, I think. It's why Brady left his job and moved back to Wisper."

"ALS," I repeated quietly, thinking of all the heartbreaking things Brady must've been going through. I couldn't imagine.

"Yes. Lou Gehrig's disease? Remember, Mom and Dad's friend had it when we were kids."

"I remember. Gary Corbett."

"That's right. It was awful."

"Thanks. I, um, I was just curious."

"Theo?"

"Yeah?"

"You like Brady, don't you?"

"I… I don't know him very well."

"What?" she said. "He's your lawyer. How do you not know him?"

"I've been a little preoccupied."

"True. But that's over now, right?"

"Right," I confirmed, and this time, I believed it. "Actually, we… Ah, I don't know if I should tell you this."

"Tell me what?"

"It's just, we've never talked about our… personal lives before. I don't want to make you uncomfortable."

"Seriously?" She laughed. "That's exactly what I want. Not the uncomfortable part, but I want to know what's going on with you. Wait. So you're dating Brady? You're dating your lawyer?"

"No. We're not dating, but we hooked up. I would really like to date him, but it's not the right time. You know?"

"You like him a lot, don't you?"

"I don't—"

"I know, I know. You don't *know* him, but come on. Be honest. You like him."

I blushed and was glad she couldn't see me. "Yeah."

"That's great, Theo. He seems like a cool guy. Oly thinks the world of him."

"Yes, but we decided not to get into anything."

"Why not?"

"Because he has a lot going on and because he's still my lawyer."

"Hm. Well, not that my opinion matters, but I think you've been through a lot, too, and I think, if you find someone you can share your life with, someone who gets you, you shouldn't ignore that."

"BOSS, THIS IS MILLIE AND OSCAR." Devo introduced me to two of her friends, a tall, thin woman with long blond hair and a shorter, fair-skinned and freckled young man with a recently cut flattop.

"Guys, this is Theo, my boss and the founder of this very community center."

"I'm not your boss, Devo," I said, shaking Oscar and Millie's hands, and I smiled at them, feeling like it came easily, which was a nice change for me.

My phone dinged, but I didn't want to be rude, so it sat in my pocket like a rock while I waited for a chance to check it.

"I know, I know, but I mean, you are kinda. And you're in charge, so… Anyway, we're here to work today. Whatcha got for us?" Devo stuffed her hands in her pockets and rocked back and forth on her feet. "Please tell me it involves sledge-hammers and screamin' 'cause that's just fun. We're knockin' down the wall today, right?"

I laughed and nodded.

"Fun for you," Millie said. "I don't want to chip my nails." She held her hand in the air, pretending to check her nail polish, but there wasn't any. Her nails were bitten to the quick.

Devo rolled her eyes. "Yeah, your manicure would defi-nitely suffer. Well, your loss. Oscar, shall we?"

"You know it," he said. "I love bustin' shit up."

I motioned with my arm for them to follow me and led them to the back wall. They all stood looking at me, waiting for further instruction, and I lifted one of the sledgehammers I'd borrowed from Finn and handed it to Devo. "You get your wish," I said, and her eyes lit up with mischief.

Oscar laughed at her.

"Are you all from Barton?" I asked.

Millie shook her head. "Originally, I'm from Toronto, but I've lived in the States since I was thirteen. My mom and dad divorced, and my mom, my brother, and I moved to Seattle. But my mom's remarried now, so I moved with my brother when he came to Jackson to pursue his dream of being a cowboy." She rolled her eyes. "He can barely ride a horse."

"What about you, Oscar?"

"I grew up in Wisper," Oscar said. "My dad *is* a cowboy—he works cattle for old man Milson—so I'm sure you can imagine how bein' trans has been. My parents are comin' around a little, but not everybody sees the light. I'm pretty excited about this center 'cause it might just be the thing my family needs to finally understand me."

"How old are you?"

"Twenty-two," he replied with a little sparkle in his eye. "What about you?"

Laughing, I said, "Too old for you. I'm thirty-four."

"Oscar, you're a horndog," Devo said, shaking her head. "Leave the man alone. Besides, he's already got his sights set on somebody else, don'tcha, boss?"

Oscar shrugged, and I dipped my head a little, glaring and warning Devo to keep quiet about my love life. Or the lack thereof. Besides, how could she know? I hadn't said anything about Brady.

I didn't think Brady was still in the closet, but I'd never actually asked him, and I didn't want to start any small-town gossip and make things harder for him than they already were. And we had our deal.

"Let's tear this wall down and go from there," I said, hoping to distract her. "Devo, you're sure it's not load-bearing?" We'd already cleared it with the contractor I'd hired, but Devo was the self-appointed forewoman, so I deferred to her.

"Positive, boss."

"All right then, go for it. Take out all your frustrations on my walls."

Devo laughed a little maniacally, lifted the hammer, and swung at the wall. She hit her mark with a loud *clack*, and plaster fell to the floor. Oscar grabbed the other sledgehammer, and together, they made quick work of the wall while Millie and I stepped back to watch.

Sneaking a look at my messages, I breathed a sigh of relief when I saw Brady's text. All it said was, "*I'm okay. Thank you.*"

I relaxed then, and we had fun. *I* had fun for the first time in a long time, and as the wall came down and the room beyond it opened to us, I could see the future I'd been dreaming of beginning to take shape. I saw families of all different shapes, sizes, and colors gathering there. I saw friends and connections being made.

"Devo, I was thinking," I said when she'd finished her gleeful wall demolition.

She was sweating and breathing hard, but she looked happy. "Yeah?"

"We need to decide on a first order of business. Once we get things situated in here, how do we get the word out"—I jabbed my thumb over my shoulder toward the front windows —"out there?"

"Oh, well, I thought we might—"

The heavy front door slammed open. It hit the wall in the foyer, and I thought I could even hear the metal hinges crack, but the door stayed where it was.

A man with an unkempt beard and long stringy hair walked in. He took off his baseball cap, and strands of it covered his eye. He flicked it away. It looked like he hadn't showered in days, and I wondered if that was what I had looked like a few weeks ago.

"Hey, man," Devo said. "You here to volunteer?" The woman was on a never-ending quest to find people she could boss around.

"No." The man laughed, like it was ludicrous that she'd ask. "No," he said again. "I was just… just looking for…" His eyes darted all around the room. "Um, I was looking for the career center. Ain't there one here? I heard y'all were startin' a community center." The man was familiar to me, but I was pretty sure we'd never formerly met. He was staring at Millie but not saying anything, so I stepped in.

"Welcome," I said. "I'm Theo, and you are?" I held my hand in front of me, hoping he'd take the cue.

Shuffling forward, he shook my hand. "Oh, uh, I'm Vern. Vernon Wexler."

"Hi, Vern," I said. "You're right. There will be a career center here, but we aren't open yet. But what is it you're looking for specifically?" I motioned to Devo, Millie, and Oscar all standing in a line next to me. "Maybe we can help."

"I, um…" Vern looked around the room, wincing a little. "I lost my job this mornin', and I gotta find another one. I had this friend, and I always just took a job wherever he was workin', but he's gone now, and I… Well, I don't know how to find a good job."

"We're not really set up yet," I said, but the look in the guy's eyes made me want to help him. "But what are you good at? What kind of jobs have you worked before? Maybe we can still help."

"Yeah," Devo said. "What job did you lose this mornin'?"

"Uh, well, I was workin' over at Bob's Feed and Tack shop, but Bob got mad at me 'cause I ran his forklift into a stack of feed bags and the shit went everywhere. Bein' fair to Bob, it wasn't the first time… or the third. Before that, I was a ranch hand for some farms around here, a day worker, but my buddy did some really bad stuff. Maybe you heard about it? His name's Doug."

Devo and I shook our heads. She didn't live in Wisper, and I'd been dealing with my own stuff, so I wasn't up on town gossip.

"Anyway, none of the farmers trust me anymore. But I used to work construction. And for a time, I was a handyman. I didn't actually get paid for that, but I can fix just about anything."

"I saw an ad in the window at José's Diner," Millie said. "They're looking for a cook."

Vern blushed. "Thank you, ma'am, but yeah, that's not

really a good job for me. I'm a klutz. I break near everything I touch, which is how I know how to fix everything. I don't think José would even let me in his kitchen, and I'm damn sure he wouldn't pay me to burn shit."

"You're not really helpin' yourself here," Devo said.

Vern shrugged.

Oscar had been silent the whole time, and if I wasn't wrong, he was trying to blend in with the wall behind him.

Finally, Vern noticed. "Livvy? Little Livvy Nichols?"

Oscar stepped away from the wall. "My name is Oscar."

"Yeah, but—"

"My name is Oscar," he repeated, looking uncomfortable. "And my pronouns are he/him."

"Oh. Well, uh… I don't really know what to say to that." Vern looked uncomfortable too.

Oscar scoffed. "I don't really need you to say anything."

"Yeah," Vern said, swinging his arm in Oscar's direction, "but you're a girl. I used to work with your daddy over at the—"

"He's a man," Millie said, stepping closer to Oscar with a scowl on her face. I certainly wouldn't like to be the guy between her and her friend. "It would be cool if you could just acknowledge what he's telling you instead of arguing."

"Oscar, you okay?" Devo asked.

"Yeah." He nodded, letting us know he felt safe with us even though his identity was being challenged. He stood a little taller, hopefully taking comfort in the fact that his friends had his back. I did too.

I was hoping Vern's ignorance was attributed to his lack of exposure to the LGBTQ community. He might've wanted to seem like he didn't agree with Oscar's identity, but more than that, he looked unsure. Not unkind.

He frowned. "I'm confused."

"I think everybody gets that," Devo said. "And maybe that's why you're here. I think you might just be the right guy for the job."

"What job?" Vern asked at the same time I did, and Devo tugged my shirt sleeve, pulling me back toward the corner of the room.

"Excuse us," I said, letting her steer me away.

When the others couldn't hear us, she put her hands on her hips. "Boss, I've seen this guy and his friend around. I'm pretty sure his buddy went to jail. But I'm thinkin', if he gets involved here, maybe the rest of Wisper will come around too. We'll have to give him a crash course on pronouns and maybe a little sensitivity reminder, but remember that destiny thing I was tellin' you about? Maybe it's Vern's destiny too."

"Okay," I hedged, uncertain about her unerring faith in people, "but Devo, there's no job. I don't have anything to offer the guy."

"But you could, right? I mean, I don't wanna tell you how to do things, so sorry if I'm oversteppin', but you could offer the guy a job. We need all kindsa things done around here. He could be like your boy Friday." She smiled, looking really pleased with herself.

"I thought that's what you are."

"Your boy Friday? Uh, well, except I'm a *woman*."

"You know what I mean."

She chuckled. "Yes, I do. And while we're on the subject, I think I'm more like your assistant director, which, technically, I should be paid for, but I'm patient and I can wait till you get your shit together. But I think Vern needs a job now. So, why not offer him one? I have a feelin' about him."

Peeking over my shoulder at Vern, I was a little less convinced, but I was willing to give him a chance. Besides, if Devo was wrong about him, I could always fire him. But she was right that I should be paying her. She worked every day on some aspect of the center, whether it was helping me reno the building or making phone calls to different community centers around Wyoming, asking them what worked and what didn't. She picked up coffee and lunch almost every day, and she was my moral support 24/7. We'd spent hours on the phone and texting about different ideas. Already, I valued her opinion above anyone else's when it came to the center.

"Hiring Vern is your first decision as assistant director, Devo, and you'll get your first paycheck at the end of next week. You shouldn't have to wait for me. I'll get payroll set up tomorrow morning."

"Really?"

"Really. I should've done it already. I apologize that it's taken me this long."

"No worries," she said. "Now, we didn't discuss numbers, but I'm thinkin' seventy bucks an hour will suffice."

I snorted and sputtered, and she tugged me back toward Vern. "Just pullin' your leg. Pay me whatever you think is fair. I don't even know how much an assistant director makes, but I bet it's better than my last job at Chick-a-Lot in Jackson paid."

"Chick-a-Lot?"

"Don't ask. And do not *ever* eat there." When we were both standing in front of Vern, she said, "Okay, Vern, there's a job for you here if you're willin' to do whatever's necessary. There's gonna be a lot of manual labor and errands we'll need you to run, and you might have to make phone calls. Does that sound like somethin' you wanna do?"

"Seriously?" Vern asked, his eyebrows creeping slowly up toward his receding hairline. He dragged his hands through his greasy hair. "I mean, yeah, I'll do anything. Wait. You guys ain't up to anything illegal here, are ya?"

"Vern," Devo said, rolling her eyes, "this is a community center. Of course we're not doin' anything illegal."

"Oh, well, it's just that I heard about..." He motioned toward me.

Now my eyebrows were rising. "You heard about me? About the man I... the man? In Nevada?"

"Yeah," Vern said, and my stomach dropped. Panic filled me. I didn't want these people to know what I'd done—or what I'd attempted to do but couldn't quite pull off. *Right*. I'd landed myself in the hospital for weeks with a broken wrist and orbital bone, and a serious concussion that had kept me unconscious for several days. There was no way I could've killed anyone.

I wasn't sure which part embarrassed me more—that I'd gone after and attempted to kill a man or that I'd failed. I supposed, though, if Vern knew about the attempted murder, it meant that the rest of Wisper did too. Did Brady? He'd never said anything.

Oh, but last night he said, "If you'd tried to kill someone to protect me, I'd love you even harder than before." I hadn't mentioned trying to protect Aislinn, so maybe he already knew.

Taking a deep breath, I lifted my shoulders, trying to remember who the old Theo was and trying to show his confidence. "I'm not sure what you've heard, but I can assure you, Vern, that your job here would not require you to do anything illegal. The man you're referring to was evil, and he was trying to hurt my sister. That's the only defense I have for my actions, but if you'll give me a chance, I'll show you I'm not a bad guy."

"Really?" Millie said, surprised. "You're gonna give him a job? Just like that? He just told you he got fired."

"Yeah," Devo said, "but I got one of my feelin's."

"It's your silver," Millie said, shaking her head. "I gotta go. Oscar, you coming?"

"Yeah," he said. "Sorry, Devo. I've gotta take my mom grocery shoppin'. Her car died this mornin', but I'll come back this weekend and help y'all with whatever, okay?"

"Thanks," Devo said. "I'll call you later, Mills, okay?"

"Sounds good," Millie said, and she and Oscar left.

Vern stared after Millie till the door cut off his view, and when they were gone, he turned back to us and said, "So, when do I start? You guys offerin' insurance? I usually need that."

Devo and I looked at each other. We both shrugged. She asked, "Do you not want the job if there's no insurance?"

"Uh, well, yeah, I still want the job."

"That's what I thought. And since it's just us here, you can bite my ass if you think I'm buyin' that you've never done anything illegal before. It's practically tattooed across your forehead—'Got a bad idea? I'm your guy!'" She snorted. "Okay, Vern. You're hired, and your first task is…" We both looked around the room kind of aimlessly. "Well, we'll get back to you on that."

Vern nodded. "Cool, cool. I'll just hang out here till y'all think of somethin'."

# CHAPTER TEN

## BRADY

"YOU ALMOST LOST the Burroughs account? Brady! And you're just tellin' me this now?"

I winced when the shrill sound of my mom's voice made my head threaten to explode.

"Oh, son." She hung her head. She was halfway hidden behind a pile of case files in her office, but she pushed them away and lowered her forehead to the desk. Since she didn't need to be in court today, she'd braided her hair, one on each side of her head, and they thunked against the desk. "We really need that account. What happened? What did you do?"

"What did *I* do? Why do you automatically assume I fucked up?"

She looked up. "Watch your language."

"I know you know I'm almost thirty years old, Mom. You did give birth to me." Plopping down into the chair across from her, I sighed. "It was some weird stroke of luck that he chose me in the first place. I keep thinkin' it's not gonna last. You know how big-time he is. He'll probably get bored, move out of Wisper. Maybe he'll go back to bein' the big corporate guy." Even as I said it, I knew it wouldn't happen. I wasn't sure why I was admitting to my mom that I'd almost lost the account—wait. Why *was* I doing that? My sex life was the last thing she needed to know about. Besides, she seemed overwhelmed enough as it was.

"Well, whatever you did to save his business, thank you."

"Mmhm." That was as far as I was going with that.

"I had a dream about him. It would've confused me if he'd fired you." She leaned back in her chair and pulled a rope of red licorice from her desk drawer, chomping off a big bite. "It's just that I don't know what we're gonna do. Mr. Burroughs's retainer is money we count on every month. All these drunk drivin' and bar fight cases don't pay, if those idiots pay their bills at all." She groaned. "I'm so tired of 'em. It feels like the more I work, the less money we make. I'm not doin' anything meaningful, and I just wanna be home with your dad, you know? I guess I've gotten used to the financial security Mr. Burroughs provides, but even with his money, it's not enough, and this new medication they gave Dad is really expensive. I don't know how—" She clicked her tongue and tossed the rest of her candy in the garbage can under her desk. Sitting up straight, she laid her hands flat out on her desk, the Mrs. Glass-Half-Full in her coming out. "You know what? We'll figure it out. We'll manage. We always do. I'm sorry I was hard on you. I was just surprised, but you've been a godsend to me, bunny. Thank you. The last three years would've gone a lot differently if you hadn't been here to help me."

"Gene Owens just hired me to work on a land dispute he's havin' with Cody Baxter. That'll help."

"Cody Baxter? Isn't that Albert Baxter's grandson? I didn't realize he'd moved here."

"Yeah. I guess he moved in after Albert passed and left

the property to him. Anyway, he and Gene are arguin' over property lines and water rights. It seems like a mess."

"Yeah," Mom said, "but you'll have that sorted quickly, I'm sure. Won't amount to many billable hours."

"No, you're probably right, but maybe it'll bring in more new business. We're doin' better than we were. The problem is, we need to charge more, but the farmers can't afford more, so…" I threw my hands up. "I dunno, Mom. I'll try harder." I didn't know what else to say.

"Oh, honey, you're already tryin' harder, and I appreciate it more than I can say. You know," she said, her eyes drifting to the side as she thought, "my dream was clear. Mr. Burroughs was lost, but a horse came to him in the night to guide him. I saw his struggles comin' to an end." She raised an eyebrow at me.

"You and your dreams." I rolled my eyes. *Ow.* My hangover was rearing its ugly head again. I would *never* tell her I'd been dreaming about Theo too. Last night, while I'd slept in his arms, I dreamt that he was standing on a really tall sand dune, and man-sized ants were poking holes in it. Theo was starting to sink, but an air balloon was waiting for me at the bottom of the hill, and all I had to do was step into it. I could've floated up to save him, but I didn't. I just stood there.

Clearly, my mom's dreams were much more elegant than mine.

A funny little smirk formed on her face. "Is there more to this than you're tellin' me?"

"What? What else could there be?" I stood, almost jumping out of the chair. "Well, I better get back to work on Gene's case. I've got a fair bit of research to do." Grabbing my satchel from the floor, I turned, trying to escape before she could see the truth in my eyes.

When she stood, I heard her chair scrape against the tile floor. "Bunny?"

"Gotta go, Mama," I called behind me. "We ain't gonna change the world sittin' here thinkin' on it. Isn't that what you always say?"

She snorted. "Change the world. Right. One idiot at a time."

---

WHEN I WALKED into the Wisper library after downing a gallon of water and three power bars, a young woman greeted me—or maybe it was more like she acknowledged my presence, kind of. She was sitting on top of the checkout desk, her legs crossed in front of her and her nose in a book.

"'S'up?"

"Hi, where's Adalaide?"

"She retired," the young woman said, flipping her long blue hair away from her face. It fell back over her shoulder, so she set her book in her lap and grabbed the length of it like she was grabbing an aggressive snake, then twisted it into a messy pile on the top of her head and stuck a pencil through it.

"Retired?"

"Yeah. You know, when you stop working after a long career of doing the same shit, day in and day out? You get old, or bored, or, I dunno, just give up? In Addi's case, she had a mild heart attack."

"Oh. I'm so sorry. I hadn't heard. Is she gonna be okay?"

"I think so, but she is eighty-two, so now she gets to live out the rest of her life watching Netflix and eating carrot sticks or oat bran." She peered at me over her pink cat-eye glasses. "Who are you?"

"Brady. So wait, are you the new librarian?"

"Yup."

"But you look really young. I mean, I don't mean to be rude, but are you qualified?"

"Qualified? To sit here in utter silence every day when the hordes of people *don't* come to check out books?"

I laughed. "It's quiet now, but it does get busy. It may be a tiny library in a small town, but we've got some book clubs, and Addi reads to the kids on Wednesday evenin's and Saturdays. We even have our very own romance author here in Wisper. She comes in when she puts out a new book and does a readin'."

"Who?" she asked, eyes narrowed in disbelief.

"Her name's Juneau Moonlight."

"Nuh uh. Really? I know her stuff. Huh. Well, maybe I underestimated this place a little. And yes, I am qualified. I'm obsessed with books. I majored in Library Sciences and just finished my master's. You're right that I look young though. It's a curse." She smirked and flashed sarcastic duck lips, if such a thing existed. "My grandpa is Jessup Anderson. He used to run the local paper."

"Oh yeah, old man Jessup. I know him."

"Of course you do. Who doesn't in this town? Anyway, he called and said Wisper needed a librarian. I didn't have any plans after I finished school, and I'm always down to help my gramps, so here I am."

"Cool, 'cause I might need your assistance with some research. You know, you still haven't told me your name?"

"Right." She hopped off the counter and extended her hand. "Sam."

"Sam?" I asked. "Just Sam?"

"Sam Russo. If you want to get technical, it's Samantha, but only my gramps calls me that, so don't get any ideas. And now that we're introduced and I am completely bored, what can I help you with? What kind of research are you conducting?"

"I've been retained for a water rights case, but I don't have experience with those, so…"

"You're a lawyer?"

"Yeah."

"Hm. Water rights? You're better off over at the County Clerk's office in Jackson. They'll have all that info."

"I know, but I wanted some background. You know, like how property lines were drawn several generations ago, how they divvied things up. Who got what and how did that effect water rights."

"Okay." Sam nodded and paused. "Good thinking. Then you'll be better able to understand what you're looking at when you get your hands on current property maps and water right distribution."

"Exactly."

"All right. Cool. You can set up at the big table by the window, and I'll pull some things to get you started."

"Thanks," I said, pulling my laptop from my satchel, but when I tried connecting to the Wi-Fi, it told me I had the wrong password. "Uh, Sam?"

"Yeah?" she called from somewhere behind the stacks.

"Did you change the Wi-Fi password?"

"Oh yeah, sorry. Addi had it set to some ridiculously long alpha-numeric code, but I think mine'll be a little easier to remember. It's 'Thistowniscraycray313'. First letter is capitalized, but the rest are lower case."

I snorted.

"What? It's true."

"You've been here, what, five minutes?"

"Yeah, so?" she said, carrying a pile of books to the table.

She plopped them down and pulled a chair out and sat. "I spent summers here as a kid though. Did you grow up here?"

"I did. I left for school, but I moved back a few years ago."

"Really? Why?" She said it like she couldn't believe anyone would come back to Wisper willingly.

"It's a long story. Anyway," I said, thumbing over the books she'd pulled for me. "I think these are a good start. Thanks."

"No problem. How come you don't just look this stuff up online?"

"I like books too. And I s'pose the library relaxes me."

"Okay," she said. "I totally get you. If you need me, just yell. I think I'm going to do some rearranging. There's a reading corner for kids, but if romance is big around here, then we should have a designated space for that too. This place is big enough, and we have that back room. Doesn't look to me like Addi was using it for anything special. Romance readers might like a bit of privacy to discuss certain scenes from their books, know what I mean?"

"I've never read one, but I can imagine."

"No? Dude, you're missing out."

"I'll take your word for it."

Sam shrugged and disappeared for a while. I could hear her moving furniture, and I offered to help, but she assured me she was fine and that I should keep working, so I did. She made her way back out to the main room after an hour or so, and I assumed she was at the desk behind me.

"Hey, Sam? I think I'm done for today. I'm gonna check this book out." I held a book published in 1972 called *Wyoming Water Rights 101* up in the air, but Sam didn't reply. "Where'd you go?"

When I found her, she was on her back under an old,

solid-wood desk in the back room, covered in dust and cobwebs.

"Sam?"

"Sorry, did you say something?"

"What're you doin' down there?"

"I found these old articles from my grandpa's paper, like from the 1960s. Did you know there used to be a club or a group here called the Mountain Misses? They were like a society group, I think, but there was some big scandal, and they disbanded. I found this folder under a pile of old papers, but look…"

She scooted out from under the desk and sat, crossing her legs like a kid, grabbing a manila folder from the floor. When she opened it, I saw yellowed newspaper clippings, but half the words on the top page had been blacked out, and the rest of the papers were in such poor condition, they were barely legible.

"What the hell?" she said. "Why would someone do that?"

"Maybe it was confidential?"

She stood, swatting the dust off her knees, but her long, black skirt was covered in it, so it didn't make much of a difference.

"But that doesn't explain why I found you sprawled out on the floor."

"Another article fell behind the desk," she said, pushing her glasses up the bridge of her nose with her index finger. "But I couldn't reach it."

"Here. Let me."

Sam stepped aside, and I pulled with my hands on either side of the desk, but it only moved half an inch.

"Bend your knees," she scolded.

I flashed her a look of annoyance. "I am." I pulled harder,

but still, the desk didn't move.

"Stop before you get a hernia. It must be bolted into place." She climbed on the desk, then lay on it, trying to see behind it. "Yep. There's a strap attached to the wall and the back of the desk. Grab those scissors on the shelf behind you."

"Here," I said, handing her the large metal scissors. "Careful, those things look sharp enough to perform surgery."

"Ha ha." Angling the scissors behind the desk, she snipped and I pulled, and the desk detached from the wall and slid toward me, and Sam landed on her ass on the floor with the scissors still in one hand. "Jeez! Watch what you're doing!"

I crossed my arms over my chest. "That's what you get for thinkin' I wasn't strong enough to move the desk."

"I never said that."

"No, but you were thinkin' it."

She smiled, holding her hand out, and I took it and pulled her to her feet. It was weird how easy she was to be around. Somehow, she reminded me of Bonnie, and it felt like I'd always known her.

"Here's the article. It's another one about the Mountain Misses. This one says, 'Scandal on Main Street—Mountain Misses President Resigns,' but look. This one's been redacted too. Seriously, what the hell? Who would go to all the trouble to do this? It's not like we can't just go look it up online."

Pulling my phone from my pocket, I searched for the *Wisper Gazette's* website, but all I could find was the "this webpage cannot be reached" message. "Your granddad must've shut the website down when he closed the paper, or he just didn't pay the bill."

"Okay, but it's gotta be online somewhere. Google it."

"Hold your horses. I am." But I found nothing. I shook

my head, and Sam frowned. "Microfiche?"

"Yeah, c'mon." She tugged on my arm, and I followed her down the hall to the "Resource Center," but it was really just a small, closet-sized room with a bare lightbulb hanging from the ceiling.

"What's so important about this?"

"It's not important. It's just that when somebody tells me I can't do something or can't have something, well, it's pretty much like giving heroin-strength catnip to a lion. Me being the junkie lion."

"That's a terrible analogy."

"Are you in a hurry or something?"

"No, I guess not." I mean, I did have a job to do, but researching more about water rights wasn't the most exciting thing I could think of. Plus, my headache was finally starting to ease, and reading more would only bring it front and center again.

"Okay, then shut up and grab that box." Sam pointed to a shelving unit covering the far wall full of shoebox-sized containers. "The one that says '1960 to 1969.'"

"Got it," I said, standing on my toes to reach the box. "Just this one box for ten years of newspaper articles?"

"Yeah, well, small town and all that. Back then, you had to send out anything you wanted to be scanned onto microfilm. Most newspapers did it regularly, but smaller newspapers had to save up and only did it every once in a while. If I know my grandpa, he probably never did, and my guess is this little library never had much of a budget, so I'm guessing it wasn't a huge priority. Who knows how much was ever even scanned. It's a shot in the dark, but I'm invested now."

"Invested? In what? It's just small-town gossip. You'll get used to that the longer you're here. It's a livin', evolvin' thing. Trust me."

"Whatever. I need something to occupy my time."

"You don't have a boyfriend? Or girlfriend?"

"Nope. Not anymore."

"There's some gossip right there," I said, lifting the box's lid.

"Ha. No. It's a dead-end story. Girl meets boy, boy acts like a douchebag, girl skedaddles."

"When was that?"

She puffed up her cheeks, her eyes drifting to the side while she thought, and then she exhaled a rushing of air, making her lips vibrate like a horse. "About a year ago, I guess. I didn't realize it had been that long till I just said it out loud. Honestly, the jerk isn't worth the effort it took to remember when we broke up. He was yet another blip on the radar of my failed love life." She shrugged. "What about you? You have a girlfriend?"

"'Failed love life'? What are you, twenty-six years old? There's still time. And nope, no girlfriend. I'm gay, but no boyfriend either."

"How come? You're attractive," she said, perusing the shelves, poking at a box or file folder here and there. She said it like it was the only attribute someone needed in order to find love.

"Um, thanks? This box is full of old receipts, by the way," I said, setting it on a shelf. "But it's what I've chosen. I mean, I'm not celibate or anything, but a relationship just really isn't a good idea for me right now."

"Probably aren't a lot of gay guys around here, anyway."

"Not many. I bet there's a few more who don't want anyone to know they're gay, but it wouldn't matter if the whole town was a daily Pride parade. My dad's sick, and I came home to help my mom take care of him. That's what I'm focused on."

"I'm sorry, Brady. That's gotta be hard. Can I ask what's wrong with him?"

"Yeah," I said, and I sighed, feeling like the air leaving my body was a weight. "It's really hard. He has ALS." I wasn't sure why I was bringing it up with this weird woman I'd just met, but there was warmth in her eyes, and I just couldn't shake the feeling that we'd known each other in another life. Stepping backward, I slumped into an old folding chair I'd seen when we entered the room. "Sometimes, it's too hard, you know? Sometimes, I don't think I can do it for one more day. Shit, one more minute sometimes."

"That's a lot of 'sometimes.' What about the other times?"

"Huh?"

"I know it's hard, and I bet there are times when you wish you could drive off into the sunset with a daiquiri in one hand and an Italian sub in the other, but what about the times that aren't so bad? Is there anything good about taking care of your dad?"

"That's a weird visual, but of course," I said, feeling like a grade-A jerk for complaining so much. "Yeah, I mean, I get to spend a lotta time with him, and our relationship now has a certain closeness it's never had before. Which is weird since he can't speak anymore, but maybe he doesn't have to. And it's brought me closer to my sister. We were kinda close as kids, but since we became adults and went off to live our lives, we've grown apart. She lives in Texas, and I was in Boise till my dad got sick, but we're both back in Wisper to help my mom. So that's nice."

"You're lucky. I'm an only child. I've always wanted a brother, mostly so I could boss him around." She smirked. "I'm just kidding. But that's cool. Plus, I bet having your sister here helps so it's not all on you."

"She does help, yeah. She's eight months pregnant, so there's a lot she can't do for my dad, but just her bein' in the same room with him does wonders for his spirit. And she stays with him when my mom and I are workin'.'"

"See? Already, you look lighter. You just needed a reminder. So—and just bear with me here—if you *were* dating, is there anyone you'd have your eye on?" She was grinning like she already knew. How was that possible?

I think I blushed. "N-not really. I mean no. No." I straightened. "No, there's no one."

One slow nod and a sly smile was all it took to convince me she knew I was lying.

Spinning in a circle on one foot, I tried to escape. "I gotta go."

Sam laughed, following me out to the main room. "Okay, but come back. You're the only person I know in this town beside my gramps, and he's in Florida for two more weeks. His house is my party pad every night. I've watched so many episodes of *The Price is Right* that I lost count. But if you have a pet, seriously, you should definitely spay and neuter."

I laughed, grabbing my satchel and facing her, hoping she wouldn't pry any further. If she asked again, I might've spilled everything, like how Theo was all I could think about. His face, his body, his voice. His shoulders. And I couldn't help wondering if maybe we *could* have something. A year wasn't that long. Was it?

"You like coffee?" I asked.

"Who doesn't? But I like green tea lattes better."

Fishing a business card out of my wallet, I handed it to her. "My cell number's on there. Text me what you usually order, and I'll bring some with me tomorrow."

"Dope. Thanks. I hope your dad's having a good day today, but if not, I'm a good listener. Just saying."

"Thanks, Sam. It was nice to meet you. I'll see you tomorrow."

But when I thought about why I was leaving the library—to check on my dad for the fiftieth time since I'd woken up on Theo's floor this morning—I realized there wasn't much hope for me and Theo anyway. He may've been getting his act together, but mine was still a shit show.

Sam's voice brought me out of my wallowing. "Do you want to come to the Duck & Bowl with me?"

"Duck & Bowl?"

"Yeah, it's this bowling alley off the highway, and they have baby ducks that you—"

Laughing, I said, "No, I know what it is, but why do you wanna go there? You like to bowl?" Doubt was making me laugh. I couldn't picture her without her long skirt and her shiny punk-rock boots, but Sam frowned.

"Well, no," she admitted. "I'm not the biggest bowler, but they have ducks, and they let you hold and pet them. Who doesn't want to do that?"

"Sure," I said. "I'll pet ducks with you, but I haven't been bowlin' since I was a kid."

"Me either. It'll be an adventure. Let's go tonight."

"Tonight? Oh, uh, lemme just make sure that's gonna work. My dad—"

"Brady, weren't you the one who just told me you needed to get out of the house sometimes? Your sister and mom will be there for your dad."

"Yeah. You're right, it's just… hard."

"I know, but I'm dying to do something fun, and I bet you are too." She shrugged. "The bowling alley's not that far, so if there's an emergency, you can be back home in a jiff. It's not a red-carpet event, but it's *something*. C'mon. Go with me?"

"Okay. Why not?"

# CHAPTER ELEVEN

BRADY

THE DUCK & Bowl really did have live ducks, and Sam was right. You could pet them. I hadn't been there in years, and the live-duck thing was new-ish. I had no clue what the owners were thinking, bringing live animals into a bowling alley. Thank God they weren't using them as pins, which had been my first disturbed thought when I'd heard about it. I suspected the ASPCA or PETA might have something to say about that, but the ducks made Sam happy, so there was that, at least. As soon as we got there, she went on a hunt for them, and I was about to follow, but I noticed Theo across the room, wearing bowling shoes and a bowling shirt that said, "The Teton County Quitters." An older man in a brown cowboy hat patted him on the back, and then he walked outside.

"Sam!" I called after her. "I forgot somethin' in my car. I'll be right back."

"'Kay. I'll be with the duckies."

When I got outside, I didn't see Theo, and I was just about to turn around to go back in, but I heard his voice. He was ending a phone call. "Okay, that sounds fine. You know the cost doesn't matter, Ace. You can have any dress you want, even if we have to fly to Tokyo to get it."

I rounded the corner of the building and smiled when I spotted him leaning against the wall. He looked happy to be talking to his sister.

When he saw me, he said, "I've got to go, but I'll see you tomorrow, and you can tell me all about it then."

He smiled at me, and my legs turned to jelly.

"Okay," he said again. "Good night." He hung up and tucked his phone into his back pocket, and when I watched him do it, I saw something next to his shoe on the ground.

"Is this yours?" I asked, bending to pick up— "Did you quit smokin'?"

I handed him the rectangular package of nicotine gum, and he shoved it into his shirt pocket quickly, like maybe he was a little embarrassed. "Yes. I never really liked it. It was just something I did when I drank."

"Good, 'cause it tasted like shit when I—"

His eyebrows popped up. "When you kissed me?"

"Yeah," I said, and I smiled, twisting my lips, trying to hide it.

"Taste me now. See if it's different."

I breathed, "Shit." He had no idea what he was asking. If I kissed him again, all bets—and deals—were off.

Someone got out of their car in the parking lot, and they locked it with a loud *beep*.

I cleared my throat. "Remember our deal?"

"Unfortunately." His eyes softened as they settled on my mouth, and the look on his face was… sultry. It was the only description I could think of.

Laughing softly, I hid my hands in my front pockets. If I hadn't, there was no way I would've been able to stop myself from grabbing him. As it was, I couldn't look away from his lips, and when he licked them, I closed my eyes, trying to remember the taste of his skin.

"If you're determined to stick to our deal," he said, "we'd better go back inside. I won't be held responsible for what I do to you if we don't. There's a clause in my retainer contract."

I opened my eyes. "No, there's not."

"Well, there should be. Since you're my lawyer, I'm demanding you put it in."

"Oh," I breathed. "I'll put it in, alright."

Now he was laughing, dragging me back inside by my hand before things took a turn, but I stopped him before he opened the door.

"I'm sorry about last night. I didn't mean to— I wasn't thinkin' straight. I'm sorry if I put you in an uncomfortable position."

He turned back to me and smiled so softly. "It's okay."

Charlie Hutchins was there when we made our way back to the lanes. He and my dad were on a league together when I was in high school, so I wasn't surprised to see him there. Charlie was in AA too. I remembered him and my dad working together years ago. I looked at the other people in Theo's party. Fred Winston was an old client, and I knew he'd been a heavy drinker. It was an AA league. *Oh, right. The Quitters. Good one.*

"Brady Douglas?" Charlie said, and he cuffed my shoulder. "Hey, kid. How's your ol' man?"

Just like that, my teasing mood was gone. "Hi, Charlie. He's uh… He's—"

Theo interrupted. I'd saved him from a hard conversation once, so maybe he was trying to repay the favor. "Charlie, how's my form?" He picked up a ball and pretty much threw it down the aisle. It hit zero pins, bounced off the gutter track, and nearly jumped into the next lane.

"Good Lord," Charlie said. "What form? Did you even watch the YouTube videos I sent you?"

Theo winced. "No."

The return spit the ball back out. Theo lifted it, holding it with both hands, and I smiled when Charlie stomped toward Theo and snatched the ball from his hands.

"Gimme the damn ball. You're liable to knock somebody out with that thing."

"Wait!" I said. "You haven't seen my form yet, Charlie." I held my hands out, and Charlie walked over and dropped the ball into them. "Oof."

He arched an eyebrow.

"Okay, now watch," I said, and I lifted up onto my tiptoes, taking quick little steps. "I call this the Fred Flintstone." Inserting my fingers and thumb into the holes, I swung my arm back and pulled it forward, sweeping my leg back and releasing the ball in just the right spot. It had been a while, but I'd never forget the technique. My dad bringing me to the bowling alley in pre-duck times to teach me were some of my best memories. The ball hit its mark, slightly to the left of the front pin, and the rest came tumbling down behind it. The loud clacking sound made me smile, and when I looked at Theo, he was smiling too.

Charlie rolled his eyes. "I see you haven't forgotten what you're doin', but that was shit form, kid." He picked his custom ball up out of his bowling bag. "Watch me," he told Theo.

Theo backed up, and when we were side by side, I bumped him with my elbow.

"Alright," Charlie said. "See how I'm anglin' my body before I release the ball?"

"Mmhm. Yes, I see it," Theo said, but he was turned, looking at me. He bumped me back.

"Okay, now watch what I do when I release the ball. See how I sweep my leg back, bend my knee, and my arm follows the ball after I let go?"

"Yes," Theo said, but Charlie caught on that Theo wasn't really watching him, so he turned just as his ball hit a strike.

"How do you two know each other?" he asked.

"Oh," I said. "I'm his lawyer."

We heard squealing, and we turned in the direction of Sam's voice. Theo laughed, and Charlie rolled his eyes again. "Go," he said, like we were his kids and we wanted to play in the arcade instead of bowling with him. He mumbled, "I think I'm gonna get vetoed if I try to vote you into the league."

We hurried over, and when we found her, Sam was lying in a blue plastic kiddie pool, with tiny, fluffy baby ducks all over her. Some were pecking at her blue hair. One pooped on her skirt, and the rest were trying to climb up. They slid and toppled over but got back up and tried again. Sam was giggling and cooing to the ducklings, trying to kiss them when they waddled by her face.

"I'm never leaving," she said. "How are you not here every day?"

Theo and I laughed, and I introduced him. "Sam, this is Theo. He's, uh, my client, and… a friend."

"Nice to meet you," she said from under more ducks. "I'd get up, but I don't want to." But she sat up, and ducks fell by her waist. "Oh, babies, I'm sorry. Are you okay?" She collected them in her arms and looked at us. "Is he the reason you needed to run out to your car?"

"What? That's—no. What?"

She smiled and winked at Theo, and I could feel him blushing beside me. I gave her a dirty look, and she shrugged.

"It's nice to meet you, Sam," Theo said. "I'd better get back. Technically, I'm in bowling school. My teacher might give me detention if I blow him off."

The word "blow" had me blushing too.

"I'll talk to you later," Theo said, and I nodded.

"Bye." I couldn't help the sigh that came out of my mouth.

"Bye," he whispered, giving me the softest smile.

"Oh my God," Sam said when Theo was back with Charlie, practicing his form.

I knew I was staring, but I didn't want to stop looking at him—at his long legs, at the hint of his ass I could see beneath his jeans and his too-large bowling shirt. The boxy shape hid his shoulders, which was a damn shame. It was the last thing I would've imagined him wearing. He'd probably borrowed it from Charlie or one of the other Quitters. "What?"

"Can you tear your eyes away, or would that kill you?"

"Funny," I said, glaring at her when I finally turned. I sat on the floor outside the kiddie pool, and she handed me four ducklings. "They really are cute, but aren't they supposed to be outside?"

"Yes. Jacinda—that's the owner's daughter—she said they're doing some work on the enclosure outside, getting it ready for colder weather, so they're keeping the littlest babies inside for now. I think it must be some kind of health code violation, but I'm not going to turn them in. Are you, Mr. Lawyer?"

"Nah," I said, holding a duck up in front of my face. It cheeped and tried to wiggle out of my hand, so I set it back in the pool along with his brothers and sisters. "Are we gonna bowl or what?"

"You just want to so you can stare at your boyfriend some more."

I pursed my lips but then smiled. "He's not my boyfriend."

"Is that because he's your client?"

"It's one of the reasons."

"Why else?"

"My dad, for one. And he's got stuff goin' on in his life too. It's just not the right time."

"Hm," she said, nuzzling a duck. "How can loving someone be wrong? When's the right time? If you wait till everything in your lives are good, then you can't really judge how you'll get along when times are hard."

Huh. She had a point.

"Do you think I could keep ducks at the library?"

"Uh, sure? If there's such a thing as a duck diaper. Otherwise, your books are gonna be covered in duck poo."

"Oh, right. Yuck."

# CHAPTER TWELVE

## THEO

"YOU DON'T DRIVE?" I asked Vern the next afternoon as I slid my truck into gear. It was a stick shift, and I still wasn't quite used to driving it, so we lurched forward a bit. I couldn't stop thinking about the smile on Brady's face when he elbowed me playfully at the bowling alley. God, I'd wanted to kiss him.

"Yeah, I can drive," Vern said, slamming back against the passenger seat. Aislinn was between us, and she was gripping my arm so tightly that I would've been surprised if it didn't go numb. "You're probably used to somebody drivin' you, huh? That why you can't drive this rig?"

Well, that cemented my suspicions about what Vern thought of me, but it wasn't untrue. "This is my first manual vehicle, so I'm still getting the hang of it, but we used to have a driver, yes." I didn't want to think about Tim. I tried hard not to, and in fact, it had been weeks since he'd crossed my mind. I still thought about wanting to kill the man who'd murdered him though. I thought about *him* every day. "But I haven't had a car for a long time. Until I bought this truck, I hadn't bought a car in, I don't know, maybe five years? Right, Ace?"

"How should I know?" She held my arm tighter. "I will say, I don't remember you being this bad of a driver. But no, I don't remember your cars. You were always getting a new one, but they were all the same to me."

"That's fair," I said. "I'm surprised you don't have a truck, though, Vern. I thought everybody around here had a RAM or a Ford."

He looked out the window. "I had one—a lifted F150. My sweet Tallulah. She was black as night with sterling rims—but I lost my job and couldn't make the payments. And then… Well, I totaled my mama's car in an accident."

"Oh, I'm so sorry. Were you injured?"

He snapped his seatbelt into place. "Yeah, broke my arm. That was a couple years ago."

"You and your mother haven't had transportation for two years?"

"Hey, you don't have to be a dick about it." To Aislinn he said, "Sorry, ma'am."

Ace scooted closer to me. I was getting the impression she wasn't Vern's biggest fan, but I thought, like everyone else, maybe she just needed to give him a chance. He wasn't so bad.

"Oh no, Vern. I'm sorry. I just meant—that sucks, is what I meant. That's all."

Crossing his arms, he angled himself away from us. He was obviously self-conscious about the subject. "Either way, it feels like you're lookin' down on me."

"No, Vern. Not at all." *Ah, damn it.* That wasn't what I'd meant at all. "Look, I have no room to judge you. I have a drinking problem. I haven't been driving myself because I was too inebriated most of the time."

"You're an alcoholic?"

"*You* don't have to be so rude," my sister said, sticking up for me.

"It's okay, Ace. I don't think Vern meant anything by it. But yes. I am an alcoholic." I was becoming more sure of the fact every day. Each morning I woke up, wanting to go straight to the liquor store, but I hadn't, not in weeks, but the impulse was still there, and my body still wanted it. I wondered if that part would ever ease, but the shaking and sweating had stopped, and the body aches were gone. "I'm in recovery."

"Hm." He turned away from his window, angling his body toward me this time, and his knee bumped against Aislinn's. "You go to AA?"

She winced, but I didn't think he noticed. He was watching my face carefully as I answered.

"I do. I just started going, actually."

He moved, turning to face forward and relaxing a little. Ace relaxed, too, and she squeezed my arm, letting me know she was proud of me.

"That's cool," Vern said. "My old daddy was a drunk. He used to go to AA, but it never did him any good."

When I was confident enough that I wouldn't crash the truck, I released the death grip I had on the gear shift and took a drink from my Cade Ranch water bottle, wiping my mouth with my sleeve. "Oh, well, I don't really know a lot about it yet. I mean, I've been doing some reading, but I'm still pretty new to the program."

"So you're a rich, drunk homo?"

I sputtered, and water sprayed the inside of my windshield.

"Oh my God," Ace said.

"Sorry. Is that rude? I mean, I was just statin' facts."

"Uh," I hedged, "well, I suppose that is all true, yes."

"What's it like bein' rich?"

I laughed. "Wow, Vern. You're really going for gold, aren't you?"

My sister scoffed, and it reminded me of when she was a teenager. "What am I even doing in this truck?"

I eased off the gas and downshifted into third as we took the exit into Jackson, then patted her leg. "You're hanging out with your brother."

"It's cool," Vern said. "I was kinda wonderin' the same thing. Anyway, you said you was a good dude. I figured that'd mean you'd tell me the truth if I asked. So, I'm askin'."

"You're right, I did say that, and I said if you gave me a chance, I'd prove it to you. That starts with honesty." I took another swig, realizing that for the first time in a long time, I wasn't wishing it was something other than water in my reusable tumbler. When Evvie Cade had given it to me a year ago, I'd thought, *I wonder how much booze I can fit in here.* I was ashamed of how far I'd fallen, and this conversation with Vern made me feel every inch of the depth, but in a way, I was glad he was curious. Making real connections with people was important to my sobriety.

We pulled into the garden center parking lot in Jackson, and I parked. "Being rich is great." It wasn't an easy question to answer, but I was trying to figure out a way to sum it up for Vern. "It's nice to not have to worry how you're going to pay your bills, though we've never had that problem, so I'm only guessing." Vern cocked his head, looking at me like I was from another planet. "But it can also be difficult to navigate. I grew up never knowing if someone wanted to be my friend because they wanted something from me, or if they really, truly liked me as a person. When I was young, I suppose I didn't really care. But after our parents died and all that money became my responsibility, it also became my burden sometimes."

"I felt the same way," Ace said.

Vern barked a laugh. "Well, boo-fuckin'-hoo."

"Are you—what?"

"You sound like a couple of whiny assholes," Vern said. "Sorry, ma'am." He tipped his hat to Aislinn, but he knew she couldn't see him.

I tried not to let his comment sting, but it bristled, settling into my thoughts like a splinter under a fingernail.

"Don't get me wrong," he said. "I think I understand. I can't for the life of me imagine what the fuck you're talkin' about, but I think I can understand. But most people 'round here struggle for money all their lives, so I wouldn't go 'round bellyachin' about your rich-guy problems. You won't get much sympathy is all I'm sayin'."

"You asked!"

"I might be sorry I did."

"How about we change the subject then?"

"Great idea," Ace said.

"Good plan," Vern agreed, lowering the brim of his red-white-and-blue trucker hat to shade his eyes from the bright fall sun while he looked up at the Gabby's Home and Garden sign. "Why we here?"

I took a breath, trying to brush his comment under my metaphorical rug. "You know the two grassy areas in front of the center, between the building and the sidewalk?"

"Yeah."

"They aren't big enough to be utilized for anything, so I thought we could remove the grass and plant some flowers and bushes, maybe lay some mulch."

Vern looked at me, his mouth turned down in a frown. "You know a lot about landscapin'?"

Ace snorted, and I elbowed her.

"Ow!"

"Serves you right," I said. This was new for us. She and I hadn't been silly with each other like this since we were little.

"No, Vern," I said, offering my sister my arm. She took it, and we followed Vern toward the store's entrance. "I know absolutely nothing about landscaping, but I remembered you talking to Millie about flowers the other day, so I thought you might know."

"Hmph. Millie."

"What about her? Millie's sweet," I said, but the scowl on his face told me he might not agree.

"No, she ain't." He scoffed. "And she hates my guts. That's for sure."

"I'm no expert on women—"

"'Cause you're a homo?" He took his hat off, pulling his long hair out the back. It fell down past his shoulders in thin strands. No one could ever accuse Vern of not having his own style. It wasn't a style anyone else might emulate, but it was a style, nonetheless.

"Uh, yeah. You know, you really shouldn't use that word. Just say gay."

He pursed his lips. "I don't really like either word."

"Well, luckily, gay people probably don't care that you don't like the word gay. But still, it's rude to call people homos. It's offensive."

"Oh." He looked at me. "Really?"

Ace couldn't help herself; she laughed out loud.

"Yes," I said, shaking my head in disbelief. Was he really that oblivious?

He winced, the side of his mouth curving up into a guilty smile at the same time. "Sorry."

"Anyway," I said, watching Vern pull a shopping cart out

of the line of them parked next to the garden center's automatic doors, and we entered the store. It smelled like wet dirt. "As I was saying, I don't know a lot about women or why they do the things they do, but I don't think Millie hates you."

He looked at his tan work boots, which were so old and worn, there were holes starting along the sides. "I ain't so sure about that. She talks to me like she thinks I'm stupid."

The defeated way he'd said it made me sad for him. "She doesn't."

"She does, and the thing is, I don't get her. I mean, why's a girl that pretty hot for other girls? She think she can't get a man or somethin'?"

"Vern, being a lesbian has absolutely nothing to do with whether a woman is attractive or not, and I can guarantee that it doesn't have *anything* to do with men—for any reason."

He stopped the cart in the middle of the first aisle inside the store and looked at me. "No?"

"No. Definitely not."

"How'd *you* reckon it? I mean, did you just know that about yourself, or was it somethin' you had to figure out?"

He seemed to be genuinely interested in my answer as he stepped closer to me to hear me better. He always kept a "safe" distance, though, like maybe he wasn't convinced I wouldn't try to stick my tongue in his mouth just because he was a man. And he didn't seem bothered by Ace standing between us. I was pretty sure Ace was bothered though. I wanted to, but I didn't laugh. She was a lot more social than she'd been after the accident, but getting to know other people besides the ones she worked with at Cade Ranch every day was good for her too. She still kept her sunglasses on around people she didn't know. It was her way of protecting herself. She didn't actually need them.

"I just knew." I shrugged. "People around me were

always talking about the opposite sex, but even as a teenager, I knew I was attracted to other boys. Never girls."

"Wasn't that weird for you?"

"No. How did you know you liked girls?"

"I mean, I just did. That was normal. You know?" He lowered his voice to a whisper, leaning in closer. "Can you close your ears, ma'am?"

"Vern, my name is Aislinn. I'm not a ma'am, and how do you propose I 'close my ears'?"

"Cover 'em, I meant," he said.

Ace sighed but let go of my arm and covered her ears with her hands. I couldn't see it behind the sunglasses, but I knew she was rolling her eyes.

When Vern was convinced she couldn't hear him, he whispered, "I got a stiffie when I thought about girls."

I didn't want to be rude, so I held in another laugh when I said, "Well, my experience was the same, only it was when I thought about men."

Vern shuddered, but he at least had manners enough to say, "Sorry."

"Can I turn my ears back on?"

"Yes, ma'am," he said, and Ace dropped her hands. She'd heard what he said but didn't react.

"I guess I'm kind of confused, though, Vern, because Millie isn't gay."

He perked up at that. "She ain't? But she hangs out with Devo."

I shook my head, watching how his face changed from a surprised expression to a tiny smile. "Millie and Devo are just friends. But she's a very beautiful woman."

Vern looked confused. "I thought you said you wasn't into girls."

"I'm not into women, no, but I can still appreciate Millie's beauty."

"She really is," he said slowly, and his voice took on a dreamy quality.

"So maybe you're frustrated because you think she's pretty, but you don't really know how to talk to her."

Scuffing his boot heel against a shelf full of ceramic flowerpots, he shrugged, and I winced, hoping he wouldn't knock it down. "That's not... Shoot, I guess maybe you're right about that."

I steadied the metal shelving unit with my hand when it wobbled. "So maybe you could approach her differently. Treat her with respect, like a friend instead of a woman you'd like to—"

"A woman I'd like to fuck?"

"Oh, jeez." My sister took my arm again, urging me to walk. She wanted out of this conversation. That was clear.

"Yes. I was trying not to be crass."

He nodded, biting the inside of his lip and thinking, like it was some huge existential question. "Okay, I'll give your way a try."

"Good."

He picked up a pair of suede work gloves, turning them over in his hand. "So, you never said how much you're payin' me."

"You're right. We haven't discussed that yet, which reminds me. I need to make a phone call. Give me a minute?"

"Sure thing."

"Ace, will you go with Vern for a few minutes?"

She squeaked, "Seriously?"

"Just a few minutes."

She sighed, a big, dramatic rush of air. "Okay."

"Why don't you go on ahead and check out the perennials. You can let me know which ones we should buy."

"You want *me* to pick?" Vern asked.

"Yes."

"Oh. Okay." He was surprised by that, but there was a bit of a pep in his step when he took Ace's arm rather brusquely and led her away. She went with him, but I knew I'd hear about it later. "We should probably get asters, ma'am, 'cause they'll come back real nice next year."

Pulling up Brady's name on my contact list, I called him, but he didn't answer, so I texted my question. *"Since you're still my lawyer, I was wondering if you might be able to help me with setting up payroll for my new employees. I've never done it before, and the taxes are different here than they are in Boston."*

When I saw the three dots preceding his reply, I felt like a sixteen-year-old asking a cute boy to go to the movies, but then I saw his answer, and the nervous ball in the middle of my chest fell further into my gut and landed with a splash. I felt nauseous. He answered immediately, so he'd seen my call but chose not to pick up. His reply said only, *"I'm not a tax attorney. Or an accountant."*

Right. Of course he wasn't. I knew that. Maybe I was looking for an excuse to see him again, but I really did need help.

A second text came through while I was contemplating how to reply. *"Call Barbara Belding at a company called Jackson Hole Account That."* He texted the phone number. *"She can help you with that sort of thing. Tell her I sent you."*

So he was determined to stick to our deal. I couldn't blame him, but he was still kind enough to offer help. Was he doing that to be genuinely nice? Or was it to get me to stop texting him?

I decided it was probably the latter and didn't text back anything other than "*Thank you*," and when I joined Ace and Vern by the asters and colorful fall mums, my face was hot and most likely red with embarrassment because I'd been shot down.

Again.

# CHAPTER THIRTEEN

BRADY

WHEN THEO TEXTED, I was in a meeting with a new potential client—a woman who'd heard about the work I'd done for Fran Morris over the summer and was hoping I could help her in a similar way—so I couldn't answer his call. He didn't text anything else, and I went over the conversation fifty times, feeling like an ass when I realized my responses sounded rude. I sat in my car after my meeting, staring at my phone and hoping those three dots would appear again, but they never did. *Shit.*

It occurred to me then that I could've used the opportunity to ask him about bringing Sam to the center to go through all the old papers in the attic. Maybe she could find more about the old Wisper society group. My new daily ritual was taking her favorite green tea latte to the library at lunch, and we'd talk while we both ate our packed lunches. She was obsessed with the articles she'd found, and some days, it was all she could talk about while she scoured the building looking for more, but listening to her go on and on was kind of comforting. It allowed me to escape the noise inside my head.

We hadn't found anything yet, though, and I usually only had a half hour to spare, and that was if I wasn't needed at home to help Bonnie. When I could, I spent hours reading through articles about the history of water rights and property distribution. It was enough to put me to sleep, but it was helping me understand my client's dispute with his neighbor. I'd spoken with the opposing council in the case, and Gene and I were set to meet with them at the beginning of the following week.

Tomorrow, though, we had a video call scheduled with the State Engineers office to make sure Gene's water permits were up to date. If you owned land in Wyoming that came with usable water bodies, even if you'd inherited the land and the rights, you still had to apply for a permit 'cause, technically, the state of Wyoming owned it all.

I had a feeling Gene's permits weren't up to date even though he swore up and down that they were. He wasn't the most organized business owner. Either way, we'd find out. And I was curious to meet his neighbor. Cody Baxter had been living next to Gene on the outskirts of Wisper for six months or so, but no one really knew him. From the gossip I'd heard, he was around my age, so it struck me as unusual that he'd be so reclusive. Everybody knew his granddad who'd lived here for years with no trouble.

Mr. Baxter had a small herd of goats, and Oly'd been out to his farm to treat them. She told me he was "cute," but that was the only piece of information I had about the guy till Gene called, freaking out 'cause his neighbor was demanding that he stay off his property and denying him use of the stream Gene had shared with Baxter's granddad.

"What're you reading?" Sam asked, and she dropped a stack of pastel-colored paperbacks onto my table. "I like this new style, by the way," she said, flicking my black button down's collar. "You look properly Western. Is that a bolo tie?"

"Yeah," I said, rolling the braided black leather between my fingers. It felt weird wearing jeans to work instead of suit pants, but there was a freedom to it too. "I'm changin' things up." I looked up. "What are those for?"

"For the library's Instagram page. Bookstack photos are really popular, especially with romance books, so I thought I'd make an account and start posting. I'd like to try TikTok, but it kind of scares me. What is that?" she asked again, picking up her sandwich, chewing, and pointing peanut butter in my direction.

"Uh, this is my client's deed, and I was lookin' over the deed to his previous neighbor's land. That guy passed away, but he and Gene had been sharin' water rights. It worked well for them, but his grandson won't hear of it, apparently. That's why I was hired."

She took a chug of her latte. "Isn't that pretty standard stuff? I mean, if the water is located on one guy's land, he gets the rights, right? I don't get how there can be a dispute."

"Well, the dispute is over land *and* water. This new guy says that the water is on his land and that the paperwork is wrong about the property boundaries. Gene says it isn't. Plus, water rights aren't so black and white. Hence, the lawyers." I pointed at my chest.

"Tricky, tricky," she said, her eyes flicking back and forth between me and the big front window. "Hey, by the way, do you know the name of that sheriff guy, the really big guy? He's older, I think. Built like a boulder?"

"Frank?"

"That's his name?" She pointed through the old, thick glass pane. "Look quickly, but don't let him see you!"

Sam backed up a few steps, like she was trying to fade

into the background, and I inched toward the window, looking out and seeing Frank trying to look in, his tan cowboy hat low over his eyes. The library was just an old, two-story house on Franklin Street, so the only thing between Frank on the sidewalk and the window was a row of bushes, but the sun was shining on the window, so I didn't think he could see in. He was a good-looking guy. Kind of scary, if you asked me. Sam was right—he was built like a boulder, the bulge of his packed muscles threatening to split his deputy's uniform in more than a few places. If you asked any other gay guy, they'd say he was a bear. He wasn't gay though. He used to be married to a woman who left him and took their dog.

"Yeah, that's Frank Sims. He's the sheriff's deputy. Why?"

When I turned around, Sam's face was as red as a strawberry. "No reason." She bit her lip, looking everywhere but at me. When I checked over my shoulder, Frank was climbing into his cruiser, and then he drove away. Was he returning books? I didn't figure the guy for a reader—he was more of a really tall deadly assassin, and his preference for not speaking didn't help—but he'd seemed pretty intent on the library.

"Why're you blushin'?"

"I'm not!" She turned abruptly, digging through a pile of books on the front desk.

"Sam, you okay?"

"Yes. Jeez, he comes here sometimes. I just didn't want to be rude by not knowing his name. You know, since he's an important person in the community. That's part of the librarian's job, to know the…" When my eyebrows began to climb toward the ceiling the longer she blabbed on and on about absolutely nothing, she said. "I mean, like, he's an elected official. Shouldn't I know his name? Why else would I ask?"

"He's actually not an elected official. Frank was appointed by Sheriff Michaels when he was elected. Frank only moved here a few years ago with his wife." She didn't say anything, and if my weird body-language detector was working properly, as it usually was, she was still embarrassed. "Sam? Am I missin' somethin'? Do you know Frank?"

"Nope. Never met the guy. He's been in here twice, and he didn't introduce himself either time, which is rude, by the way. I was just curious. Get over it." She scrunched her lips. "He's married?"

"Uh, no, divorced—" My phone buzzed in my bag, and I reached over Sam's bookstack to grab it.

"Hey! Watch it. Those are new. I ordered a bunch of really popular romances, but if you bend the covers—"

"Hold on." I cut her off when I saw my dad's nurse's number on my screen and answered, "Britt? Is my dad okay?"

"Hi, Brady. Listen, I tried calling your mom, but I think she's in court. Everything's under control, but we need to have a conversation, and I don't think we can put it off any longer. Can you come home? It's important."

"Y-yes. I'm on my way, but shouldn't we wait till she can be there?"

"I'd rather not. My shift ends at three, and since I'm your dad's primary nurse, I think it should be me you discuss your options with. I can go over it again later with your mom, but…"

There was a bomb ticking in my stomach. I was sure of it. "What aren't you sayin'?"

She sighed, and the bomb dropped. "It's just that I've been here before, you know? And I don't wanna wait to talk about these kinds of things since the future is unknown. It's better to have everyone be informed and prepared as soon as possible. I think that time is now."

"The future?" A weird echoing noise was weaving its way in and out of my head. I knew the end was coming, but I wasn't ready yet. Dad wasn't ready. Mom and Bonnie weren't.

"Your sister's here, but I don't think I should give her this information when she's by herself."

"I-I'm on my way. Five minutes."

"Thank you."

My phone slipped from my hand and landed on the table, and my eyes fixed on it, like if I stared hard enough, I could make the whole conversation not exist.

"Brady? Is your dad okay?"

I was dizzy, and it felt like the library was spinning all around me. "I have to go."

"Okay, but let me drive you. You're shaking."

I looked at Sam. "You can't leave. There's no one else here."

"Please, I had one patron yesterday. I'll just put a sign on the door. No problem."

"You don't have a car."

"I'll drive yours. I can walk back."

"It's too f—"

"Don't worry about me," she said. "C'mon. Let's go."

---

SO THAT WAS how my dad would die. He'd drown in his own saliva, or he'd aspirate enough of it and die from complications from pneumonia. I'd always worried it would be some kind of cardiac event. Because ALS affected the brain's ability to communicate with a person's muscles, I figured his heart would give out at some point.

Britt was very professional while she explained all this, keeping only to the facts, though she loved him. He was her favorite patient, and they had a special bond, but Dad had had two choking episodes before she'd called me, and it was clear he'd finally lost what little swallowing ability he'd had left. It was important to Britt that we understood that he could go at any time. It wasn't a surprise since he hadn't been able to eat for a year—we fed him with liquid nutrition from a tube in his stomach—but it truly had never occurred to me that this would be how he died.

I was angry at myself for not considering it. Somewhere deep inside, I knew that was stupid. I'd never met anyone with ALS before, so how could I have known? But I was berating myself 'cause I should've known. I should've researched more. I should've been prepared.

And now, when she was trying to teach Bonnie and me how to suction my dad's spit, my hands were shaking and I didn't want to do it. I didn't want to force his mouth open and stick a tube in there. I wanted to run away. I didn't want to—

"Bunny?" Gently, my sister placed her hand on my arm, and the warmth from her skin stopped my frantic thoughts. Her eyes were filled with understanding when I looked into them. "It's okay. I can handle this for now."

But when I looked back down at my dad, at the fear and sadness I saw in his eyes, I knew I couldn't leave. He wouldn't want me to force myself to stay, but leaving him wasn't an option. He was stuck. He couldn't go anywhere, so why should I have the choice?

"No, I'm fine," I said, and I willed myself to calm down, trying to force my hands to stop shaking. I needed to be steady and dependable for my dad. If I wasn't, and he died because—

"Brady, I think Bonnie's right," Britt said, and a piece of her dirty-blond hair fell out of the purple scrunchie holding it in a loose ponytail. It swept the side of her neck and hung limply by her ear, and I focused on it. "Go take a breather."

Dad blinked rapidly, letting me know he agreed. He could see how hard it was for me. He saw everything, and it made me feel like the worst son. If I couldn't handle this one small thing, how could he feel confident that I could take care of things when he was gone?

"You sure?" I said, looking at my sister. She was right; I wasn't helping. She nodded, and I kissed Dad's cheek, whispering, "I'm sorry."

My mom was climbing the porch stairs when I stepped outside, her purse slung over her shoulder and a stuffed laptop bag dangling from her fingers, papers bursting out the top. She looked tired and put out, but when she saw my face and the tears trying hard not fall, she dropped it, and it made a loud *thunk* against the wood at her feet.

"Is he…? Did he?"

"No, he's okay. For now."

"What's wrong? What happened?" Her eyes flicked between the door and my face. She wanted to go to him, but she was afraid to, afraid of what she'd find.

"He can't swallow anymore, Mom. He was choking on his own saliva. We have to suction his mouth now."

She hung her head, collecting herself and trying to slow her breathing. "Oh, honey, we knew this was comin'."

"I didn't, but I should've."

"Stop." She stepped forward to hug me. "This isn't all on you, you know? Bonnie and I are here too. Don't forget that. I've asked a lot of you, I know, and I'm sorry I've had to, but you stepped up. I'm proud of you and grateful, but you can't save him. None of us can." She took a deep breath and stepped back, and I sat on the porch swing as she leaned back against the railing across from me. "Maybe it's time we start to think about hospice."

"Mom, no! He'd hate that. All those strangers, a sterile room, monitors beepin' all the time?"

"I know, but they're better equipped to handle what's gonna happen."

"Yeah, but they're not us. They can't replace us."

Really, I was only thinking about how it would feel when he wasn't at home, when it *wasn't* my responsibility to make sure he was still breathing. She said it wasn't mine alone, but it felt that way sometimes. And if I gave up, passed the responsibility to someone else, someone who didn't know my dad, who didn't love him, maybe they'd miss something. Maybe they wouldn't handle his care with the best intentions if they were having a bad day or they hated their job.

They weren't family.

She sighed. "We need to think about it. I *am* thinkin' about it. You can't fight this, Brady. You can't fix it. He has a Do Not Resuscitate order. You know this. We discussed it as a family, and you have to prepare yourself." She pushed off the porch railing and took a steadying breath. She was crying softly, but I couldn't look at her. "You think I like admittin' this is what's meant to happen? He's the love of my life. But you can't fight God."

I watched her walk away out of the corner of my eye. I wanted to scream at her. How could she betray him like that? How could she give up?

"Brady?" Theo's voice was a surprise, and I gasped when I heard it.

He was standing on the sidewalk in front of my parents'

house, and he looked different. He looked like he used to before his life had gone to shit. Handsome and powerful. I wondered what he saw when he looked at me. It was my turn to fall apart.

"I'm sorry." He looked at my front door, then back to me. Maybe he'd heard the conversation with my mom. "Is this a bad time?"

"What're you doin' here?"

"I got your address from Kevin Cade. I wanted to apologize for my text earlier. I know tax law isn't your area. I just…"

"You just what?"

"I-I, I'm kind of alone here. I didn't know who to ask."

I laughed. "Right. There's not one person in your life you could ask about tax law or settin' up payroll? Please."

"You're right," he said, and he nodded and took a step back.

"Yeah, no shit. You know what, this *is* a bad time. Go cry about your entitled problems to somebody else. I've got *real-life* problems here. I don't have time for—"

I didn't say the thing I wanted to, that he was spoiled, pampered, and feeling sorry for himself. I didn't say it 'cause what I really wanted to do was throw myself in his arms. I wanted to feel their warmth. I wanted him to hold me the way he had the night I showed up drunk. I still remembered it.

"Certainly," he said. "Of course, I apologize." And he walked away, climbed into his truck, and I cried then, when no one could see.

# CHAPTER FOURTEEN

### THEO

I WATCHED him breaking down in my rear-view mirror as I drove away.

The change that had come over his face when he snapped at me was clearly one of pain. Every other interaction I'd had with Brady Douglas had been pleasant at the very least, and when we were together, he was… This—this was the opposite of that, and the anguish displayed so clearly on his beautiful face was building up inside him like an imminent storm, the clouds darkening and swirling, the pressure beginning to drop. I knew it had to do with his dad's illness, and I ached for him.

I remembered acutely what it felt like to lose a parent. I'd lost both of mine on the same day, and I still felt the rip it had caused in me. In my soul.

And then there was regret. I still wanted to punish myself when I thought about the man I'd tried to kill and all the lies I'd told to try to accomplish that insane goal, and I knew with everything inside me that my parents were disappointed in me. I'd spent my entire life doing everything I could to *not* disappoint them, so it was no surprise to me when I found myself parked in front of the Liquor Depot on the outskirts of Wisper.

The scene was like a bad movie in my head—my sister's face when she learned that I'd been lying to her for years, the pain and betrayal she'd felt when she found out the truth about her birth mother. Those hurt the worst, but I also vividly remembered chasing the blackmailing lowlife through California and Nevada, luring him behind a building, and trying to shoot him.

Brady's "entitled" comment rang true, because who else would possess the arrogance to do such a thing? And the quick way that man had disarmed me, turned the gun on me, then hit me with it, knocking me to the ground—he'd beaten me within an inch of my life.

That was the cost of my arrogance.

And I was still paying it. The price kept increasing.

I'd been to this liquor store many times over the last couple of years, but this time felt different. At least now I was aware of what I was doing, fully aware that if I walked into the store, I'd be making yet another bad choice, no matter what my intentions were.

I didn't want that.

I didn't want to feel ashamed of myself today, and I didn't go in, but I sat in my truck, staring at the door, like if I just walked through it, all my problems would disappear. They probably would, actually, but only until I sobered up again, and then they would be waiting for me, like they always were.

The sounds of that night in Nevada were loud in my head —the banging of my body against a dumpster when Blake Ormand had thrown me against it. The sound of his feet shuffling in the gravel behind an old gas station a second before he kicked my ribs so hard it felt like a blow to my head. And then he did kick my head, again and again. And then the sound of a trunk thudding shut above my body when he'd thrown me into it as I passed out.

The sounds were screaming at me, and I squeezed my eyes closed, trying to force them out of my mind. My heart was racing, my breath coming faster, and they just kept bouncing around my skull, over and over. Louder and louder.

Nothing would make them stop.

Certainly not alcohol. It had taken three years, but I'd finally realized this undeniable fact, but the urge to find a way to forget was intense, and slowly, it was taking over my whole body.

For the first time, I didn't give in to the impulse. Instead, I called Charlie.

He answered his phone with a grunt. "Yeah?"

"Um, hello, Charlie. This is Theo. I'm sorry to bother you, but you gave me your number at the bowling alley."

"Yeah, kid, I know who you are. Your name's flashin' all over my phone. I ain't so old I can't remember a week ago."

"Of course, I apologize."

"You've never called before. What's up?"

"I… I want a drink." *Desperately.*

"Have you had one?"

"No," I said, trying to hold onto that word with every-thing in me. My voice dropped, and the low, rough truth of it scared me. "But I'm parked in front of a liquor store."

"Where? I'm on my way."

"Wisper. The Liquor Depot."

"Can you drive away?"

"I'm in my truck. I-I haven't gotten out yet, but I can't seem to make myself leave."

"Okay. Talk to me then." I heard the jangle of a set of

keys, and a door slammed shut. "What's been goin' on with you?"

My voice was shaking. "Uh, well, I've been getting a lot of work done on the community center. Did I tell you about that?" I asked, so fucking thankful for the chance to change the subject.

"No, sure didn't." Charlie's vehicle rumbled to life, and there were muffled noises over the line, but then his voice was clear. "Go 'head. Tell me now. I'll be there in ten minutes."

So I spoke to Charlie about dreams. My dream, specifically, the dream I'd had forever about a community center where anyone from any walk of life could feel safe and comfortable, and by the time I was done, he was pulling up beside me in the Liquor Depot parking lot, and then he opened the passenger door, removed his cowboy hat, and climbed in.

"Cool idea, man. You need somebody to teach woodworkin'?"

"Woodworking? You do that? Wait. Shouldn't you be at work?"

"Yeah, well, I took a smoke break. I'm an electrician by trade, but in my spare time, I like to carve stuff. Wolves are my specialty."

"You don't smoke."

He shrugged.

"My friend's dad—well, actually, he's not really my friend, but this guy I know, his dad was a furniture maker before he got sick. Do you do that kind of thing?"

"He live around here?"

"Yes."

"Wait. You talkin' about Brady? From the bowlin' alley the other day?"

"Yes."

"I know Brady's daddy. Foster Douglas, right? Married to a nice Shoshone lady?"

"Yes, right. I forgot you knew each other."

"Yep, that's ol' Fossy." He chuckled. "Known the guy for ages. He was actually the one who helped me get sober. Has Brady said anything lately? I wonder how his dad's doin'. I think about him a lot."

"Not well, I think, because Brady seems to be having a hard time with it."

"Aw, yeah, he and Brady have a special bond. They always did. I'll call Jeanine, see if there's anything I can do to help." Charlie sighed and clapped his hands on his thighs. "Well, so?"

"So?"

"You want me to teach at your center?"

"Sure," I said. "I'd actually love that." A small part of me wondered what kind of teacher Charlie would be. He wasn't the most patient person, from the little knowledge I had of him, but he was a local and… a friend.

"I can teach ceramics, too, but that'd take a lot of space. Plus, you probably don't have a kiln."

"A kiln?"

"Yeah," he said, "to bake the ceramics."

"Oh, well, no, I don't have one of those, but if there's enough interest from the community, I could buy one."

"Just like that? Those things ain't cheap."

"Yes, I mean, if you're serious."

He thought for a minute, then turned toward me, angling his body in my direction. "You got a sponsor yet?"

"No. I suppose I do need a sponsor, but I guess I've been a little hesitant to ask anyone because I'm new to AA. And I'm a mess. Who would want to deal with that?"

Charlie blinked, a confused expression growing on his face. "That's the whole point of bein' in AA, genius. Everybody's a mess, but some of us have been functional messes for a long time. Bein' a sponsor's part of my sobriety, just like havin' one is part of yours. So you want me to be your sponsor?"

"You'd do that for me? I guess I thought we might be… I don't know, too different."

"Different? Because you're black and I ain't?"

"No, of course not, but I'm… Well, I'm different than you."

"Different age? Different social class? Oh," he said, understanding finally dawning. "'Cause you're gay?"

"Well, yes, I mean, it did cross my mind. You seemed a little surprised by that when we met."

"Yeah, I admit it. I was. You're the first gay friend I've ever had, but differences ain't a big deal, kid. Plus, it's good for people to get outta their comfort zones. Helps you grow. So, you in?"

He put his hat back on and pushed his hand toward me, offering it up for a shake.

"Thank you, Charlie." I shook it. "Yes, I would like you to be my sponsor."

He tsked and adjusted the brim of his hat. "Alright, then our first order of business is for you to tell me what made you drive to a liquor store in the middle of the day."

# CHAPTER FIFTEEN

## BRADY

WHEN THEO ARRIVED at the center, he parked his truck behind the building, and I was sitting cross-legged like a kid, waiting on the loading dock in the alley.

He got out, but he hung his head, then leaned against the driver's-side door. The drawn look on his face and the slumped set of his shoulders hinted pretty loudly that he was having a bad day, and I was ashamed that I was probably part of the reason why.

"I'm sorry," I said, standing and swiping old sawdust off my ass, and he turned quickly.

There was only the truck between us, but he felt miles away.

I'd surprised him, but he recovered quickly. "Why?"

He walked around the truck bed, twirling his keys. They were dangling from his fingers, and the tinkling song they were playing made me think his hand might be shaking.

"I was rude earlier when you texted, and I yelled at you when you came to my parents' house. I didn't mean to."

He shook his head. "No, I'm sorry. I shouldn't have bothered you. You have a lot going on. You don't need to apologize, Brady. You didn't do anything wrong." He stopped and looked right in my eyes. "You're going through something difficult. I get it. I understand."

I nodded to the clinking keys. "So are you, and you didn't deserve what I said."

Laughing softly under his breath, he said, "You can tell?"

I nodded. "Yeah. My granddad—my dad's dad—was a heavy drinker for a long time, and I still remember him gettin' sober. I was ten."

"Is he…?"

"Still sober? He passed away a few years ago, but he was pretty stubborn. Once he made a habit of somethin', it was hard for him to break it. Worked *with* the alcoholism and against it."

His head bobbed up and down a few times. "I'm sorry you had to go through that."

"Me too. I mean, sorry you do too."

"Have you noticed we're always saying we're sorry? I'm getting tired of it."

I smiled and said again, "Me too."

"Did you need something else?" The exhaustion in his voice made me feel it in my soul.

"No, I… That's it. Just wanted to apologize. But now that I'm here, can I see inside? I've heard the place has been through a makeover in the last couple weeks. I think I might've missed that last time I was here."

The instant smile on his face made mine grow bigger, and it was the first sign of light in his eyes. "Sure. I'd love to show you."

Walking up the dock, his smile grew the closer he got to me until he was a foot away, and I was sure he was blushing, but his smooth brown skin and the dark stubble on his cheeks was hiding it. I stepped behind him onto the platform by the back door as he unlocked it.

When I followed him inside, he turned to shut and lock the door, and we were face to face again, three inches apart.

But I was drawn to the brightness behind him. The change in the place blew me away. "Wow."

He took a step back and turned. "Big difference, isn't there?"

"You ain't kiddin'," I said. The inside of his building was light and airy feeling. The walls had been opened up and painted a soft white color, and the floors had been shined. The windows had been reframed and repainted, and they had fancy new wooden blinds. "How'd you get so much done this fast?"

Smirking, he turned to me. "Elbow grease. Isn't that what it's called?"

I laughed. "Yeah. You did all this yourself?"

"Oh God, no. I had help. A lot of help. We're not finished yet, and I hired a local artist to paint murals on these white walls, but Devo and her friends have been amazing. James Brockovich helped, and Vern. He's been great. He's a hard worker."

"Vern? Are you talkin' about Vern Wexler? You can't mean him."

"Yes," Theo said. "Devo and I hired him. He's kind of like a handyman, but he did the landscaping, and I guess he does whatever needs to be done. Huh. I should probably give him a better job title."

"Vern Wexler?" I said again and laughed. "What happened to the guy who said, 'I vet everyone, Mr. Douglas'? Vern's been in jail more times than I could probably count on both hands. I know 'cause my mom's represented him a few of those times. He's always gettin' into some kinda trouble."

"Well, everyone deserves a second chance, don't you think? And so far, I haven't regretted hiring him once."

"I s'pose they do. Just keep your eyes open, though, okay? I'd hate for him to mess this up for you."

He smiled at me. "Thanks for looking out for me, Mr. Douglas, but I think Vern will do just fine." He seemed sure about his decision, and I hoped he was right. Dropping his keys on one of the old desks in the back corner of the front room, his voice echoed through the empty space when he said, "Would you like to see upstairs? It hasn't been painted yet—we're doing that tomorrow—but the third floor is done. It's completely different than the last—"

The last time I was here? When I'd had his cock in my mouth?

"Love to," I said, and I smirked this time.

WE RODE the elevator to the third floor. He backed against one wall, and I leaned against the opposite wall, and then we stared at each other. I wondered if he could read on my face that I was using all my self-control not to rip his clothes off and take him down to the floor.

It was the longest minute of my life.

When we were in his new apartment, it was hard to picture what it had looked like that first night, though it was impossible for me to forget because the memory had been burned into my mind. Specifically, I remembered the floor and the ancient metal printing press he'd held onto while I gave him head. My face was probably the color of a beet, and I was trying to slow my breathing.

"I didn't even know this buildin' had an elevator."

"Surprisingly, it's in great condition." He scuffed the floor with his shoe. "So this will be my new place. I'm just waiting on furniture to be delivered." He shrugged. "It's a lot different than anywhere I've ever lived before. Much… smaller."

Yeah, probably miniscule compared to the luxury condos and vacation homes he was used to. But it was nice. It was only one large room. There was plenty of space for a couch in the middle, maybe some kind of bookshelf or storage shelves. A kitchen took up the length of the north wall, with room for a small dining nook next to a window that looked down onto Main Street. The sink and fixtures looked old, so the kitchen must've existed before he'd claimed the third floor as his apartment. I hadn't noticed when I was up here before, but then again, I hadn't really been in the mood to contemplate real estate.

"I don't know," he said, uncertainty in his voice. This was new for him. No billion-dollar investment company, no staff, no sister to take care of. Just him and a room.

"I love it. It's got a real urban vibe, you know? Which is weird since it's in the middle of a small country town, but the brick walls are cool."

He bobbed his head again. "Thanks." This relaxed posture was new for him too. I was used to a very buttoned-up business tycoon or the complete opposite of that—a falling-down drunk.

"What'd you do with all those old papers that were up here? Sam would love to get her hands on 'em. She's lookin' into some big thing that happened in Wisper in the '60s. It's kind of a mystery."

"A mystery?" he asked, his eyebrows dipping down.

"Of sorts, I guess. We found all these old articles at the library—Sam's the new librarian. Anyway, there was some kind of society group here, but apparently there was a big scandal and they disbanded. She's kinda obsessed with the whole thing 'cause the articles were all blacked out. You know, like the CIA does? Black lines all over the place. So I was thinkin' maybe all those old papers might help her solve it."

"Huh, that's interesting. Uh, I didn't throw them away. They're boxed up downstairs. I'll take them over to her. I'm glad someone can get some use out of them."

"Thanks. You know," I said, walking over to stand in front of the window, "you'll have prime seatin' for all the parades and festivals Wisper puts on and the fireworks on the Fourth of July. They had to cancel it this year 'cause of that big storm, but—" I turned and smiled at him, watching how sudden child-like excitement filled up his eyes, the light green color almost making them glow.

"Oh, just wait. I haven't shown you the best part yet. Come with me."

When he took my hand, it was almost like I'd been zapped with electricity, and a warmth traveled up my arm, settling in my chest as he dragged me to a staircase behind the bedroom. At least, I assumed it would be his bedroom. It was the only part of the apartment that had any kind of privacy. There was a wall blocking off the area, which was just big enough for a bed. It was only a half wall, so it wouldn't hide much, but I imagined him lying in that bed, and I imagined myself next to him, snuggled up under a blanket in the winter, waking up and making out while our coffee was brewing.

I liked that image, and I could see it so clearly. It made me hard, so I was really trying to push it out of my mind. Staring at his ass on the way up the stairs didn't help either.

When we got to the top, he pushed open a heavy, gray

metal door, and we stepped onto a huge open rooftop covered with flat black shingles.

"Whoa," I said. "This is incredible. Look at that view."

He stepped next to me. "Yeah. It's my favorite part of the building."

We stood there, looking out over my hometown and beyond, to the farms and fields in the distance. The mountains were beautiful from this vantage point, surrounding us in all directions. They were like grumpy rock giants, guarding Wisper, shielding her from anything that would ever dare to hurt her.

There was a rainstorm brewing in the distance. I could see a far-off wall of showers to the northwest, but the sun was still forcing its way through from the southwest, and it lit up Theo's face. I didn't mean to, but I reached for his hand again and held it for all of two seconds, but I heard his soft gasp and dropped it. "Sorry."

"No. Don't be sorry. Don't ever be sorry with me," he said, threading his fingers through mine. He turned, pulling a little, and I looked in his eyes. "This is nice. You being here. I like it."

I nodded, and he kissed me.

I'd known it was coming, but it still took my breath away, maybe because it felt so good so fast. There was no buildup —it was full-on right off the bat—but it was still soft and gentle and quiet.

Wrapping my arms around his neck, I pulled him closer, feeling his body against mine, his chest rising and falling quickly, and his hands settled on my hips.

I wanted to lose myself in him, wanted this feeling to last forever—his mouth on mine, his shaky breath. There was a nervousness between us, but also a peace I'd never felt with anyone before, and I hadn't once thought about my dad since we'd walked into the building. But it wasn't reality. It wasn't possible, this thing between us, and when his hands moved up, caressing me, sliding up my arms, working their way to my face to hold it between them, *actual* reality slammed back into my mind.

I pulled his hands away, kissing one palm softly, but then I dropped them and took a step back. He didn't say anything. He knew why I'd stopped the kiss, but something about him was making me feel safe enough to talk about my dad. I wanted to tell him, wanted to confide all the things I'd been having such a hard time putting into words these last few months.

"It hasn't been a year yet," I said.

There was a ratty old lawn chair behind me, and I sat, or more like fell into it, and he took two steps away, giving me the distance I kept claiming I wanted and needed, but maybe it was an excuse. Maybe I was just scared.

I opened my mouth and everything I'd been feeling poured out. "My dad won't live much longer. That's what the doctors and nurses are tellin' us. It's gettin' to be the end now." I looked at him. "That's what I was talkin' to my mom about when you stopped by earlier. That's why I was rude to you. I don't... I don't know how to handle it." I shrugged, gripping the chair's arms with both hands. "I don't know who I am without him in my life, you know?"

He nodded once and then stepped closer and held out his hands. I took them, and he pulled me up and led me back down to his apartment.

# CHAPTER SIXTEEN

## THEO

I SMILED OVER MY SHOULDER, but something was different.

The air around Brady was different. He wasn't usually the loudest guy, but now, there was a quiet stillness about him that I hadn't noticed before.

"Are you okay?"

"Yeah," he said when we were standing in my future bedroom. Suddenly, I was more than disappointed that my new bed hadn't been delivered yet. "I'm just tired. Exhausted, actually."

Pulling my phone from my pocket, I clicked on the piece I'd just been reading about him from the *Jackson Hole Daily*. I'd found it when I looked him up online. I wanted to see his face after I'd spent the afternoon telling Charlie my life story. Brady's smile eased the ache in my chest.

The article was about how he'd helped a single mom get out from under her abusive husband's thumb. He'd set up a trust for her daughter and put safeguards in place for the little girl in case anything bad ever happened to her mom. Doug Morris was the father. He was in jail now, and in the back of my mind, I wondered if it was the same man Vern had mentioned. He'd been arrested by the FBI for all manner of bad deeds, but some people from the Wyoming legal community were praising Brady for his use of certain case laws he'd cited to win his case. He was brilliant, and he was a good person. The case was pro bono, and there was only one quote from Brady in the article. When they asked him how he could keep his family law practice afloat if he gave his services away, all he said was, "That's kind of a dumb question, don't you think? When someone needs help, you help them."

"Look," I said.

He blushed when he noticed the article on my phone, the bright light illuminating his face in the dark space. The sky outside was growing darker by the minute.

"This is who you are."

Shaking his head, he said, "That's nothin'."

"It's not nothing. You're amazing. I-I'm proud of you."

He shrugged, looking in my eyes, and then he was shaking his head. "Look, I know we were only together that one time, and it hasn't been anywhere close to a year…" His eyes darted around the room while he remembered that night. Mine did too.

The time we were together was a scorching-hot memory in my mind. When I thought about it, all kinds of things happened to my body—and my heart, if I was honest with myself.

He looked at me. "But—"

Ah. Here was the let go. I was surprised by how much it hurt already.

"But," I said, and I nodded slowly, acceptance tugging at the edges of my pride. I didn't *want* to accept it, but I knew what he was going through, and he knew that I was… whatever I was. Working on myself? Was that the right description? Or maybe he could see the weakness in me, and it had turned him off. Maybe he felt sorry for me.

That would be the worst. I couldn't take that.

"Maybe you should just go." I tried to smile. I wasn't sure what it looked like, but the way my face contorted didn't feel like a smile. It felt awful.

When I turned, I clicked off my phone, shoving it in my back pocket, but he grabbed my hand and pulled. "Hold on. You didn't let me finish."

I'd lost him before he was even mine. "I'm not sure what more there is to say."

He stepped forward, resting his warm hands on the sides of my neck. "I can't speak for you, but this"—he looked down my body and back up—"sex is a part of who I am. I miss it. And it doesn't mean we're jumpin' into anything. Or it doesn't have to. We both need it. Why are we tryin' to live without it? Nobody has to know."

He was right. Now that I was waking up from my three-year stupor, sex was very much on my mind. Sex with him.

He kissed the edge of my lip. "We said we'd wait a year, and part of me thinks that was the right call. There's so much I need to deal with. I don't even know who I'm gonna be in a month. If my dad—when my dad… It's gonna change me. And you… Well, I can't even imagine what you're goin' through."

"I'm not who everybody thinks I am," I said, admitting the truth finally to another person. "I'm not powerful. I'm not in charge. And I'm definitely not in control. I was all of those things for a long time, and now, I'm none of them. It isn't who I want to be. But where I've fallen to? It's going to take a *lot* of climbing to get back up."

His thumbs were caressing my jaw, and he was looking so deeply into my eyes that I wanted to fall into him. I wanted him to be inside of me so that warm feeling would never go away.

"I know. But…" he said.

"But?" That was the second but. I didn't really know where he was going with this.

Or maybe this was the part where he was going to tell me a year wasn't enough, that I was the classic "right guy at the wrong time."

He said, "You know we'll see each other every day. We work a half a mile apart. We go to the same coffee shop every mornin'. It's gonna be torture. I want you. I want you *bad*. And maybe this is what we both need." Wrapping his hands around my hips, he pulled me closer. "I want this, this thing we feel when we're together like this. Don't you feel it?"

Relief flooded my whole body. "I do. God, I really fucking do."

He kissed me. It was a light peck on my lips, but he didn't close his eyes. "Good, 'cause I can't wait any more. But we *have* to find you new representation. Promise me you'll call the lawyers on the list I gave you?"

"I promise."

He smiled, but it turned into a serious expression quickly, his eyes darkening and his lids getting heavier by the second.

"Oh, thank God," I said. "I thought you were going to tell me a year wasn't enough time, or that you were leaving Wisper." Thinking for a minute, I wondered what waiting would be like. I was certain it would be hell, but—"I will though," I said. "If it's what you need, I can wait—"

He pulled me even closer, shaking his head. Our bodies were so close, even air didn't exist between us. He whispered, "I think boundary number one was no kissin'," and he kissed me again.

I laughed but closed my eyes when his tongue snaked into my mouth.

He barely detached his lips before he said, "Number two, no touchin'."

Reaching around, I grabbed his ass with both hands, feeling him clench when I squeezed, and he moaned into my mouth.

Breathlessly, he said, "Three and four: no datin' and definitely no fuckin'. Actually, I think that was my one and only rule." Opening his eyes, he was resolute. "I've waited long enough for that."

"I don't know," I said, pulling back and grinning. "Maybe we should still give it a month—"

His breath quickened, and I felt his pulse in his jeans. "Now." So fast that I lost my breath, he slammed me back against the brick wall, pushing his hand down the front of my jeans, and his mouth was on mine again.

To say I was surprised was an understatement, but I didn't argue. I let all the remorse, self-hatred, and guilt go from my body, feeling it flow from my hands and fingers. It allowed the rest of me to feel *him*, his tongue in my mouth, the short hair over his lip scratching my face.

It was intoxicating, and I tilted my head and took over the kiss. Holding his face in my hands again while I kissed him deeper than I'd ever kissed anyone, I pulled him back with me toward my kitchen counter. I couldn't get enough of him, of the way he tasted, and the kiss became a hardcore smashing of teeth and tongue. He bit me at one point, and I bit back.

"Where we goin'?" he asked, panting, trying to breathe through my kiss.

"Kitchen counter."

He moaned, probably imagining what I was: me bent over

the old, yellowed laminate countertop while he pounded into me.

"I have condoms. I ordered them just in case you—"

He stopped the kiss, smiling while I pulled him further backward. "Got lube?"

"Under the bathroom sink."

When we reached the counter, he crowded me against it, rubbing his dick against mine through our jeans. "Stay right there," he said, and he backed away toward my small bathroom. There was a toilet, a sink, and a skinny shower stall in there. It was enough for me, but I was imagining taking a shower with him, and I wasn't sure if we'd both fit.

When he was a few feet away, he turned and ran the rest of the way, and then tore through the cabinet, looking for lube. I could hear him frantically knocking around in there.

"Snap cap. Got it!"

He hurried back and nearly skidded to a stop when he noticed my bare chest. My sweater was in a heap on the floor, and my nipples were hard and pointed toward him.

"Now your jeans," he ordered, staring at the place where the denim was covering my erection, and I obeyed. I wasn't wearing underwear, which elicited a glint in his eyes and a smirk on his lips.

"Your turn."

"I've been dreamin' about this," he said as he pulled his shirt over his head so quickly that it got stuck, and I stepped closer, trying to help him untangle himself. As soon as his lips were free of the shirt, I kissed them, pulling it off the rest of the way. His hands were warm on my body, wrapping around my ribcage while I unbuttoned his jeans and pushed them down.

He kicked them off, and his voice was strained when he asked, "Are you—do you want me to fuck you?"

"Yes," I groaned. "Is that what you want?"

"Yeah," he said, his voice only a whisper, but it was full of lust. "Do you want that too? I mean, do you want to do that to me?"

I shook my head. "No. I want you to take me and make me come with your hand."

"Shit."

"Yes," I said while he kissed me again and made his way south, planning to prep me before he did just what I'd asked.

He spent some time on my chest, and I loved the way he held his breath, sucking a nipple into his mouth. I groaned, and he wrapped his arms around me, pulling me closer. He seemed to love the sound of my voice, which was ironic since the sound of his was what I fell asleep to every night when I replayed our conversations in my head. It spurred him on while my hands found their way into his hair. Pulling my fingers through it, over and over, I let it fall between them, and then I'd start over at the roots again.

Slowly, my hands made their way to his shoulders, and I applied pressure, pushing him down. He knew what I wanted, and I watched as he kneeled in front of me. I was looking at his face, but he couldn't take his eyes off my cock.

"You're really sexy," I said, and I smiled as he looked up, then he opened his mouth wide and took me inside. "Oh."

He got to work then, sucking hard and rolling my balls in his hand. It felt amazing—the warmth and the rush of blood through my veins in places that had only felt my hands lately —and I gripped the sides of his head, using the leverage it gave me to fuck further into his mouth. I was thrusting hard, and every pull out made my low back hit the counter. It hurt, but I liked it.

He'd barely had time to use the tricks he'd promised he had before I was trying to pull out. I tried to move away, but he held me there, letting the angle of my cock do the work for him. Pushing forward and sliding back, he tightened his lips, and now I was pulling his hair too hard, trying not to come.

"Brady, stop," I begged him. "I'm almost there."

"I know." He chased my body, sucking me down again and pressing me hard against the counter so I had nowhere else to go.

"I want you to make me come when you're inside me."

That stopped him cold, and he looked up. "Like I'm gonna argue with that?"

He stood, licking his lips, his tongue collecting the little bit of cum I wasn't able to hold back. I was about to burst, and I closed my eyes, moaning when I saw it. I couldn't look at him, or things would explode.

Noticing the condom I'd placed on the counter, he grabbed it, holding it between his teeth as he turned me. I watched him over my shoulder, barely holding onto my sanity while he rolled the condom into place, and he leaned forward, kissing me while he spread my ass cheeks apart.

His tongue was wicked, and he was opening his mouth wide enough to devour me. It was the sexiest kiss I'd ever experienced, and I almost didn't want it to stop, but his dick was an inch from my ass, throbbing between my legs, and that was what I really wanted.

I needed the physical connection.

All the dizzying emotions I'd been trying to avoid were buzzing in my head. They were swirling all around me like a storm, and that was when I heard thunder crack outside, like it was the soundtrack to our imminent fucking.

While he squeezed lube over himself, rain smacked and crackled against the roof tiles, and when lightning flashed outside my window, he entered my body.

Warm arms wrapped around me, and he covered my chest

with his hands, rubbing my nipples with his palms. I covered his hands with mine, then pushed my ass further onto his dick. I was in ecstasy as he began to move slowly.

The feeling of falling came back, and I gripped the countertop, but he was still holding me. I knew I couldn't fall.

Lube was dripping everywhere, running down the backs of my thighs, but the warm glide was everything, and he worked carefully to quicken his pace, in and out, again and again while his breath washed over my neck.

Bending his knees, he was driving me wild, rubbing my prostate with every thrust. I couldn't stop my body from shaking every time he went deeper. His hand slid down my chest slowly, the hair there pulling and stinging, but it felt good.

I couldn't take much more when he finally covered my cockhead with his fingers, letting them slide down as cum began to flow, and when he squeezed, I started to shoot.

"Wait." Breathlessly, he begged, "Wait for me."

# CHAPTER SEVENTEEN

## BRADY

HOLDING his cock in my hand, I didn't pump. I didn't want him to come yet, but I couldn't stop touching him. He was shaking, trying with all his might to hold back, so I fucked him faster, attacking the back of his neck and shoulders with my mouth, loving how wide and strong they felt. I licked them, and he shuddered.

He whispered, begging me, "Brady."

"I know," I breathed. "Fuck, you feel so good. I'm…" I was panting now while his tight ass cheeks slapped against my stomach, and I watched myself moving in and out of him. It was too much.

I coated my hand with his cum and punched my body into his one last time. He must've known I was coming 'cause he tensed, and the inside of his body clamped down on me. There was no more holding back after that.

Biting down on his shoulder, I came, jacking his dick with my hand while I emptied myself into the condom. Lube was everywhere. There was so much, and it was warm. It ran back down, dripping through my pubic hair, wetting it and turning me on all over again.

When I pulled out, he turned and gripped my arms with his hands when I staggered 'cause I was a little woozy from coming so hard. That turned me on even more, and nothing could've stopped me from kissing him again.

But he was still in it too. His eyes were darker, his eyelids heavy over his sage green irises. "We need to clean up, but my shower's really small."

"We'll fit," I said. "If I don't let go of you, it'll be like we're one person."

He moaned and captured my lips again, fucking into my mouth with his tongue. There was just no end of the heat between us, and my dick was trying to harden again while I followed him to the shower, watching how the soft black fuzz above his ass dipped down between his cheeks. I wanted to lick it.

Pushing the knob to hot, he tested the water with his hand. "Takes a minute."

I tossed the condom into his little plastic garbage can by the john, and my eyes raked over his body as we stood there. He was hard again.

"You plannin' to do somethin' about that?" I asked, my mouth slowly forming a sly smirk.

"I—I want to, but I haven't in a long time. And I think… I think maybe that was the old me. You know? The guy in charge. The boss. Maybe it isn't who I should be anymore."

"Why? How you fuck has nothin' to do with who you are as a person."

"You don't get it. That was my identity. I was demanding and unforgiving, and that was how I related to men with sex too. I guess I'm scared to be that way again. Look where it led me."

"You don't have to dominate me to fuck me, Theo. Turn the water off. C'mere." Taking his hand, I led him out of the bathroom, back to the kitchen, grabbing another condom from the counter and the bottle of lube, and then I motioned to a hardback dining chair I'd seen sitting next to the Main Street window. Thankfully, he hadn't taken down the busted blinds that were hanging precariously in front of it. I could see out, but I was hoping no one could see in.

Gently, I pushed him into the chair with my hands on his chest, feeling for a second how the hair there was soft but really curly, and he sat and spread his legs, his cock reddened and jutting up toward me.

I climbed over him. "Put this on," I said, handing him the condom.

He did, and I opened the lube while he looked in my eyes. There was something in his that was breaking my heart. Was it fear?

Pouring lube into my hand, I leaned down and kissed him. I was getting addicted to his mouth. It was slow this time, my tongue teasing and pulling his, mixing our saliva, our breath. It was the most sensual thing I'd ever experienced.

I was hard again now too.

Reaching between us, I coated the condom with lube, rubbing with firm strokes slowly, and then I stood, angling my ass over him, jacking myself off with the leftover lube. He slid two fingers over his cock, collecting more, and pushed his hand between my legs, fingering me, getting me ready for him.

My head fell back at the invasion, and I rode his finger slowly till he added another.

"Yeah, just like that. Go slow."

His breath was unsteady, and I focused on it 'cause it meant this was just as intense for him as it was for me. When I looked at him, his head was resting back against the wall while he watched me. His mouth was open, and I swore I could hear his heartbeat thundering in his chest.

Kissing him again, I said, "I'm ready."

He didn't speak, only nodded, and I lifted up. When he squeezed his hands around my hips, I slid down slowly, taking him all the way in, and his face scrunched like he was in pain.

"Am I hurtin' you?"

He shook his head.

"Theo, talk to me. Tell me what you're feelin'."

Breath rushed from his mouth. "It feels so fucking good, but I don't know if I can hold back."

"You can because I need you to. It's been a while for me too."

He nodded, his eyebrows dipping down in concentration, and I lifted up again and lowered myself slowly, feeling his cock swell inside me.

It was… so fucking erotic, this connection between us. Where had it come from?

All I could do was breathe, and finally, he took over, pushing me up and pulling me back down with his hands still on my hips, his fingertips digging into my ass cheeks. He didn't look away from my eyes once, and that was the hottest part of it all.

This time was unhurried, and sweat began to bead on our bodies the longer he fucked me. I felt it on the back of my neck, wetting my hair, dripping down my back.

The storm was raging outside while he found the pace he liked. I could tell because he made sexy groaning noises in the back of his throat, and he blinked slowly, his body becoming more and more relaxed the longer he was inside me.

The lights in his apartment kept flickering on and off, but we were quiet.

We didn't speak. We just fucked slowly.

It felt like a few minutes had gone by, but the night outside the window was black. Maybe it was the storm, or maybe we'd been at this for hours. Time had stopped for me. Everything stopped except for the beat of my heart, the blood rushing through my body, and this heavy energy between us.

And then it wasn't fucking anymore. He was making love to me. The way he touched me was intimate, like no one had ever touched me before, caressing me softly, like he was worshiping my body, his hand now tangling in my hair.

"Kiss me again," he said. "Kiss me and make me come."

My cock throbbed when I heard those words, and he felt it against his stomach. He reached down, wrapping his fingers around me, rubbing me slowly up and down as I kissed him, and I moaned when his tongue touched mine.

He whispered into my mouth, "I'm coming."

And then he was leaning forward, hugging my body to his with one arm while he pumped my cock with the other. He shouted his release, and that was all it took for me to reach my own climax. Just the sound of him letting go.

SILENTLY, he pressed me against the shower wall, dragging his soapy hands over my body, between my thighs, over my chest.

His bathroom was tiny. He was right that we barely fit, but I wasn't about to complain. We were still kissing—I wasn't sure we could stop—so I was right, too, that we were more like one person instead of two. He washed my hair, pulled his fingers through the dripping mess over and over, massaging the back of my head.

"I know this is gonna sound ludicrous after I was the one sayin' we should stay away from each other, but… I want you to—would you… like to meet my dad?"

It was absolutely the wrong time to bring up the subject, and there was a sadness that crept into me when I brought my dad into the quiet space between us, but suddenly, I *needed* Theo to meet my dad. I wanted him to meet the man who raised me, who made me who I was. I needed him to see how amazing my dad was so he could believe that maybe someday, I'd live up to that.

I wanted him to believe I could.

"Yes," he said.

Maybe I wanted to believe it too.

# CHAPTER EIGHTEEN

## THEO

WHILE I DROVE TO HIS PARENTS' the next day, the eerie stillness that had descended over Wisper after the storm as we'd said goodbye in my foyer was starting to burn away with the morning sun. He left the center late, so I promised to meet his dad when he had a break in his workday today. He left with my kiss on his lips and hope. Secret hope, maybe, but still hope.

The neighborhood his parents lived in had been built at the edge of Wisper, and it was small. There were maybe fifteen homes in total, each ranch-style house a varying shade of a sunset—muted gold, burnt orange, sage green. There was even a salmon-colored house. I hadn't really noticed them the first time I was here because as soon as I'd noticed Brady sitting on a wooden porch swing, he was all I could see, but now it was registering that his house was a medium, almost periwinkle blue.

The views of the mountains to the north were incredible but somehow oppressive, the tall peaks towering over me like judgment, and a nervousness was working its way through me, manifesting in a tremble that was settling in my hands.

I imagined Brady playing when he was young, running around in his front yard with bare feet, the Tetons like a movie-set backdrop to his childhood. I could imagine his house covered in Halloween decorations in the fall, with piles of crunchy colorful leaves everywhere, and Christmas lights in December, shining through the falling snow.

It was mid-October now, and when I pulled into the driveway, I noticed his neighbors' houses all decked out for trick-or-treating. I got the feeling that the glaring lack of pumpkins and fake cobwebs at Brady's house was about his father and the pain he and his family were going through. Who gave a shit about holiday celebrations when the person you loved the most was dying right in front of you, day by day.

Brady loved his father fiercely. It had been easy to see in his eyes when he'd asked if I wanted to meet his dad. He was nervous, but he looked hopeful in a way that made me certain he really wanted me to say yes.

I wasn't sure if he was anxious about me meeting his dad or his dad meeting me, but either way, I knew it was important to him. We hadn't really come to an official decision, but last night proved he was having as hard of a time as I was trying to keep our distance.

It was the best sex of my life, and now, as I parked and shut my truck off, the way he was smiling at me from his front porch and the excitement I could practically see coming off of him was electric.

The air crackled with something almost like first-date energy, but this was bigger. More serious, certainly, and definitely different, but still exhilarating. Any time I was near him, I felt it, and now that I was sober and was more aware of *everything* around me, it was inescapable.

Looking at him, I wanted him again. He was the first person to understand the struggle I was feeling—the pull inside me to be the old Theo pushing against this new, less dominant Theo.

A part of me felt bad that I was thinking about sex. This—meeting his father—wasn't about that or about whether we could be together or not. Brady was sad about what was happening to his dad. He was struggling with it, but he was still so proud of his dad, still enamored with him, like I imagined he'd always been, and for some reason, he wanted me to see it. He wanted someone else to know just how wonderful his dad was and how much he loved him.

I'd loved my father, and there wasn't a time I could remember when I wasn't doing something in pursuit of his pride and acceptance, but I'd never felt that way about my father, never got excited just to introduce him to someone.

I got out of my truck, and he came to meet me, but he stood on the other side. Across the hood, he said, "He's… He's not what he used to be. I mean, that's okay. What I mean is, he doesn't look the same. I guess that won't matter to you since you've never met him before, but he used to be a lot stronger. He was a big presence, you know?"

I only nodded because I knew he was trying to pump himself up, like it was hard for him to see who his dad had become when he used to be a superhero to Brady, and now he was a sick, dying patient.

"Anyway, he can't talk or move. But he blinks. Twice for yes, once for no. And sometimes you can see the smile in there." He took a big breath. "You ready?"

"I'm ready," I said, and I followed him into his childhood home.

The house was quiet, the slow ticking of a wall clock the only sound my ears could register. There didn't seem to be anyone home besides a nurse wearing black scrubs with orange bats all over them. When she greeted us, she wrapped a stethoscope around her neck, and while she and Brady spoke, I noticed a long line of photographs hanging on the living room wall. I started at the beginning. They were school photos, the kind the school photographer took in the fall but you didn't bring home till spring, with a blue background and a goofy smile.

Brady'd had a little bit of an overbite as a kid. It was always the first thing my eyes went to as I moved from one image to the next, and I wondered if he'd had to wear braces to correct it. There were pictures of a girl, too, and with her straight, black hair and Brady's same nose, I assumed she was his sister.

As he grew in the photos, he became more and more beautiful. Most children seemed to go through an awkward phase during middle school, but not Brady, even when he did get braces in the sixth grade. He was wiry and skinny, but he was gorgeous, even then. His wide cheekbones and straight nose pointed to a pair of full, dark pink lips, and I laughed to myself, thinking that if I'd lived in Wisper then, I would've been in love with twelve-year-old Brady.

At the end of the long wall, his larger high school photographs were displayed, and there was no other word for it: he was breathtaking. His hair was longer then, like now, and I was almost jealous of his handsomeness.

It made me want to kiss him again.

When the nurse finally left us alone, Brady was watching me as I admired the evidence of his happy childhood. I stood in front of his senior-year picture, completely enamored and maybe swooning a little on the inside. He looked *alive* in that image—wholly happy, excited for the future, and like he had not a care in the world.

Looking from that Brady to the one standing next to me in the middle of a comfortably decorated middle-class home with Southwestern accents here and there, the similarities were there, but the differences were arresting.

The roundness of boyhood was gone from his face. He had filled out and was taller, but that bone-deep happiness was missing. And now, he was achingly and hauntingly beautiful. I wasn't sure if it was purposeful, but he was changing in front of my eyes, day by day. No more suits. He wore jeans to work now, usually black, and he still wore a button-down shirt, but they were getting darker as the days passed, and he'd gotten rid of ties. I'd seen him walking to Coffee Shot or to his office while he talked on his cell, and the briefcase he'd sometimes carried had disappeared. Now, he wore a distressed leather satchel across his chest.

He was becoming a different man, and I wanted to know that man.

He blushed when he noticed me studying the difference, and I knew that he was absolutely humble. He probably had no idea how much I was attracted to him because he would never believe himself to be that alluring.

But he was, and if we weren't about to walk into his dying father's room, I would have had a hard time not touching him.

I didn't now, though, because after last night, I wasn't sure where we stood. Did he really want me, as more than a client he'd had sex with, or was it just sex? Sex that we needed to hide from the world until I could find a new lawyer. We'd made a deal. Obviously, that was over, and he was okay being friends with me, but other than that, I had no reason to believe I was someone he would want to be in a relationship with. In my experience, men didn't discuss such things. You fucked, you hung out, or you didn't, but we didn't have long drawn-out conversations about it. At least, I never had.

But he'd invited me to meet the person he loved most in

the world, so what did that mean? And now that I was nervous to the point of being nauseated, I followed him into his father's room to meet the person who'd shaped Brady into the incomparable man that he was.

"Dad, this is Theo," Brady introduced me to his father, who lay motionless in his bed. There wasn't a lot of obvious hospital equipment in the room except for an IV and its stand, an oxygen sensor on his index finger, and wires leading to what I thought was probably a heart monitor, but I didn't see one. "That's my sister, Bonnie," he said, motioning to a very pregnant woman sitting in a chair on the other side of the bed.

Bonnie smiled and gave a little wave.

It was awkward, but I said, "Hello, Mr. Douglas. I'm Theo Burroughs, Brady's… friend."

Brady nodded, acknowledging the truth of that statement. Odd friends though we were, still, it was true on some level.

I wasn't sure what to do, so I looked at Bonnie, and she was smirking now.

Brady didn't seem to notice. "Theo's buildin' a community center downtown. He bought the old newspaper building. I don't know if you remember, but Mr. Anderson sold it a few years ago, and Theo bought it. It looks great. They're almost ready to open the place up. Isn't that cool?"

Brady's father blinked twice, but he wasn't looking at Brady. His eyes were fixed on mine, and it felt like he could see inside me. Like he could see every dark thing I'd done, every lie I'd told, and all my faults.

I was terrified that with one look he would know that I wasn't good enough for his son.

"Tell him about Boston, Theo," Brady said. "Theo used to run this huge company, Dad. He's been all over the world. He's an angel investor. Pretty interestin' stuff, huh?"

Mr. Douglas blinked two more times, but I wanted to run

away. The lack of life in his eyes was about me. It had to be. Or it felt like that. And suddenly, I needed to get away from Brady. I needed to be far away so I couldn't hurt him. So I couldn't drag him down with me into the muddy mire I'd been drowning in.

Brady deserved better, and his father deserved to die knowing that his son wouldn't be with me.

"I'm sorry, but I-I have to go. I just remembered I have a delivery scheduled today, and if I'm not there, they'll take it back to the warehouse. Apologies." I looked at Brady. "I'm sorry, Brady. I forgot." It hurt to lie to someone I cared about. I'd vowed to be done with that, but to protect him from the mess that was my life, it was the only choice in the moment. It wasn't like I could explain in front of his father.

Bonnie frowned, and Brady froze. "Okay," he said, but it was clear from the flat tone of his voice that he didn't believe me.

THE LIE FESTERED. It ate at me, and I kicked my door before I got in my truck to escape. Slamming my hands against my steering wheel over and over didn't help either. I knew I needed to distract myself so I didn't run for the first bottle of vodka I could find, so I drove back to the center and packed the boxes of old newspapers into my truck and took them to the library.

I wanted to drink. I wanted to drown myself in alcohol, but… But I didn't. I couldn't. I'd come so far. The person I used to be was in the back of my mind, and he wouldn't let me.

The new librarian, Samantha Russo, or Sam, as she demanded she be called, was a little odd. She looked like a

Gen Z punk rock kind of person, but she was wearing a long, floral skirt over her combat boots, and there was a tenderness about her. She was halfway through a hard copy of *Pride and Prejudice* when I entered the library, and I pictured her being the sort who believed wholeheartedly in true love. It was funny, but just being near someone like that made me feel like I might be able to believe in it too.

If I wasn't such a fucking liar.

After reintroducing myself and explaining why I was there, she said in a loud voice, "Oh, I remember you. You're that awful bowler."

I laughed, though it did nothing to ease the ache in my chest.

"Brady's mentioned you. Aren't you the investor everyone's always talking about?" Her fifties-looking cat-eye glasses were low on her nose, and she pushed them up. "You're the guy who bought my grandpa's building."

"Your grandpa? You're Jessup Anderson's granddaughter?"

"Yep. Gramps called and said Wisper needed a new librarian when the old one retired. So here I am."

"That's generous of you."

She shrugged.

"Brady thought you might be able to get some use out of these old papers, but if you can't, I can recycle them. I don't want to dump them on you."

"Oh no," she said, popping the top off one of the boxes. "I was hoping they existed somewhere, but I didn't think my gramps would've saved them. Thank you. And whatever I don't use, I'll try to organize, and maybe we can get them scanned, then we won't need the physical copies."

"Great. I'm happy to pay for that. I can't imagine you have much of a budget here."

She laughed. "You imagined correctly. Thanks for the offer, but I can't take money from you. You would have to donate it to the library."

"Done," I said. "I'd be glad to."

"That's really sweet. Thanks." She held a paper up and folded it carefully in half. "Look at these old ads. I kind of love them. They're so different than the ones we see today, and really, who gets the actual newspaper anymore? We see all our advertisements online now. The old-school feel of these makes me... I dunno. Happy. You know? Makes me feel like I was a part of a better time. I wasn't even alive when these were printed, but holding them makes me feel like I was." She set the paper back in the box, leaning over it. "God, look at their clothes. These ladies had style, I'll give them that. I mean, sure, they weren't actually allowed to wear pants, and that pisses me off to no end, but still, these skirts and hats are amazing." She pointed to the paper. "And the shoes? Ugh. I wish."

I was standing there with my hands at my sides, feeling like I knew exactly what she meant. I wished I could go back to my childhood. I wanted to start over.

Getting sober was the hardest thing I'd ever done, and with everything in me, I wanted to go back and make different choices.

It was a dangerous way of thinking. I knew that, had been told that by the people at AA meetings. Wishing and dreaming were a waste of time. All we had was the here and now, and the best thing for our sobriety was to get on with life, to move forward, not back.

Dreaming of a different life would only lead to bad places and bad decisions, which would eventually lead back to drinking.

*Tell that to my heart.*

"Are you busy right now?" Sam asked. "You wanna help me look through these?"

"Sure," I said. "No. I'm not busy." I had a mountain of tasks to check off my list, and I was sure there was someone or something needing my attention back at the center, but right then, none of it mattered. I wanted to be anywhere else doing anything else, and Sam's hunt for information about some 1960s mystery seemed like the perfect distraction.

# CHAPTER NINETEEN

### THEO

"DUDE! I was right. It's all here. All the saucy details." Sam jumped up from the floor, waving a front-page article in her hand. The large black-and-white image gave it away. We'd spread the newspapers out over the floor in the library's main room, and there wasn't one inch of the weathered 1970s parquet pattern clear, so she landed on a paper, and her shoe tore it in half when she slid back an inch. "Shit."

"What did you find?"

"Look," she said, leaning to hand the paper to me without moving so she wouldn't damage any more. They hadn't been properly stored, sitting for years in the open air and sunlight on the third floor of my building, so they were soft and delicate. A few looked like they'd suffered water damage, and those were stiff, almost crunchy, and touching them resulted in rips no matter how carefully we handled them.

I had no clue what I was doing with this woman, investigating some town secret, but it gave me something to do that didn't have anything to do with me, with my sobriety, my obligations to the center, or anything else that was stressing me out.

Or Brady, although not thinking about him became harder and harder the longer I sat there.

For a little while, though, I was able to focus only on Sam and her papers, and it felt good.

"What am I looking at?"

"It's all right there. The Mountain Misses spurned a member because she was gay!"

"Really?" That definitely would've been big news in Wisper in 1968. I could imagine the gossip. I looked over the article, and sure enough, Sam was right. The Mountain Misses had been absolutely scandalized when one of their members—Sissy Melton, the president no less—had been caught kissing another woman. "The article doesn't say who this woman was. Did you find anything else?"

"No, but I think I know where we can go for answers."

"We?"

"Well, yeah. I mean, you're in this now too. Don't you want to know?"

"Yes," I said, shrugging. "Guess I do."

"C'mon." She reached for my hand and hauled me up to standing. "You've already met my gramps, right?"

"Jessup?" Brushing dust off my ass, I said, "Uh, yes, I did meet him once when the sale of the newspaper building was going through, but I doubt he remembers me. It's been three years."

"Are you kidding? Closing the paper's all he ever talks about. There's no way he *doesn't* know who you are. And he'll have all the dirt. He's been out of town, but he just got home today." She twisted her lips to one side. "Uh… I don't exactly have a car. Can you drive?"

"Of course, but how did you get to work?"

"Walked."

"But aren't you worried about getting into a stranger's car?"

She scoffed. "Please. We can bet at least five people saw you hauling those boxes in here, and I doubt there's a person in Wisper who doesn't know who you are. They know who I am. People talk to me like I've been here my whole life. So if you murder me, they'll know where to look."

"Good point."

***

"HELLO, HELLO!" Mr. Anderson called when Sam opened his front door. When we stepped over the threshold, I felt like I was following her into a museum.

There were clocks on every surface. Old cuckoo clocks hung on the walls, and on top of every available side table, coffee table, or open spot on a bookshelf sat small, round metal alarm clocks, each with two bells on top with a dinging metal hammer between them. Jessup had them in a myriad of colors. The furniture looked like it had come straight from a 1950s showroom, or what I could see of it anyway, because there were at least four knitted blankets thrown wherever there was a place that could hold one.

I could smell the dust and could see it floating lazily in the air where the sun was shining in through a big bay window facing Park Street. The pillows decorating the window's bench seat were covered in green and orange canvas floral pillowcases. Jessup Anderson seemed to be confused about which decade he liked best.

"Samantha, my sunshine," he greeted Sam with a big smile on his face, walking into his living room and hugging her. "My darlin', I gotta say, it's so good to be home. How are you settlin' in at the library? I've missed you, but you know

Florida calls us old folks like a relentless telemarketer." He patted her face. "It sure is nice to have somebody else afoot since your grandmama's gone. I was actually glad to see dirty dishes in the sink when I got home."

Sam threw me a look over her shoulder. "Yeah, yeah, I live with my gramps. Get over it."

I laughed. "It seems like a lovely place to live," I said. "Hello, Mr. Anderson. I don't know if you remember—"

"Mr. Burroughs. How are you, son? How's my buildin'? You know, I've been hearin' the talk around town, and I was plannin' to drop by to see what you'd done with the place now that I'm home. It'll warm my heart to see it restored. I was so sad to let it go, but it was just too much for these old hands to handle." He held his hands up, the skin wrinkled and the joints set at not quite the right angle.

"I'm well, Mr. Anderson," I said, shaking his hand. "Thank you for asking. Things are really taking shape down there. Please, I'd love it if you'd come to see it. You're welcome any time."

It touched me a little that he still thought of the center as "his building." I was hoping the rest of Wisper would come to think of it that way too.

He smiled, the skin around his eyes creasing upwards. "That's wonderful. I'm sure glad to hear it. And you call me Jessup."

"Thank you, sir."

"Ah, ah," he warned, wagging one finger in my direction.

"Thank you, Jessup."

"Better. So, what brings you kids here in the middle of the day? Samantha, who's watchin' the library if you're here?"

"Oh, Gramps," Sam said. "You're so funny. No one. No one is watching the library because no one *comes* to the library." She rolled her eyes. "Like, for real. No. One. It's sad. I'm gonna have to do something about that. Ooo," she said, looking at me with some kind of sparkle in her eye. "Maybe if I had a little help from someone with, well, a lot of money…"

"That someone being me?" I asked.

"Exactly. Maybe we could set up some kind of library fundraiser to raise money for new books, new furniture, and some library events. Oh! We could have a fall festival. And then maybe people would sign their kids up for the Saturday readings like they used to do with Addi."

"Samantha, it's rude to talk about a man's money in front of him."

"It's fine, Jessup, really," I said. "And it's not a bad idea, Sam. Maybe we could do a joint event for the library and the new center."

"Oh my God, yes! Genius." She elbowed me in the side. "See? I knew I liked you." To her grandfather she said, "Now, I know you have the gossip, so we're here to get it outta you."

"Gossip about what?"

"About the Mountain Misses and Sissy Melton."

"Oh now, there's a story. But that's old news." He waved her away, and we followed him into the kitchen.

"I found some articles at the library, but they were blacked out. Theo brought me a bunch of old *Wisper Gazettes*, and I found one that said Sissy was caught kissing another woman and that the club disbanded after that, but that's all I could find, and I *need* to know what happened. Why'd they disband? What was the big deal?"

Jessup tsked. "Why do you wanna know? I'm sure you have plenty of other things to do."

"I don't," Sam said. "Now, spill."

"Would you like coffee?" Jessup asked me. "Samantha

doesn't drink it often, but I have some brewin' if you'd like a cup."

"Grandpa! Quit stalling."

He laughed, and I declined the coffee. Coffee Shot was way too close, and I'd stopped off for three shots of espresso before I showed up at the library. That was plenty, and besides, my hands had just begun to stop shaking.

"Alright, alright. Come sit here with me at the table. We have a grand view of the mountains, and I have cookies!"

His enthusiasm for entertaining visitors was endearing, so I sat at his kitchen table and helped myself to two store-bought chocolate chip cookies. That made him smile, and then he began to tell us about the big scandal that had rocked Wisper to its core in a bygone era.

"Well, lemme start off by sayin' that I think you can imagine how unusual it was back then. We have all kinds of people livin' in Wisper nowadays, but back then, there was only farmers, ranchers, their wives, and their kids. Maybe a single man here or there. A few widowers. But there was not one woman who lived alone, until one day, Adora Friedrichsen moved into a little house about two blocks away from the courthouse. It was one of the white cottages we still have here in town. They're a little worse for the wear these d—"

"Gramps, you're getting off topic," Sam said, nudging him back to the point.

"Right, right. Anyway, everybody was talkin' about this woman, Adora. She was German, moved here from Berlin, I do believe. This was long before the wall came down. She wasn't a widow, never been married, and she had no kids. She was just a single workin' woman. She applied for a job at my paper."

"At the paper? You were sitting on that bombshell this

whole time, and you didn't lead with that?"

Jessup chuckled. "Get a grip, Samantha." He turned his attention toward me. "I hired her from a town over in California. She called to inquire about the job, lookin' for a fresh start after a bad relationship, and I'd had myself a fair few of those, so I gave her a shot."

"Grandpa, you had relationships with women other than Grandma? What the heck?"

"Oh, c'mon now," he said, and Sam laughed. "When I was younger."

"Go on," Sam told him, and she stuffed a whole cookie in her mouth. Crumbs fell down to the wooden tabletop beneath her elbows, and she swiped them away with a sheepish look.

Jessup shook his head, tsking at his granddaughter again. She seemed to exasperate him, but it was clear he loved her. "Anyway, Adora had several years' experience workin' at a bigger newspaper than mine, so I was hopin' she could help me to get and stay organized. And she started to. We worked well together. Even your grandma liked her. They became fast friends, and we had her out to the old house for dinner several times. Grandma asked her about her life—why she wasn't married or didn't have kids—but Adora never really did answer. We thought she might just be shy, or maybe she'd had a hard time and didn't wanna talk about it.

"That was until Birdy Mason and her daughter caught Adora one afternoon lip-locked with none other than Sissy Melton in the alleyway behind the newspaper."

"The paper said Sissy was the president of the Mountain Misses, but, like, who was she?" Sam asked.

"Oh, well, she's been around forever. She was married to Howard Melton for years and years till he died. She's a farmer, has a booth at the farmers market."

"So she was married to a man, but she was kissing a

woman?" Sam asked.

"Yes."

Curiosity was getting the better of me. "What did her husband think about that?"

"Well, now, that's somethin' you're gonna have to ask Sissy herself. I didn't get involved then, and I ain't gonna do it now."

"How could you not be involved?" Sam asked him. "You wrote about it in the paper."

"Well," he said, "I did. I had to. It was all anyone could talk about, and all kindsa rumors were spreadin' through Wisper like wildfire. I tried to set the record straight, but I asked Adora's and Sissy's permission before I took it to print. Sissy was fine with it, but Adora was hesitant. In the end, she agreed 'cause she thought the truth was better than the most popular rumor at the time—that she was really a Russian spy, come to induct our young men into the Soviet army." Jessup rolled his eyes.

"Sissy's still alive?" I asked. It would be rude to show up on an old woman's doorstep and ask her to talk about something that was probably intensely private, right?

"Oh yes. That woman will never die. All her friends and family died years ago, but she's still kickin'."

"What's her address?" Sam said, pulling out her phone to look it up.

"Samantha, you can't go stormin' over there, demandin' Sissy tell you all her secrets. That's rude."

"I don't want to be rude, but I have to know what happened. Where's Adora now?"

"It's not my place to say," Jessup said, and he looked down. It was a clue that something sad had happened to Adora, or to Sissy, or to both of them.

And now, I needed to know just as badly as Sam did.

# CHAPTER TWENTY

## BRADY

SURPRISE, surprise. Gene's permits weren't up to date. We resubmitted his application, but we had to wait for his water rights to be regranted back to him, and in the meantime, I needed to try to manage the feud between him and his neighbor, so I met with Gene and Cody Baxter and Baxter's lawyer, Collin Ames.

I'd met Collin before. He and I had run into each other at the courthouse in Jackson from time to time. We'd never gone up against each other, but I already knew he was more practiced in litigation than I was. I'd heard he was good. Good enough that I couldn't gauge if I was better.

He was dressed in an appropriate suit, but they were losing their appeal for me. Taking care of them was an added chore, and I just didn't give a shit anymore. Nothing seemed important compared to what was going on with my dad. Why not wear what I wanted? So I was dressed in black jeans and a black button-down, with my favorite bolo tie my auntie had given me for my eighteenth birthday tightened around my neck. The turquoise slide had been shaped into an oval and polished till the stone shone and glinted in the sunlight.

This was me, or it was who I was slowly becoming. It was a part of myself I'd denied for a long time, never wanting to claim my heritage because for so long, it had been another thing that made me stand apart from everyone else. My mom's family had been a point of shame in my life because of the stigma attached to being an "Indian." But now that I was losing the one person who I'd thought had shaped my identity, it seemed less and less important what people thought of me. And I knew this new version of me would make my dad happy. He was proud of my mom's heritage, and it had always disappointed him when, as kids, Bonnie and I tried to disguise the Shoshone in us.

I thought about that and about what Theo thought of me, of the changes I was making. Maybe a polished lawyer was more his style. He'd left my parents' house in a hurry. He'd given an excuse, but I saw in his eyes it was a lie.

After the sex we'd had, I thought we were on the same page. We hadn't said as much out loud, but there was a reason he bailed, and I was driving myself insane, trying to decide what it could be.

Was my family drama too much for him? Maybe now that he was getting his life back, I wasn't what he wanted anymore. The thought had me freezing, trying to replay our conversations in my mind for any clues. It took Gene almost shouting my name to bring me back to the present.

Gene and I had met in front of Mr. Baxter's farmhouse, and then the four of us took golf carts out to the land and the stream in question. Baxter refused to ride in the same cart as Gene and me, like a cranky pre-teen, so we took two. And when we got there, he hopped out and stomped over to the edge of the water.

"Do you see this?" Mr. Baxter asked me. He wouldn't even look at Gene. "I have no idea how you can make a claim on *my* stream when it's clearly on *my* property. It doesn't even touch his land."

When he finally scowled at Gene, Gene took a deep breath, his large chest expanding. He was holding his hat in his hands, but he smoothed his hair back, then climbed out of our cart and fixed the Stetson back on his head. He was wearing denim overalls with a brown flannel shirt underneath, and he was covered head to toe in dirt, or maybe it was cow shit. I had no idea, but Mr. Baxter was looking him up and down, like Gene was just some country idiot, and he couldn't believe he had to lower himself to deal with the situation.

Gene said slowly, "See that tree right there?" He pointed to a lone aspen standing guard over the stream, shading it and setting it in its yellow-leafed glow.

"What about it?" Collin asked, speaking for Mr. Baxter.

"That tree marks the property line," Gene continued. "It always has. The stream has changed and moved over the years so it looks like the stream's on your land, but it's on both. Which means, accordin' to the state of Wyoming, we both have the use of it as long as we've both applied for the permit."

*Shit.* I winced, hoping no one had seen my face. I'd asked Gene not to mention the permits. It was clear Collin and Mr. Baxter knew Gene didn't actually have a permit anymore. They'd done their homework. Our new application was likely to be approved, but if Mr. Baxter decided to dispute it, which, clearly, he would, then there was still a chance Gene could lose his rights permanently.

Collin said, "Unfortunately, Mr. Owens, your permits haven't been kept up to date, so technically, you have no water rights. But let's just say for the moment that you do. You are also claimin' that your land includes an entire mile along this water body that is definitively owned by my client. How do you plan to prove that?"

"Hey now," I said, stepping forward, and Mr. Baxter fixed his glare on me again like a hungry dog. "The assessor hasn't been out yet. We have to wait for his findings before you can go accusin' my client of land theft." Cocking my head, I raised a brow at Collin, and he smirked. He knew he was getting ahead of himself, and he was doing it on purpose. He could bet I wouldn't give up, but he had to try. I would've.

"Cody, your granddaddy and I worked together for years and years, sharin' the land and the water. We never cared who owned what. It worked well for both of us. Now, I just don't understand why you and I can't do the same."

"Because it's mine," Baxter said. "I don't owe you a goddamn thing, and I have no desire to 'work' with you." Folding his arms over his chest, he said, "I don't need your business messing with mine, and I sure as hell don't want your animals' filth contaminating my water. I've seen your operation. It's antiquated and dirty."

Oly had been right that he was attractive, physically, but Cody Baxter's attitude made him ugly. His clothes looked like the usual jeans and T-shirt ranchers and farmers wore around here, but they were stiff and brand new, like he'd bought them yesterday just to fit in. But it was his lack of friendliness that showed him to be an outsider. He really was an asshole. Even if he and Gene didn't agree, that didn't mean the guy had to be purposely cruel.

And Gene was right. The stream could be mutually beneficial to both farms, so I had no clue why the guy was being so difficult, other than the fact that he was just a dick. Plenty of people shared water rights around here. The problem was, Mr. Baxter was claiming that the stream started on his property, so even if it did cross over onto

Gene's, if it was true, Baxter would have first rights either way we cut it.

It was looking more and more like I would probably lose this case.

Trying to let that possibility sink in, I looked around, trying to think of an angle I could use to try to barter an agreement between the two men. It occurred to me as I looked at the stream, following it south and into the trees at the base of the mountains, that maybe I was like that stream, straddling two different lives. Strait-laced corporate lawyer Brady, holding onto an old dream, was warring with whoever this new guy was.

But who the fuck was he?

Whoever he was, like the stream, he was flowing to somewhere, rushing to a place I had no control of. A new place I'd never been, full of uncertainty and anger and—

My phone buzzed in my pocket, and when I looked at it, my heart dropped into my stomach and the thought dissolved. Somehow, I managed to say, "Please excuse me. This is an urgent matter. I have to take this call."

"G'on ahead, Brady. Take your call," Gene said. "We'll be right here when you get back." And he crossed his arms too.

When I'd walked far enough away that they couldn't hear me, I answered. "Britt? What's wrong?"

"Brady? I'm sorry. I know you weren't expectin' this, but I've called an ambulance to transfer your dad to hospice. It's time. I can't keep up with what he needs here at the house. Things are happenin' quickly now. He's in pain, and he's gettin' weaker by the hour. He *needs* hospice. He's developed some kind of infection. From the sound of his lungs, it's pneumonia. You should come home."

*Fuck. Not yet. I'm not ready.*

"Brady?" she said when I didn't respond. "I already called your mom. She was really flustered, and your sister's a mess, so I told them I'd let you know. Your mom's on her way. Head home, okay?"

"Okay," I said, but it was more like a whisper. I cleared my throat. "Okay."

DAD WAS in and out of consciousness when I got there. His fever had shot up to 102 degrees, and when the transport came to take him to hospice, he was out, and I was worried he'd wake up in a strange place and be scared.

The people at hospice were nice, but that didn't make it any easier. They were careful with him, and they were helpful and accommodating to my mom, Bonnie, and me. They fed us, gave us pillows and blankets so we could camp out there in his room with him, and they even went searching for a charger for my phone 'cause I'd forgotten mine and I needed to know when the assessor had made his determination about Gene and Mr. Baxter's property lines. While I waited, I lay there on a pile of blankets on the floor so Bonnie could have the cot, crying silently, wishing I was anywhere else.

"Bunny," Mom said softly.

Would she ever stop calling me that? I was thirty fucking years old. "Yeah?"

"Have you met the new librarian yet?"

"What? Why're you askin' me that now?" My mom's attitude was pissing me off. Yet again, she wanted to let the earth and the universe make important decisions for our family. What a load of bullshit. And now she wanted to talk gossip? Right now?

"I just thought of it. Besides, we have to talk about somethin'. We can't just sit here cryin'. You know your dad wouldn't want that."

*He wouldn't want hospice.* "Yeah, I've met her," I said, pushing the wet mess off my face with the back of my hand. I lifted up and tried to punch the pillow a nurse had given me into submission. It was too lumpy. "Why?"

"I couldn't believe it when I saw her at the market. That's little Sunny. Don't you remember playin' with her? You were probably five years old. She was a little younger, I think, but she used to come here during the summer to stay with her grandparents. Remember? Jessup and Josie Anderson used to live down the street from us, and you two kids had the run of our neighborhood."

"The librarian's name is Sam."

"Yeah, her grandparents called her Sunny. It was a nick-name 'cause Jessup called her Samantha Sunshine. You really don't remember?"

"No. I don't remember," I said, but I did. A little girl with dirty blond hair flashed through my head, dressed in a pink Sunday school dress, white ruffled-edged socks, and shiny pink shoes, but we'd been out in my backyard, digging in the dirt, burying dead frogs we'd found 'cause they made her sad and I'd wanted to make her smile, so she was covered head to toe in it when she went home. I could still hear her grandma screeching when she saw the state of Sunny's dress.

So Sam was familiar to me because I *had* known her in another life. I wondered if she would remember me if I told her.

"I can't believe you don't remember her," my mom said. "Y'all used to be glued at the hip. I can still see your little faces, stained purple from popsicles. Oh, she used to drive her grandmama nuts. She was such a stubborn little thing. She stopped comin' when she was five or six 'cause her parents moved far away. Her grandmama told me all about…" My mom kept droning on and on, but I wasn't listening 'cause I was remembering my dad. I'd come home later that evening, and I'd sat with him in the back yard, watching how the late afternoon light faded slowly while he was making a new piece. He was really getting into it, letting his body and the movement of his strong arms guide him.

He was the strongest man in the world in my eyes back then, and I had been in awe of him, of his ability to create something so beautiful out of a boring piece of wood.

It was a one-of-a-kind dining table he'd been making, and after he'd crafted six chairs to match, he sold the set to a couple out of Seattle, and they'd driven down themselves to pick them up.

I remembered my dad lifting me in the air, twirling me around after they left. They'd paid him two thousand dollars, which was a lot of money for us back then. He'd never made that kind of money on one set, and he was so happy.

He'd taken us out to dinner at an Italian restaurant in Jackson that night, and I still remembered the way the pistachio gelato had tasted after dinner, melting in my mouth.

Before I gave into sleep on the cold hospice floor, I licked my lips, tasting it, trying to cement the sweet, nutty flavor in my memory so I'd never forget the proud smile on my dad's face while it dripped down my five-year-old chin.

---

BONNIE SHOOK MY SHOULDER. "Bunny, wake up."

I swatted at her, landing a blow on her arm. "Quit fuckin' callin' me that."

Hitting my pregnant sister wasn't my finest moment, but she wasn't mad. Her voice was quiet and soft, and she smoothed my hair away from my face. "He's awake. They said we should spend this time with him, in case…"

In case he never woke again.

"I'm sorry."

"It's okay," she said.

Opening my eyes, I watched a nurse's off-brand running shoes squeaking across the floor as she adjusted my dad's IV. She injected medicine into it, tucked his blanket tighter around his body to keep warmth in, and then she left us alone.

My mom was holding my dad's hand, looking in his eyes, tears streaming down her face while they gazed at the person they loved most in the world for maybe the last time. They were such different people, but they'd been in love my whole life, and my stomach hurt when I tried to imagine my mom living without him.

It was the middle of the night. 2:47 a.m., to be exact. The round, old-school clock on the wall was ticking away, counting the last moments of my dad's life, one by one, and instead of rushing to him to spend every second I had left with him, I watched that damn clock.

I was angry at the clock. What fucking right did it have to time us like that? Like we were some items on a list the universe needed to check off. It was the same universe my mom believed so strongly in. *Fuck her universe. And fuck God.*

*Tick*—say goodbye. *Tock*—remember the good times. *Tick*—let him go. *Tock*—fuck off.

I stood, letting the cheap, scratchy blanket someone had laid over me fall to the hard tile floor. Tying my hair back with a loose piece of fringe from the edge of the throw, I kicked a chair toward the wall, then climbed on it and yanked the clock down. My mom and Bonnie were watching me like I'd lost my mind, but I didn't care, and nobody said anything.

I took the stupid thing out of my dad's room, down the hall-way, and out the back door, and then I set it carefully on the sidewalk.

It was battery powered, and I watched the clock hands do their slow, one-way shuffle for a long time, long enough that I began to panic that my dad would die before I'd had a chance to say goodbye, but I couldn't go back inside.

I couldn't face the time I had left, and it made me *hate* that clock.

I jumped on it. The clear clockface cracked, but still, it kept ticking, so I jumped again and again and again until all that was left were broken plastic pieces and black hands that looked like they'd been put down a garbage disposal.

Somehow, that satisfied me, and I left it, broken and busted apart on the sidewalk, and walked back inside to say goodbye to the best man I would ever know.

---

"I KNOW YOU'RE HURTIN', son," my mom said softly in the hallway outside my dad's room while Bonnie stayed with him, telling him made-up stories about what her child would look like and all the things she'd do with him, the traditions she would carry into the baby's life that our dad had brought into ours, like cutting down our own Christmas tree and then using the wood after the holidays to make something our family could use every year. We had a whole set of weird-looking hand-carved wooden Christmas elves our dad put out in front of the house the day after Thanksgiving. Or Sunday morning hashbrown casserole. It was our dad's favorite. My mom hated it, but she made it nearly every weekend of their marriage because he loved it.

My mom spoke louder, and I admired that. I admired that

she could be so sure about anything when everything was falling apart. "But you need to go in there. If you don't say goodbye, you'll regret it for the rest of your life."

I stared at the floor, not wanting to see the pain on her face, counting the veins in the ceramic tiles under my feet, begging and hoping and wishing as hard as I could that I was still sleeping and this was just a bad dream. I'd wake up and be back in Boise at my boring job, in the crappy apartment I'd rented on the edge of town 'cause, as much as I wanted to pretend like I was some hot-shot attorney, it had been all I could afford.

"I know," I said. I kicked at the tile, and the sole of my boot left a black mark as I turned and walked into my dad's room.

When I was by his side, Bonnie leaned over him to kiss his cheek, her breath hitching and tears leaking down her face to land on his. She wiped them softly away with a tissue, and I heard her sobbing silently as she left the room, leaving my dad and me alone.

He was awake, but the light in his eyes had gone. The doctors were keeping him drugged with pain medication so he didn't have to suffer while he died.

Slowly, those eyes turned to mine, and he waited for me to speak.

I couldn't.

Looking at the short white hair on his chin, all I could see was when that had been a full, proud beard, and the words just wouldn't come, so I laid my head on his chest, careful not to let its weight obstruct his breathing. His arms lay rigidly by his sides, but one twitched, and I looked at him. He was trying to reach for me, and I knew I had to do this. I knew my mom was right, and if I didn't say goodbye, I would never forgive myself.

Scooting my chair closer, I said, "I'm sorry, Dad."

He blinked once. *No, don't be sorry.*

"I haven't handled this very well. You deserved better from me."

He blinked again.

And then it all came out because he was the person I loved and trusted the most in the world. Who else could I tell? "But I don't know how to do this. I don't know how to be strong. I know I'm s'posed to tell you that it's okay for you to go, but it's not. None of this is okay. I'm *angry*." Tears dripped down my face. "You didn't deserve this disease, and I'm pissed off. It's not fair. You're my best friend. You're the best man I've ever known, and I've worshiped you my whole life. Everything I've done, I've done to make you proud. What am I gonna do now? How will you know to be proud of me? How will you know I love you?"

He closed his eyes, and a tear fell down onto his shoulder. I lifted his hand and pressed it to my face, and I cried.

Panic was building inside me again, like I was wasting our time being weak. That wasn't good enough for the man who'd been strong my whole life.

When I was done, when there were no more tears inside me, that was when I knew what I had to do. For him. I was sorry it had taken me this long.

"Forget everything I just said, Dad. It will be okay, because I'm your son. You've taught me how to be good, like you. You've taught me how to be strong. I don't feel like that right now, but it's in me. It has to be, right?"

He blinked twice.

"I love you," I said. "I will miss you every goddamn day when you're gone, but I'll be okay."

It was a lie, and he knew it, and he blinked once.

# CHAPTER TWENTY-ONE

## THEO

"THEO, this place is really taking shape," my sister's best friend and future sister-in-law said when she'd driven Aislinn over so I could show them the newest renovations. They were waiting for Oly to meet them after work and were planning to go to dinner in Jackson.

"Thanks, Billie," I said. "We've been working hard on it."

"Did you hire someone besides Vern?" Ace asked.

"Yes, Devo is officially my assistant director, and the three of us have done a lot of the work. But I did hire someone to reframe where Devo and her friends knocked down a couple walls. A guy named James Brockovich."

"Oh, really?" Billie said. "Yeah, we know ol' Brockie." She was being sarcastic somehow, but Brock had been great. He helped clean up the mess we'd made knocking the walls down, and then he'd gotten to work right away, reframing small areas that had needed it and installing new drywall. He'd even helped us paint the downstairs walls. All that was left was the second floor. I'd already painted my apartment. Some of the walls were exposed brick, so I left those as they were but painted the interior walls a dark shade of grayish blue, like a stormy sky.

"But, other than that, we did most of it ourselves. We painted miles' worth of new baseboards. We'll install those after we finish painting the rest of the place. The apartment is ready upstairs. I'm just waiting for a bed and a refrigerator to be delivered before I officially move in. I know you haven't quite warmed up to him yet, Ace, but Vern's been really help-ful. A little… unorthodox, maybe, but great. He did all the landscaping out front. It looks good, doesn't it, Billie?"

"Yeah," she said. "Looks professional."

"We planted the mums and asters you two picked out, Ace," I said, describing them for her. "He planted the purple and orange on either side of that deep crimson red you chose. Vern said he'll plant some tulips there, too, and they'll bloom in the spring. He really knows what he's doing."

"I'm excited for you, Theo," my sister said. "How's AA? Are you still going?"

Billie choked on the iced coffee she'd just taken a gulp of. "Oh, uh, why don't I go check out those mums," she said, uncomfortable after Ace's question, and she coughed the coffee from her throat.

"It's okay, Billie," I said. "I'm not very hung up on the anonymity thing. You're Ace's best friend, so I'm okay talking about this in front of you. Unless you'd rather not hear about it."

She shrugged and led Ace to sit in a metal folding chair. I'd ordered a truckload of furniture for the center—comfy couches and armchairs so people could feel like they were in their own homes—and it would be here in less than two weeks, which was perfect timing because the roof would be finished, and Devo and I would be done painting the rest of the building by then. Our new sign would be delivered around the same time too.

Things were really coming along, and my excitement and pride were growing every day. The All & Sundry Collective was almost a reality, and we would open our doors to the public in a month.

"Yes, I'm still going to AA. I try to go every day, if I can. And I'm already organizing meetings that we'll hold here once the place is open."

"That's wonderful, big brother." Ace smiled, a true, genuine smile, and I crossed the room to hug her when she stood.

"Thanks for not giving up on me," I said.

"I never will. You didn't give up on me, not once in ten years. I love you."

"Love you too."

Her phone rang, and I let go of her so she could answer. "Hello?"

Billie and I chatted while Ace took her call, but she hung up in less than a minute. "Oly can't come tonight."

"Damn it! We planned this, like, two weeks ago. You guys were the ones who said I needed to get out of my office for a night." She groaned. "I washed my hair and everything."

"I know," Ace said. "Sorry. We can still go, but her friend's dad just passed away, so she wants to be there for him."

"Which friend?" I asked, and my heart began to race. *Please don't let her say Brady's name.*

Ace turned toward me, her voice aimed at me. It seemed like she was looking right through me. "Brady Douglas." Somehow, even though I'd only mentioned him to her briefly, she knew he meant something to me.

*Ah, Brady.* I was almost in a panic. I wanted to go find him. I wanted to hold him.

And I wanted to drink when I realized none of those things were possible because I didn't mean anything to him. We'd screwed, but I'd kind of blown him off, and his stiff reaction told me I wouldn't be welcome. How presumptuous would it be for me to show up on his doorstep now?

"I need to go to a meeting."

"Are you okay?" Ace asked.

"I… Yes, I think so. It's just that hearing about parents dying still isn't easy for me. And I'm sad for Brady."

"Well, that's good, man," Billie said. "I mean, that you recognize that instead of giving into those feelings, you should reach out to your AA peeps. Don't let us stop you. C'mon, Ace. Let's go find some pizza. I'm not wasting this outfit. I look hot."

Billie walked outside, and Ace reached out for me, pulling me in for another hug when I touched the back of her hand.

When she let go, she extended her walking cane and turned toward the door. "Go to your meeting, but call me if you need me, okay? I'm always here for you."

"I know, thank you," I said. "You don't know what that means to me."

"I do, silly. I know exactly what it means."

---

"WHO WANTS TO START?" Cora asked the room, and I stood. I wasn't usually one to jump on the chopping block first, but tonight, I needed to.

"Hi. I'm Theo. I'm an alcoholic."

This time, twenty voices greeted me, "Hi, Theo."

"My friend's dad died today," I said, and I looked at Charlie. I'd told him about Brady's dad when we met in the parking lot outside the church. He hung his head, and I went on. "I didn't know him well, but his son has become important to me, and it hurt to get that news. It wasn't my first thought, but I wanted to drink. I didn't want to think about how my friend must be feeling. And I *really* didn't want to think about how I'd felt when I lost my own parents.

Would Brady ever forgive me for missing out on the chance to get to know his dad? I wasn't sure I'd ever forgive myself. The best I could do was try to be better. To love myself more so I wouldn't go around hurting people by attempting to protect them from me.

"But then I realized that trying not to feel all those things is what led me to drink in the first place, so I knew I needed a meeting, and I guess, if it's okay with all of you, I'll tell you how it felt."

People were nodding, and Charlie actually smiled at me, which was a first.

"I was in college when both of my parents were killed in a car accident in Boston. My sister was only sixteen, and she was in the car with them. I don't want to go into details, but she was badly injured. She lost her sight. They told us we were lucky that she hadn't suffered a traumatic brain injury. A lot of people don't come back from those."

Looking around at the faces in the room, I let the despair I'd felt back then settle inside me.

But I was ready to give it a voice.

"It didn't *feel* lucky. I've never been so terrified. She and I weren't close—I'd been away at school, and before that, she was a bratty teenager—but after the accident, she couldn't do anything without my help. I had to move home. I had to leave my life.

"I tried so hard to help her, to make her happy, to give her the things I thought she wanted. All *I* ever wanted was for her to smile. I thought if I could make that happen, then maybe I'd feel like it was worth it, you know? Maybe then I wouldn't feel so damn guilty for being angry about having to give up everything for her."

I laughed at how easily the truth was flowing out of me now.

"And then we came here for my business, and she met a man, and he made her smile like no one had ever been able to, and it *pissed* me off. I've hated that man because he did what I never could. But now I'm realizing that, really, it was me I've been hating this whole time. I was mad at myself because I missed the bigger picture. Who cares who makes my sister happy? As long as she's happy. I mean, her world was turned upside down and inside out too. I'm sure I wasn't the easiest guy to be around. She had to put up with me just as much as I had to put up with her.

"And all of that jealousy and anger was stopping me from facing what I was really feeling, which was… loss. I lost both of my parents on the same day. I lost my family, my life, my stability. We lost everything except for money. And what good has that ever done anyone?"

Vern's whiny asshole comment was bouncing around my head, and there were some doubtful faces in the room after that, but no one interrupted.

"And then someone tried to blackmail me for all that money. He threatened my sister's life, and I tried to kill him." I stopped, waiting for any reaction. I'd been certain there would be at least one, but there wasn't. People continued to look up at me, waiting for me to finish. "I *wanted* to kill him. I didn't, but not because I came to my senses. I couldn't kill him because he was bigger and stronger than me, and when it came down to it, I was weak, and *he* almost killed *me*.

"I've been struggling with that," I said, "with trying to accept that I could still be a good person if I'd had those thoughts and desires. I mean, taking another's life… That's—it's not normal, and maybe it meant that I didn't deserve good things in my own life anymore."

The next bit would take some courage, but I'd already told them I'd wanted to murder someone, so why not?

"I've told you all that I'm gay, but I never got the chance to tell my parents. I guess that's why it's so important for the people around me to know."

I looked at Charlie again, and he nodded, encouraging me to finish my share. "It's not *who* I am, but it's a big part of what makes me, me. And I've been avoiding that too. Not letting myself even think about loving someone, because how could I deserve that? A selfish, spoiled kid pretending to be a man?" I shook my head. "No, I convinced myself I wasn't worth having that. But I'm tired of apologizing for living. I'm tired of saying sorry. People kept telling me I deserve good things in my life, and now, finally, I think I agree."

When I sat, everyone clapped for me, and Charlie said, "Good share. Now, I think it's time for you to start your steps. Here." He handed me a fake bronze chip with a big "30" in the middle, and I held onto that thing like it was a rare precious metal that held all the answers to life within.

Maybe it did.

"THE NEW SIGN CAME EARLY," Devo said when I returned to the center. She'd just revealed the huge thing from under the biggest piece of bubble wrap I'd ever seen.

"'Al's Sunday Connection'?" I said. "What the hell!"

"Yeah. They messed this thing up royally."

Pressing my finger between my eyebrows, I tried to rub the headache I felt there that was threatening to spread. "I'll have to call them and order a new one, but I don't know if it'll be ready before we open. Damn it."

"Maybe we can get a printed sign for now," Devo said, trying to pep me up.

"Yeah, maybe."

"We can," Vern called over his shoulder before he opened the back door to the alley. "I know a guy over in Jackson who can print that shit quick. He'll make a sign big as you want. I'll call him."

"Wait, Vern," I said. "Now I'm thinking the name sucks. If the sign guy got it so wrong, maybe everyone else will too. I think we need something simpler than 'The All and Sundry Collective.' I don't even know what I was thinking."

Devo cocked her head. "Like what?"

"I don't know yet. Maybe it'll come to me. Let me think about it for a day or so, and then we'll call your friend, Vern. Thank you."

"Sure thing, boss. I'ma go out back and put that coffee cart together. Lemme know if you need me."

Devo smiled at him. "Thanks, Vern."

"Can you handle things for an hour or two? I'm supposed to meet a friend, but we're expecting the nursery delivery today. Toys, shelving units, art supplies, oh, and that padded puzzle flooring is coming today too. That should be fun to install."

"Yeah, I got you. I'll see you later. I still have a mountain of phone calls to make. I put calls out to job centers around the area. And we still need someone for the daycare. We can't really depend on volunteers for that since daycares are pretty regulated. You don't really want the crazy dude from down the street who never showers watchin' your kid." Devo snorted. "Did you think any more about the festival idea? I think it's a good one, and it sounds like a great way to connect with other businesses and locals."

"Let's go for it," I said on a whim. It wasn't like I couldn't afford it. "What's stopping us? And Devo, thank you. Seriously, I don't know what I'd do without you."

"Right on," she said, blushing a little. "Okay, I'll start makin' a list of things we're gonna need. Will you see the librarian chick again? If so, tell her to call me. We can coordinate."

"That's who I'm meeting. I'll give her your number."

Devo kicked her foot in my direction, shooing me away. "Alright, now get outta here."

"Yeah, yeah," I said. "See ya."

# CHAPTER TWENTY-TWO

THEO

WE DROVE to the farmers market after I picked Sam up at the library. The market took up a whole block downtown behind the courthouse, so I could've walked from the center, but Sam whined until I said I'd drive. She and I had become some kind of weird quick friends, kind of like I'd become with Devo and with most people I'd met in Wisper. There was some kind of small-town connection between everyone here, and it was just accepted. It was normal, and I was really thankful for it, because it meant that I had people in my life who cared. If I needed help, I knew these people would be there, probably with food, and that was a comfort. I smiled while I drove the two blocks, thinking about it, making a mental note to invite every single person I'd met here in Wisper to the center's grand opening.

Would Brady come? I hadn't spoken to him since his father passed, and I was starting to doubt that he wanted to see me.

I called him, but he didn't answer, so I sent him a text. *"I'm sorry, Brady, so very sorry for your loss. And I'm sorry I left the other day. I shouldn't have. I was scared."*

He didn't reply, and I couldn't blame him.

I couldn't obsess about him though. There was so much work to be done before the opening, and if he didn't want to see me, I didn't want to force the issue. Hopefully, he'd come to me when he was ready. Hopefully, I hadn't ruined everything between us.

To keep moving forward and to keep my mind off of things, today, I was focused on Sam and the Mountain Misses mystery that was "driving her bonkers." She couldn't reconcile that a woman would kiss another woman if she was married to a man. I'd tried to point out that bisexuality wasn't a new thing, but she said she knew there was more to it and she needed to find out from the source.

Sam's grandfather had told us if we wanted to find Sissy Melton, the farmers market was where we should look. She'd either be there at her homemade jams and honey booth or somewhere out on her farm. We started at the market because Sam said she'd heard there was a custom perfume booth there, and she was looking for a scent you couldn't find in normal stores—blackberry with a wild-flower type of scent mixed in, which seemed oddly specific and definitely weird—but that was where we found Sissy, sitting at her booth, napping in the afternoon sun, an over-sized gardening hat shielding her face from its rays. The brim was so wide, if she tucked her knees up, she'd disappear completely.

The fall market wasn't bustling. It was quiet, like maybe it was winding down for the season, and I could've probably counted on both hands how many people were milling around, shopping for what was left of fresh vegetables, flowers, or hand-poured candles. Some of the booth-owners had already closed for the day, so there were only five open, and Sissy's was one.

"Mrs. Melton?" Sam asked. To me, she whispered, "You don't think she's dead, do you?"

Sissy tilted her head so she could see us and cracked an eye open. "I ain't dead, girl. You here for some honey? Harvest it myself."

"No, ma'am," Sam said. "We were wondering if we could talk to you about… about the Mountain Misses."

Sissy laughed, sitting up in her chair. "Whoowee. If that ain't ancient history, I got no idea what is." As she took her hat off, revealing long gray hair that she wore loose around her shoulders, she was eyeing me like she recognized me, but we'd never met.

Sam picked up on it. "This is Theo Burroughs. He's dating Brady Douglas." Turning toward me, shading her eyes from the sun, she cocked her head and smirked at me. "Please," she said. "Give me a little credit. Besides, it's so obvious you like each other. You should see his eyes twinkle when he talks about you."

I smiled at that. Couldn't help myself.

That seemed to satisfy Sissy's curiosity, and she motioned to a bench behind her booth. I tried to carry her folding chair over there, but she smacked my hand. "Do I look like I need a man's help?"

"No, ma'am. You don't."

"Alright then," she said, and she lifted the chair. She was fit for an eighty-something year old woman. It was evident that she was still active and she worked hard, and there was mischief in her eyes, but her skin gave her away. It was tanned, thin, and paper-like, and she was covered in brown age spots and wrinkles, but her smile was kind when she finally sat and settled into her chair.

"I know who he is," Sissy said, nodding toward me, "but

who're you, and why you wanna know about the Mountain Misses?"

"I'm Sam, the new librarian. Hi." She extended her hand toward Sissy, and they shook. "Samantha Russo, but only my grandpa calls me Samantha."

"And who's your granddaddy?"

"Oh, right. Jessup. Jessup Anderson. Do you know him?"

Sissy laughed again while Sam and I sat on the bench across from her. "'Course I do. We came up together. And I knew your grandmama, Josie. She was one of my best friends. She was one that stuck by me back then, after it all came out."

"What came out?" Sam asked. It sounded more like a demand, but she caught herself and smiled at Sissy.

"What's a little girl doin' diggin' through the past? What good you expect to come of this?"

"I don't know," Sam said. "I came across some articles at the library, and I've been trying to find out more about it. Theo's been helping me look through a bunch of old *Wisper Gazettes*. We just really want to know. Is that okay? Would you mind telling us?"

"S'pose I wouldn't mind too much," Sissy said. "I like talkin' about Adora. I loved her."

Sam tried to hide her gasp behind her hand. "You did?"

"Well, yeah. Why else would I kiss her?"

"But—"

"Girl, you're gettin' ahead of me."

Under her breath, Sam said, "I'm not actually a little girl. Jeez. I'm a grown woman with a freaking master's degree."

"What's that you say?"

"Nothing, ma'am. Please, continue."

Sissy looked at me, sitting on the bench with my hands folded together on my lap. She was seeing something Sam and I couldn't, and I was jealous of the love she was remembering.

"The year was 1968, and I was a young bride. I married at fifteen, I'll have you know. My mama and daddy signed off on it, so we was allowed to do it back then. And that was what every level-headed girl wanted. Or what they were s'posed to want.

"But I wasn't like the others my age. Never had been. And Howard knew that. He said it was part of what made him wanna marry me. We loved each other, but we weren't *in* love, and we accepted that. Lots of folks did back then. Now, don't you go thinkin' I was cheatin' on my vows. I did not. Howard knew. He knew my quirks, and still he loved me. We had ourselves what you kids today might call an open relationship.

"Well, I s'pose that's not *quite* true. It didn't apply to just anybody. I'd never kissed another woman till Adora. And not one since, but she was special, and Howard knew that too. In fact, after it all came out, he asked me if I wanted to bring Adora to live with us, and he told me if I wanted her, then he'd accept her. She could live with us, and we could be a family, peculiar family though it woulda been. Howard wasn't like most people in Wisper. He understood."

"Understood what?" Sam asked. She was getting a little impatient, if the tapping of her foot was any indication.

"When I met Adora Friedrichsen, I was… I dunno what to call it. Mesmerized. Oh, she was beautiful in a way I'd never before seen. Her accent was intriguin', but that wasn't the only thing. It was the shape of her face, her eyes, and the way her brown hair fell down around it. It was the way she spoke about books and art and music. Things I knew nothin' about. I was a farm girl through and through, but Adora knew these things, and she talked about 'em all the time.

"Lord, how I loved listenin' to her." Sissy inhaled deeply and breathed a sigh. "And then, one day, I walked her back to the Wisper Gazette after we'd had lunch at the diner. It wasn't called José's back then. It was just 'The Diner.' Hm." Sissy chuckled. "Ain't that weird?

"And that's when I kissed her, and that's when Birdy and the rest of them stuck-up ladies had a fit. They woulda tarred and feathered me if they coulda. They demanded I step down as club president, and all their husbands gossiped about me like a bunch of little ol' ladies. I heard what they was sayin'. They talked bad about my Howard, too, and that wasn't fair because he hadn't done nothin' wrong 'cept love me."

Sam frowned, trying to understand. "But who blacked out all the newspapers?"

"I suspect that was Birdy. She used to work at the library. She was embarrassed, I s'pose, 'cause we'd been friends and she hadn't known me as well as she thought she had."

"But *why* did you kiss Adora?" Sam asked. "I mean, if you knew people wouldn't accept it, that it could ruin your life, why'd you do it?"

"Who said it ruined my life? And, well," Sissy said, swiping at her pants like she was trying to swipe away her memories, "I suspect you've never been in love before, have you?"

"No," Sam said quietly, seeming reluctant to admit that. "I guess that's why I need to know. I need to know a love like that can exist because I want that kind of love. I believe in it, but I can't find it."

Sissy laughed. "Child, what are you, twenty years old? You got all the time in the world."

"No." Sam scoffed. "I'm twenty-eight."

"Oh, well, sorry. You look young."

"Thank you," Sam said, accepting Sissy's compliment

like it was a foregone conclusion. "And I've been in relationships where I *thought* I was in love, but now I know I wasn't."

"I've had that too," I said. With Tim, before he died. "So, Mrs. Melton, how did you know you loved Adora? How did you know you were willing to risk everything for her?"

She thought for a moment, inspecting us, determining if we were worthy of her knowledge, and I supposed at her age, she had that right. She twined her long fingers together, and I noticed the line of dirt beneath her nails. More evidence of her hard work.

She must've finally decided we were worthy, and maybe she wanted to put Sam out of her misery, because she was sitting cross-legged with her feet up on the bench, her body leaned forward toward Sissy, hanging on her every word— definitive proof that Sam was a hopeless romantic, no matter how tough she seemed on the outside.

"I just knew. When she looked at me, smiled at me, I felt this… desperation inside my body, you know? It was a pull, a… yearnin'. I'd never felt like that before, not even with Howard. I loved him, wanted a life with him, but things were so different back then. If you had a husband, you'd already won the lottery, and if he worked hard, put food on the table and children in your belly, you were rich, no matter how much love or money you had. So I was satisfied in that way.

"But when I met Adora, I felt things I'd never known possible. She made me laugh so hard, my toes would curl. And when she touched me?" Sissy cleared her throat. "Well, now, that's private. But I woulda done anything to protect her. And in fact, I did. I gave her up."

"What do you mean?" I asked.

"She wanted to stay with me, but with the way people were treatin' us, Adora couldn't handle that. She was afraid that the taunts and the bullyin' and the makin' fun would turn into somethin' dangerous. People were threatened by what they didn't know. It scared 'em, and that scared Adora. I guess I'd figured it was a good thing people knew about us so we didn't have to hide, but Adora didn't think so. And when we were together after that day, she could barely look at me 'cause she was always lookin' behind us, tryin' to see what was comin' our way.

"Finally, I told her to go. I gave her up because that was what was best for her. I couldn't leave. I had my husband and our farm. My brothers were still livin' in Wisper at the time, so there was nowhere else for me. Wisper was my home. It was where I'd always planned on raisin' my kids, and I did. But Adora didn't have those ties, so she could go somewhere she'd feel safe. Which was just what she did."

"Did you ever see her again?" I asked.

"I did, yes," Sissy said, and sorrow settled in the lines around her eyes. "I was at the state fair a few years later, and I saw Adora there, on the arm of another woman. Passersby woulda thought they were only friends. It wasn't unusual for a girl to hold her friend's hand, but I knew the truth. I saw it in her eyes. They were together. She looked happy, and I tried to take comfort in that."

Sissy stood. "You know, this world's come a long way." She looked pointedly at me. "I'm proud of you, sonny. Proud that you don't hide who you are. I bet your parents are real proud."

I tried to smile, but I shook my head. "They never knew. They died, and I hadn't told them yet." But I could feel their pride in Sissy, in the look she was giving me, the way her eyes were warm and familiar though we'd never met before today.

She nodded. "Well, you look here, my kids have all

moved on. Hell, they're old now, too, and I don't see 'em but a few times a year. A woman can get lonely, so if there's ever anything you need, young man, you just ask. And if you ever feel like you need to get away, I always have iced tea at my house. I set it out to steep in the sun. Gives it an earthy flavor. You're welcome to come and share a glass any time."

"Thank you," I told her, trying not to let the women see the tears forming in my eyes, but Sissy's acceptance reminded me of Aislinn's. It was unconditional. It always had been, even when she was acting like a jerk.

And just like that, I had the new name for the community center: Ace's House.

# CHAPTER TWENTY-THREE

### BRADY

SITTING IN MY OFFICE, I stared at the text notification bubble on my phone. Seventeen messages. They were probably all from Oly. She'd been checking on me every five minutes since she'd stopped by the house to hug me. She was sweet, but I was past tired of people asking me, "Are you okay?" It was enough to drive me mad. So I was grateful when my phone rang and I saw the county assessor's name flashing on my screen. I flicked the texting app closed and accepted the call.

"Jim? Do you have good news for me?"

"Yeah, sure do, Brady. But how're you doin'? I heard about your daddy."

I hung my head and repeated mechanically, "I'm fine. Thank you for askin'."

"He was a good man. I'm sorry for your loss. Will you give your mama my condolences?"

"Of course."

"Well, on to business then," he said, like that was it. As long as he brought it up once, we could dismiss the subject of my dead father and move on. If only it were that simple. "Gene Owens was right. That is his land. Mr.... Uh..." I heard shuffling while Jim searched through his paperwork for Cody Baxter's name. "Shoot, gave myself a papercut." A sucking noise came through the phone. "Oh yeah, Baxter. Mr. Baxter is incorrect in his claim that Gene's encroachin' on his property. So, technically, since the water starts on both their properties—there really is no way to determine anything else in this case—they're gonna have to share water rights. Now, I can tell you got your work cut out for you. I spoke to this Baxter on the phone and to his lawyer. The lawyer was nice enough, but Mr. Baxter was anything but. Good luck with that."

"Yeah, thanks. And thanks for gettin' back to us so fast. I appreciate that."

"Alright then. Cara and I'll see you at your daddy's service. You know when that's gonna be?"

"No," I said, feeling numb. "He didn't want a funeral. My mom's having a celebration of life thing over at the Lodge next Sunday. One o'clock."

"Alright, kid. We'll see you there. Let us know if there's anything we can do."

"Thanks. Will do," I said, but what I really wanted to say was, "Shut up!" Or how about, "Can you bring my dad back? No? Then fuck off."

Next, I called Collin. "Hey, Collin. Did you speak to Jim?"

"Yeah, I did. But why are you workin' on this today?"

"Why wouldn't I?"

"I heard your dad passed away. You can take a day off, you know? It's not like the land or water's goin' anywhere. And besides, you won, basically. Other than some paperwork, this is a done deal. Sorry for your loss, by the way."

How the hell did Collin know my dad died? He didn't even live in Wisper.

I repeated my *heartfelt* thanks, but again, what I really wanted to say was, "You didn't even know him! I don't even know you! What right do you have to bring up the most painful thing I've ever experienced?" But instead, I focused on work, trying not to sound like an asshole. "I don't know that it's over though. Your client seems hellbent on keepin' his rights separate from my client's."

"Well, there isn't much he can do. We both know that."

"Right, but I don't see this endin' amicably."

"Well, you may be right about that, but seriously, there's nothin' much you can do today. I'll speak to Baxter. Take some time off. Go be with your family."

Right, exactly what I was hoping to do. Seriously, there was still time to leave, to run screaming out of Wisper. Celebrating my dad's life wasn't a bad thing, but standing around listening to my mom pass his death off as part of God's plan or fate or whatever literally made me want to vomit. And if I had to accept one more condolence, I was going to scream.

My dad dying from a disease that had decimated his body and his dignity wasn't God's plan. It wasn't fate. It wasn't the universe's will.

It was cruel and unfair, and nobody was going to convince me otherwise. What fucking good could come from him dying like that?

There could be no good to come from that.

None.

My phone rang again. *Would it ever stop?*

I answered, "Brady Douglas," though my hand was itching to chuck the damn thing out the window.

"Such a strong name. Hello, my Toko-a." I could hear the smile in my grandpa's voice, and I could picture it, the lines creasing in his cheeks and around his eyes. Bonnie and I were his only grandkids, and he and Grandma had always been a positive part of our lives before she passed.

"Hi, Grandpa."

"How are you, my son?"

"I'm… fine."

"Don't lie to me. I've been dreamin' about you."

"Toko, I'm sorry, but I don't have time for—"

"Make time."

"Yes, sir," I said, sighing, and I clicked speakerphone, tossed my cell on my desk, and put my feet up next to it, leaning back in my creaky desk chair. I'd never believed in the dreams he and my mom were always going on about, but just the sound of his voice was soothing. It took me back to a time when everything felt right and good, when I was innocent and the world still seemed bright and open to me. Toko was someone others had always listened to and looked up to. "Tell me about your dreams."

"There are two men in your life. One you know, and one you've never met."

"How can you dream about someone I've never even met?"

"He spoke to me. He wants me to tell you to hold on and let go. You must choose your path now. A stream may split, but it returns to its river in the end."

"Right. Yeah. That makes sense." I shook my head, glad that my grandpa couldn't see me, but c'mon.

"The other man doesn't speak to me, but I've seen him more than once in my dreams. He's protected by a horse. She comes from another tribe, but she is strong and good, and he's lucky to have her."

"Who is this horse-man person? How do I know him?"

"You will love him."

I straightened and took him off speaker. *Theo?*

"He's finding his way home from a dark place. He needs you, and you need him. Do not deny that. Don't believe what they tell you about time and needin' love. We all do, and there's nothin' bad about that. He is the earth, and you are the lightning. Neither can exist without the other."

"Okay. Good to know." How the hell was I supposed to decipher any of that? "Thank you for callin', but I gotta get back to work."

"I love you, Toko-a. I'll see you Sunday. We will eat and dance to celebrate your father. He speaks to me, too, and he wants you to let go of your anger. He says that you are in the eye of the storm. If you look, you will see the destruction it's causin' all around you. You must stop it. You must let the winds die down."

I rolled my eyes but held in another sigh. "Okay. Sure."

"Goodbye. I will forgive you for that face you're makin' because I know what you're feelin'. Grief is harder on you because you don't have my practice."

WHEN I WENT BACK to my parents'—to my *mom's* house, I tossed my satchel on the kitchen table, and the strap knocked over her beloved, handmade bighorn sheep salt and pepper shakers. They both landed on the floor, and the pepper sheep exploded into pieces, a brownish-gray pile forming beside it.

My mom whipped around, the fridge door still wide open because she'd been rearranging condolence casseroles. There were at least twenty in there already. "Brady!"

"Sorry."

She hurried to the mess, crouching and lifting the still

intact saltshaker, inspecting it for damage. "These were a gift from the chief's wife. She gave them to me at the last Sun Dance." She tsked, her disappointment in me clear.

"They're salt and pepper shakers, Mom. It ain't the end of the world."

Her voice was terse. "Of course not, bunny, but they were special."

"Seriously?"

"What?" She stood, and her hands on her hips told me she was irritated with me.

"That's what you're concerned about right now? You didn't show this much heartbreak about Dad dyin'. You're actin' like it didn't happen."

"Brady, that's not fair. You don't know what I'm feelin'."

"I don't think you feel *anything*. Dad dyin' was just some kinda divine plan, right? And now, his body will be given back to the land. He'll be food for the trees and animals, and we should all be grateful for his service to Mother Earth." I shook my head, whispering, "It's bullshit."

"What did you say?"

"Nothin'."

"No, please, say your piece. It's no secret around here that my beliefs and religion embarrass you. So tell me. Go ahead and tell me what you think about the way I'm dealin' with my husband's death. Brady's smarter than everyone else, isn't that right? He knows better?"

Her anger at me pushed me over some edge. And she was right. She did embarrass me. Nothing she and Toko said made any sense. It was all bullshit. It wasn't who I was or who I would become.

"I said, it's bull*shit*."

"Why does that make you so mad? What does it matter to you how I process this?"

"Because! Because you're makin' it seem like him dyin' was just some predetermined event. Like he existed just to be a part of your journey, and now that he's gone, we should all just move on. We should all act like he never existed."

"Guys?" Bonnie came into the kitchen, rubbing her eyes after a nap. "Why're you arguin'?"

I ignored her. "Well, he did exist! And he didn't believe in all that crap. Yeah, he went along with it 'cause he loved you, but if he could hear you right now? You're turnin' his death into a joke, into some kinda Shoshone religious bullshit. It's all bullshit! He was our dad! He was the best man any of us will ever know, and you're reducin' his life and his... his impact on this world down to nothin'. You're makin' it seem like he was just part of a stupid vision quest."

My mom gasped, and as soon as the words left my mouth, I regretted them. The look on her face was one of deep hurt and betrayal, and I wanted to beg her forgiveness, but instead, I stormed out of the house and got in my car.

I'd never spoken to her like that. I'd never felt so much anger.

She didn't deserve it. We didn't deserve any of this. Why? Why, when we'd lived our whole lives trying to be good, trying to help people and make a difference in the world—why would God or the universe or whatever, why would they punish us like this?

I couldn't give a name to how I was feeling. It made no sense.

Nothing made sense anymore.

I wanted to call Theo. I wanted to see him. I wanted him to wrap me up in his gentle embrace and never let go. But he'd left. He'd lied and bailed.

What the fuck was I supposed to do with that?

My phone rang as soon as I put my car into drive, but I

didn't answer it. I just drove, winding my way through Wisper because I was too messed up to pay any attention to where I was going. But then it rang again and again and again.

"What!"

"Brady?"

"What, Bonnie? I'm sorry, but I can't deal with Mom right now. I'm not comin' back there. I need time."

"My water just broke."

"What?" I pulled to the side of the road. "What's that mean?"

"It means the baby's comin', and I want you there." I could hear the worry in her voice, and I was sure she was crying. "Gerry might not get here in time, and I need my brother."

*Shit.* "Okay." I nodded. "I'll come get you."

"No, that's okay. We're halfway there already. Just meet us at the hospital."

"I'm on my way."

She sniffled. "Thank you."

"I'm sorry, bonbon. I'm sorry for everything."

"I know. Everything's gonna be okay, little brother." She panted through a contraction. "You'll see. Just get to the hospital."

She hung up, and as soon as the connection was cut, my phone rang again. I figured it was my mom calling right back. She'd probably tell me that it was my anger that had made Bonnie's water break. The weight of the way I'd been behaving was immense, and I wanted to tell her how sorry I was.

"Mom?"

Gene's voice sounded weird. "Brady?"

"Gene? What's wrong?"

His breathing was shallow and rapid. "I'm over at Cody Baxter's place. I came to talk to him, to try to work things out, but he wasn't happy about losin' our case..."

There were muffled noises in the background, and I thought I heard Gene grunting.

"Gene? What happened? Are you okay?"

"I'm pretty sure he's havin' a heart attack. I'm doin' CPR."

*Shit!* "Gene, why're you callin' me? Hang up. I'll call an ambulance. Is he still breathin'?"

"No, stay on the line with me, kid. Cody was sayin' somethin' about contactin' his lawyer. Somethin' about his family. He said somethin' about his daughters. I don't know."

Slamming my car back into drive, I punched the gas. I had to be there for Bonnie, but the least I could do was send help to Gene. "I'm callin' the sheriff, and I'll call Baxter's lawyer."

The line went dead, and I tried to dial the sheriff's number. It wasn't easy 'cause my heart was beating a mile a minute and my hands were shaking, but I finally got through without running my car into an innocent pedestrian or a tree.

I heard bubble gum smacking when Shelley, the receptionist, answered. "Sheriff's Department."

"Shelley! This is Brady Douglas. Gene Owens just called me. He said Cody Baxter's havin' a heart attack. I think it's bad."

"The sheriff is already in route with paramedics."

"Oh, thank God."

"You know your sister's in labor, right?" More gum smacking.

"Yeah. How do you know that?"

"She joined my mommy-and-me class 'cause she wasn't sure how long she'd be in Wisper, so she's on my labor phone tree. And I heard your mama on dispatch when she called for an ambulance. She thinks somethin's wrong with the baby."

No. This couldn't be happening.

"Get your butt to the hospital. Your sister needs you."

Only in Wisper, Wyoming. In what other town would calling the sheriff's office result in getting scolded about your family by a random receptionist?

# CHAPTER TWENTY-FOUR

## THEO

"BOSS, YOU'RE BLEEDIN'. A lot," Vern said. "You need stitches."

"Oh shit." Devo turned and let out a low whistle when she saw the state of my hand. "How'd you do that?"

Holding it up in the air to slow the trickle of blood that was fast becoming a stream, I said, "Yeah. I think you're right. Can you drive?" I reached in my pocket with my right hand and tossed Vern my keys. "I was trying to open that box of coffee mugs with scissors." I nodded toward the offending tool. "Ah, damn. It's really flowing."

"Whoa." Devo laughed. "Told you we shoulda gone with paper cups. You a little woozy? You look like you might fall over. Not a fan of blood, eh?"

I groaned. "No. I don't mind it if it's not mine, but…"

"Alright, off we go." Vern hooked my right arm over his shoulder, carrying the bulk of my weight, and the three of us made our way outside.

"Thank you, Vern, but I can walk."

"Yup," he said, "but I can't tell if you're gonna fall on

your face. Be a shame to mess up that pretty mug." He winked.

Devo locked the door behind us. "Damn, man, you left a trail of blood a mile long. That thing's really leakin'."

"Thank you for that commentary, Devo. Can we please go to the hospital now before I do pass out?" Vern helped me into my truck, and Devo slid in beside me. There were a few people on Main Street, shopping and slurping lattes across the street at Coffee Shot, and every single one of them was watching us, trying to discern what had happened, ready to gossip when we drove away. *What has the drunk done now?*

"Sure thing." She laughed. "Sorry, it's just that it's kinda funny to me that such a powerful dude can be brought down by a little bit of blood. You watch all those shoot-'em-up army movies, so it never occurred to me you'd be scared by it."

I ignored her "powerful" comment. I was anything but. "Like I said, as long as it's not *my* blood, it doesn't bother me."

"It's a good thing you quit drinkin', or you'd need a transfusion by now."

"Devo."

"Sorry. Shuttin' up."

The town doctor was on vacation, so the local clinic was out of the question. Vern was quiet as he drove with focused concentration to the hospital in Jackson. It was a sign that he and I really had become friends. He was concerned for me, and he took his job seriously.

When we got there, the hospital was a flurry of activity. The woman behind the check-in counter gave us white towels to sop up the blood, which just made it look all the more gruesome, and she warned me to keep my hand in the air until the doctors could get to me. So we hung out in the waiting room, and Devo pulled up *Saving Private Ryan* on her phone and stuck one of her earbuds in my ear and the other in hers.

"Why you like these military movies so much?" she asked, placing her phone in my right hand and adjusting the volume as the movie's opening credits rolled across the screen.

"I don't know," I said, and I shrugged one shoulder. It had something to do with being in a boardroom my whole life. The only action I'd ever seen were arguments between businessmen. It had come to blows in one meeting when I was a teenager, and that had been kind of exciting, but still, I'd wanted a different life, even at fourteen.

Looking around the waiting room at men in cowboy hats, women in jeans, T-shirts, and cowboy boots, and kids with dirty hands and faces, and then looking at Vern and Devo, I realized I'd gotten my wish. This was an entirely different life than the one I'd been born to lead, and I loved it.

This place, these people, they were my family.

Wyoming was finally my home.

---

"FIVE STITCHES," Devo said proudly. "You want a lollipop?"

"Funny." I rolled my eyes but nudged her with the arm that wasn't blood-soaked. My left sleeve was wet with it, and it was still grossing me out. "Where's the gift shop? Maybe I could buy a shirt to wear."

"Uh, I dunno," she said. "Maybe they'd give you scrubs if we asked. Here, sit in that chair." She pointed to a long row of chairs pressed up against a wall in a walkway that led from one end of the hospital to the other. Daylight was streaming in through its many windows, and the sun felt good on my face when I sat. "I'll be right back. I'm gonna go see if I can find you somethin'. I really don't wanna have to sit next to your bloody arm in the truck."

She wandered off, and Vern sat next to me. "How's it feel?"

"Oh, it's not so bad. Still kind of numb from the shot they gave me. It is starting to throb a little though."

"Yeah, well, ibuprofen's a man's best friend. I can tell you that from experience." He held up his hand, and I noticed a long scar down one finger that led onto the palm of his hand.

"How'd you do that?"

"Don't ask. It wasn't my finest moment."

I nodded. "I've had a few not fine moments—"

"Theo? Not you too. Are you okay?" Suddenly, Brady was standing in front of me, looking from my bandaged hand to Vern's face and back. "What happened?"

"I cut my hand. It's not a big deal. I needed stitches, but it's fine."

A loud sigh escaped him, and he hung his head.

"Brady?" He looked up. "Are *you* okay?"

"I-I'm not sure. Actually, no. I don't think so."

"Why are you at the hospital?"

"My sister's in labor. She's upstairs, but my client's neighbor just had a heart attack—"

"Who's your client?" Vern asked, and he stood. He might not have wanted anyone to know, but Vern was just as big a part of the Wisper community as anyone else, and it was endearing to see him showing concern for his neighbor.

"Gene Owens," Brady said. "His neighbor, Cody Baxter, had a heart attack. He's in surgery, but Gene was really shook up, so I wanted to check on him."

"Is your sister okay?" I asked.

"She's, um… I don't know. There was something wrong with the baby, and they had to take her for an emergency C-section. Her husband's on his way. I hope he gets here soon."

"May I wait with you?" I asked, needing to be close to him. There was so much turmoil in his eyes, and I didn't like what that was doing to the expression on his face. I wanted to stay with him so maybe he'd talk to me. Maybe talking would help. "Vern, why don't you and Devo head back to the center. I'd like to wait—"

A door slammed in the distance. It hit a wall, making a loud *bang*, and a large man exited the restroom down the hall. The guy was well over six feet tall and loaded with muscles. I thought he looked familiar, but—

Memories came flooding back, and somehow, the whole scene changed. The man I'd seen was standing above me, but his face morphed into one I definitely recognized. I was on the floor, except it wasn't a tile floor anymore. It was gravel. And it was nighttime. There was only one streetlight, and my vision was becoming hazier with each blow from Blake Ormand. He kicked and kicked, then leaned over to punch my head, and I was starting to black out. I heard my sister's voice. She was screaming, "No! No!" but she wasn't really there.

My attacker was twice my size. He was angry about something, and his swollen muscles seemed to be vibrating, and every single one of them was being used to kill me. I couldn't breathe. I couldn't speak.

I tried to get up, but I couldn't move.

I lay there, taking each punch, thinking, *This is it. I'm going to die, and my sister will never forgive me for the lies I've told. I will have failed completely at taking care of her,*

*protecting her, which was the only thing my parents ever
wanted from me.*

In reality, I knew that what I was seeing and feeling
wasn't actually happening, but I felt the pain, saw what that
man was doing to me, and I clutched my stomach, wishing it
would stop.

"Theo!" I heard Vern's voice, but I couldn't see him.

There were other voices, too, a low, gruff, male voice and
a high-pitched woman's voice. But still, all I saw was gravel.
I felt it under my back. It was digging into my skin, and I
thought I could even taste it.

"Hey, hey, Theo!" Brady was shaking me. I felt his breath
wash over my face. I was moaning and crying, but his low
voice was like a lifeline. I grabbed hold of it. "Theo! Wake
up. What is this? What's happenin' to him?"

"Move out of the way, sir," someone said, and then hands
were lifting me onto a bed or stretcher.

I opened my eyes.

At least ten people were standing around me when I came
to, staring at me, looking extremely concerned.

Brady stepped forward. "Are you in there? Can you
hear me?"

"Yes," I said, clearing my throat when my voice came out too
quiet for him to hear. Looking at him, at the warmth in his brown
eyes and the way they were inspecting my face, was the only
thing tethering me to reality, but it felt like it could slip away at
any moment. I was shaking, and I couldn't catch my breath.

"What was that?" he said. "Where'd you go?"

"I-I… Who was that man?"

Brady looked over his shoulder. "What man? Frank?"

"There was a man—the man who—never mind." I shook
my head and the world spun.

Looking back at me, his eyebrows shot up. "It's happenin' again."

"I don't feel so well," I said, and then all I saw was darkness.

---

WHEN I WOKE, I was lying in a bed in a private examination room, and Brady was there, sitting in a chair against the wall with his head in his hands. His hair was covering his face, but from the set of his shoulders and the deep way he was breathing, it was clear he was upset.

"How long was I out?"

He looked up. "Oh, thank God. They said you were fine. I mean, your heart and pulse and all that were good, but nobody knows why you keep passin' out. They wanna run tests. I told 'em I was your lawyer so I could stay, but I called your sister. She should be here any minute."

"Thank you," I said, "but that's not really necessary."

"Theo, you fell down. You were on the floor, and it looked like maybe you were havin' a seizure or somethin'."

"I wasn't. I was—it was a memory. Do you remember when we first met, right here in the hospital? You were dressed in a gray suit with that awful briefcase."

"Yeah," he said, chuckling. "You remember what I was wearin'?" He stood and came closer to my bed.

"The man who put me in the hospital back then, it—he… What he did to me, I guess, I've never really dealt with that. I saw a man in the hallway who looked kind of like Blake Ormand, and it all came back." I shook my head, not really believing what I was saying. It had felt so odd, like I was outside of my body, looking down on myself. "There was so much going on—my hand, your sister, your dad. I think it was all too much."

"That was just Frank Sims. He's a deputy for the Sheriff's Department. But… are you sayin' what just happened to you was *my* fault?"

"What? No, that's not what I said."

"But it is what you meant." He took the last step toward me, leaning his hip against my bed, and he lifted my hand. He held it in his, caressing his thumb lightly over the top of the bandage. "I unloaded all my problems onto you, and it made you relive the worst moment of your life. It *is* my fault."

"Brady, that wasn't the worst moment of my life. Not by a long shot. And I'm the one who didn't deal with what happened to me. I'm the one who became an alcoholic trying to repress those memories. I guess now that I'm sober, they're there. You know?"

Pursing his lips, he nodded. "It wasn't the worst moment?" He sat, nestling himself next to me, and it felt like a drug, like the warmth from his body was the medication I needed to be okay. His shoulder pressed against mine was grounding.

"No," I said, looking at our legs side by side on the bed. His jeans were a faded black, and mine were blue. "The day my parents died was the worst day of my life. The moment I was told they were dead and that Aislinn was hurt was the worst. I don't think anything can ever compare." He reached for my unbandaged hand, and my eyes moved over his knuckles, at the way they were turning white while he held on to me so tightly. "Are you okay?"

He looked in my eyes. "My dad…"

"I'm so sorry. If I could, I would take that pain from you."

A tear welled in the corner of his eye, then slipped out and fell, streaking his cheek. "You would?"

"In a second."

"I… I'm just so fuckin' angry, Theo, and no one gets it. There are people in this world, like the guy who assaulted you, and they're walkin' around, breathin'—they get to live, and my dad can't? He was the best of us. He was good and strong, and it's just not fair."

# CHAPTER TWENTY-FIVE

## BRADY

"YOU'RE RIGHT," Theo said. "It's not fair."

"I sound like a whiny kid, don't I?" I felt like one. Even-keeled Brady the lawyer seemed to have disappeared.

A small smile formed on his face, and I noticed the lines around his eyes. I'd never noticed them before, and I was ashamed that I'd been so focused on my own misery that I wasn't seeing what the people around me had been going through.

"No. You sound like someone who just lost his father to an ugly disease. You sound like someone who's hurting." He pulled his hand from mine and lifted his arm, draping it over my shoulder and scooting as close to me as he could. I loved it. I loved that we were both falling apart, but when we were together, somehow, we held each other up.

"What're you doin'?"

"I'm holding you. That's a thing, you know? People who care for other people hold them when that person is sad or scared."

"Yeah, but I didn't know you felt that way about me. Not really. You left. You walked out, and I thought that meant… I mean, I hoped, but—and I meant your hand. Be careful."

"How could you not know? When we were together—you felt it, didn't you? That wasn't just sex to me."

"Yeah, but I just thought you had no clue what the hell you wanted."

"I had a clue," he whispered.

"Why?" I was such a mess. How could he want me?

"Why what?"

"Why do you… care about me?"

We weren't looking at each other, but he said, "Because you're beautiful. You have a beautiful soul, and you're kind. You go out of your way to help people, and I've seen the respect the people in this community have for you. I don't think I've ever felt that. I've been surrounded by fake people my whole life. People respected me because I had money, because they thought they could gain something from me. I've never met anyone like you before. Do you know that?"

"No. I—what do you mean, 'like me'?"

"You're honest, and you aren't afraid to be who you are. You accept yourself, and you forgive yourself. I know what you're feeling right now is hard, but you'll survive this because you're strong, and you refuse to see life any other way than hopeful."

"How do you know that?"

"Which part?" he asked.

"That I'll get through it."

He pulled me closer, and I felt his breath on my cheek when he leaned in, resting his head on my shoulder, and then he tucked it against my neck. His voice was a quiet lull. "You tell me," he said. "What is it inside you that allows you to know that you're good and that you're a fighter? I wish I had that. It's taken me a long time just to see that I deserve to breathe. I can't even imagine knowing myself that well, knowing that there's always another side of things."

I thought about it, and I smiled when I came to the answer in my mind. "I guess it comes from my dad. He was that way, always findin' a silver linin' somewhere. He was the best person, Theo. There's no way for me to make you understand. I wish you could've gotten to know him."

"Me too. I was thinking the other day about what it would've been like if he and my father had met. They were very different, but I bet they would've gotten along. My father would've been so impressed with your dad's creativity." He laughed. "I'm not kidding, he would've commissioned a whole house-full of furniture. He was loud about his money, but he used it to help a lot of people. That's where I got the idea to become an angel investor. It's what he did before being an angel investor was even a thing." He kissed my neck. "I'm sorry I left like that. I was scared. I'm still scared. Scared to let you down."

We sat there for a few minutes, both of us thinking, just listening to the other breathe. Finally, he said, "But there's a storm inside you, Brady. I can see it changing you. Let it out. You *have* to let it out.

"I didn't. I held everything inside. I tried to tell you, but it was too hard. The day I came to your office last summer? That's why I was there. I wanted to admit to you what I'd tried to do. That I'd tried to take someone's life. It's been eating at me, turning me inside out. How can I be good? How can I be worthy of anyone? How can I be worthy of you?"

His hand was warm on my jaw, and he pulled, asking me to look at him. When I did, he said, "I thought I was a monster. It's why I've been hiding. Why I've been drinking. Does that make sense?"

"Yeah," I said. "I wish I would've known that's what you

were strugglin' with, 'cause I knew right after we met. When I left your hospital room that day, I called Oly. She told me what happened in Nevada with you, Jay, and Billie. I'm sure I didn't get the whole story, so if you want to, when you're ready, you can tell me, but I knew you were tryin' to protect your sister. And Theo, no one faults you for that. But I understand what you're sayin' about not feelin' like you deserved good things. I know how that feels."

"I should've guessed everyone already knew. Even Vern heard about it."

We both laughed, but then he sighed. "If I'd just talked to my sister, I would've known it was common knowledge. But Brady, you aren't that person. You won't think it's going to change you, but it will. You're not meant to go through the darkness you'll feel if you let your anger take over. You've got to find a way to let it go. Trust me."

And the thing was, I did.

---

I WANTED to stay with him, but Theo's sister showed up with Finn, and there wasn't enough room for me. She was really worried about her brother, and I couldn't blame her. Everything he'd said made sense, but it didn't stop me from worrying about him too.

My sister needed me, though, so I left them and found my family, and I slid in through my sister's open door, hoping my mom wouldn't notice me. She did, of course, but she gave me half a smile and nodded.

Bonnie's husband had already been at the airport in Houston when she went into labor. He was heading to Wisper to be here for her after Dad died and had planned on staying until after the celebration of life service…?

Party? I didn't know what the hell to call it. The point was, Gerry had just arrived when I got to Bonnie's hospital room.

He attacked me in a hug before I'd even had time to notice the baby. "Brady. Hey, man. I'm sorry about Dad," he said, slapping me too hard on my back.

"Thanks, Gerry. You okay?"

"I'm good. But you look…" He pulled back, inspecting me. Could he see the exhaustion on my face? The anger? Was it that obvious?

I waved him away. "Ah, it's not important."

My mom stepped forward, her eyebrows slashing down in concern.

"I'm fine, Mom. Promise." That seemed to satisfy her, and she relaxed, for the moment at least. I knew she was worrying about me, and I felt awful for making my anger about her.

Turning my attention to the bundle in a very woozy Bonnie's arms, I said, "Are we sure she should be holdin' a live human baby? She looks like she might fall over. And is anybody gonna tell me what we got? The blanket's yellow. That tells me nothin'."

My brother-in-law punched my arm. "Bonnie's a warrior. She's got this. Just look at that kid. He's so strong and hand-some." Gerry leaned over, kissing my sister's cheek and making goo-goo faces at his baby.

So it was a boy.

Bonnie held the little blanket-wrapped bundle a little higher in the air, wincing from the pain and turning him so I could see. "His name is Foster Douglas Eisenhower." The smile on my sister's face was like none I'd ever seen. She was in love. She could barely take her eyes off the kid, though all he was doing was making squeaking noises and turning his own face red while he tried to poo his diaper or something. Maybe it was gas. "Wanna hold him?"

Tears were trying to form, and a knot was swelling in my throat. I was so proud of Bonnie, and so sorry for all the things I'd said and how I'd been acting. "'Course I do."

I stepped forward, and she transferred the little burrito into my arms as carefully as if he was the sound of silence itself, like if we disturbed him, nothing would ever be right again.

"Support the back of his neck and head," she said.

"Okay. He doesn't weigh very much." Lifting him up and down a couple times, I was feeling for my nephew's heft, but there was none. Honestly, it was like holding a stuffed animal. I assumed it would at least feel like holding a cat.

And then that mysterious tiny human opened his eyes. He was staring up at me, and I saw my dad. I saw the same twinkle in his eye, the same love, the same joy for life. Yeah, I knew he probably couldn't see a damn thing, but it was nice to feel like someday he would. He'd see the world the way my dad had 'cause Bonnie and Gerry would teach him to. My mom would, and I would.

And that was okay. It was more than okay.

It was perfect.

He was perfect, and I realized Toko had been right. There were two men in my life, and little Foster was the one I hadn't yet met. But now I had, and it was clear in that moment that things would never be the same, but in a good way.

---

"*I HAVE A NEPHEW*," I texted Theo when I got to my mom's later that night. I was sitting on the porch swing, watching the sky. A fall thunderstorm was threatening again, turning the night sky to a tangle of stars and gray swirling clouds that were starting to choke out the moonlight. *"I came back to tell you, but you'd already been released."*

When I hadn't been able to find Theo at the hospital, I stopped off at Cody Baxter's room. He was out of surgery and doing well, and Gene was there with his family, watching over his neighbor even though all the guy had ever done to Gene was make his life miserable. But we talked, and I got Cody to agree to sit down with Gene and me when he was recovered so we could map out their issues, so we could make it work for both of them. Cody even smiled at Gene. He was probably feeling grateful that Gene had saved his life, and I hoped that could at least start to bridge the divide between them.

Theo texted back thirty seconds later. Had he been waiting for me? *"Congratulations. What's his name?"*

*"Bonnie named him after my dad: Foster Douglas Eisenhower."*

*"Wow. What a strong name."*

He texted again a second later, *"Bonnie's okay?"*

*"She's good,"* I replied. *"Her blood pressure shot through the roof. Apparently that's really dangerous for her and the baby, but they got him out safely. Bonnie's sore, but she's happier than I've ever seen anybody. How's your hand?"*

*"I'm glad,"* he texted. *"My hand is fine. I feel foolish that I cut it so badly trying to open a box."*

Three dots appeared again as he wrote something else, but it took forever and a day to come through. I leaned back as I waited, watching how the dark clouds were flying past the bright yellow moon now, like they were trying to run away from it. It was a moon fit for Halloween, though most of the trick-or-treaters had gone home by now. All that was left were teenagers running through the streets, looking for pranks to pull and houses to decorate with toilet paper.

Finally, my phone dinged with a new text. *"Thank you for being there for me today. I hope I'm not crossing a boundary, but I miss you."*

*"If you are, you can meet me on the other side cuz I crossed that line days ago."*

*"Can I see you?"*

*"I'll stop by, but first, I need to talk to my mom. I've got some apologizing to do."*

*"Ok. Good luck. Let me know when you're coming."*

*"Oh, baby,"* I texted back, *"you know I will! ;)"*

---

"MAMA?"

My mom was on her knees by my dad's bed with her hands clasped together on top. She twisted around when she heard my voice from the doorway. "Come in, bunny."

"Mom, can we please discuss this nickname? You've *really* gotta stop callin' me bunny. Where did it even come from?"

She smiled and stood, then sat on the edge of the therapy bed she'd shared with my dad for the past year and a half. She patted it, and I sat next to her. It felt weird to see it empty, but I was starting to feel peace about it, too, 'cause it meant my dad wasn't in pain. He wasn't stuck anymore.

"Promise you won't be mad?" She hung her arm over my shoulder, and I reached up, lacing my fingers through hers.

"No. I absolutely do not promise that."

Mom smirked. "You had a really big overbite when you were young, and you always had so much energy. You know, your dad asked you to help him in the backyard all those times as a way to get you to learn to focus. You always looked up to him, and he knew you'd pay attention if he taught you what he loved to do."

I let go of her hand and crossed my arms over my chest. She knew I was kidding. "Wow," I said. "I can't believe you're admittin' that I got my nickname 'cause I had buck teeth!"

She laughed.

"I'm sorry, Mom," I said, twisting my lips and wringing my hands together like a kid. I'd been acting like one. "You don't embarrass me."

"I do, but I think I'm s'posed to. I'm your mama." She chuckled and squeezed my hand, pulling it onto her lap. "But I understand. Bein' part Shoshone hasn't always been easy on you. It was different for me 'cause I grew up in that culture, surrounded by it every day, but you and Bonnie were raised in a different life, and sometimes people can be cruel. I'm sorry you had to go through that."

"Yeah, that sucked, but it was more that it caused me to question who I was, you know? I'm nothin' like you. But I shouldn't whine about it. I should be stronger."

"Brady Douglas, I've just about had it with that crap. Where do you get the idea that you have to be this pillar of strength? Who told you that?"

I shrugged. "No one, but I wanted to make Dad proud. He was strong, and I wanted to be like him."

"You are. You're *so* like him. You're so like both of us. You have my tenacity, and you have that thing Dad did, the thing that made everyone love him and talk to him. He was such a big part of this community. It's a little overwhelmin' how many people are callin' and textin' me. The fridge is chock-full of casseroles and pies. There's no room left for regular food. Even the freezer in the garage is full. The Celebration of Life ceremony is gonna be huge Sunday." Mom looked at me, swiping a strand of hair behind my ear. "You really do look like Toko." She hesitated before she asked, "You'll be there, right?"

"'Course I will."

"Good. And then next week, we'll take Dad's ashes up near Wind Cave. He always loved it up there. Remember we used to hike to the caves with a picnic when you were little?"

"Yeah," I said. "Some of my favorite memories."

"Mine too." She paused. "Listen, maybe it's not the right time, but I've been wantin' to talk to you about somethin'."

"Okay," I said slowly. "What about?"

"You aren't happy at work."

"What? No. I mean, I…"

"It's okay, Brady. You've been there for me, and now I want to be there for you. So you're fired."

My head snapped back. "What?"

"Not right away, but I think you should look for a job that fulfills you. One that you'll love goin' to every day."

"Mom, I like workin' with you. I'm sorry if I made you feel like I didn't."

"I know you do, but you're not bein' challenged. You do it 'cause you have to. And I'll be honest, *I'm* not happy. I used to love workin' with the community, but lately, all I'm doin' is bailin' people outta jail. I'm not makin' a difference. I wanna do *that* again."

"How?"

"I'm not exactly sure yet, but a friend told me about an opportunity to work out at the reservation, and I think I could be really helpful there. It would mean traveling a lot, which would be new for me, but I think it could be good for me. We're gonna have a lot of free time on our hands now. I need a way to fill it."

I was nodding before she'd even stopped talking. She was right. Happiness wasn't something you should give up on. Living life with a "this is fine" attitude was wasting life. Wasting time. We'd be doing my dad a disservice if we lived like that now.

"Okay," I said. "You're right. I'll start lookin' for somethin' else. I kinda think I'd be a good mediator, and I'd like to find an opportunity where I could do some more pro bono work. That was really satisfyin'."

"Good," Mom said. "There are a lot of folks around here that could use your services." She kissed the back of my hand and stood. "Alright, well, we'll figure this out. We just have to communicate and support each other."

"Yeah."

She turned to leave the bedroom, but I called her back. "Maybe I could help you out at the reservation once a month or somethin', once I get situated?"

A smile grew on her face, bigger and bigger till she was all teeth. "I would love that."

"Me too."

She nodded and turned again.

"Oh, hey, Mom?"

"Yeah? What is it?"

"You mind if I bring a date Sunday?"

Her eyebrows shot to the ceiling. "To your father's funeral?"

"You're the one who said it wasn't a funeral, and… yeah. I think I might've found someone who—"

She came at me, full-on mama, hugging me like I was five and had just won my first soccer trophy. "Nothin' would make your dad happier, baby."

# CHAPTER TWENTY-SIX

## THEO

"AGAIN," I said. "More."

"How much more?" Devo whined. "And how come I'm up on this ladder and you ain't? You're way taller than me. And where the hell is Vern?"

A crisp wind blew, wobbling the ladder, stirring up leaves. I watched them swirl down Main Street, and a childhood memory popped into my head. The leaves made a scuffling sound against the road, and I remembered standing outside of a fifties-style diner somewhere in Maine with my parents and Aislinn. I was maybe ten. My dad was holding my hand as we finished our milkshakes before getting back into the car. We'd driven north to see the fall foliage. My mom loved it, but Ace wasn't happy being stuck in a car for so long, so we'd stopped to give her a break. I wondered if she remembered the trip, if she could still remember the brilliant colors of those trees, the way they shaded the road and tinged the light inside our SUV to a warm golden glow.

I remembered how happy we'd been as a family back then, and I was smiling as I realized that, even though we weren't related, the friends I'd made, along with my sister and Finn, were all the family I needed. I'd always miss my parents, but I felt in my bones that they were proud of me.

"I deserve a bonus for this," Devo griped, grabbing the sides of the ladder, trying to steady herself.

"Sorry," I said, holding up my bandaged hand. But if she fell, I'd catch her, even if it ripped out my stitches. "I sent Vern and Millie on an errand. Move it up on the left side again, please. Just a little more, and then it's perfect."

The Ace's House sign had been delivered, and it was beautiful. Perfect timing, too, with one day before the grand opening. It was a chic, round birchwood sign, with "Ace's House" written in an easy-to-read, bold, metallic font. There was a hint of a rainbow in the metal letters, with an ombré effect across them, fading into a deep black. It was pretty cool and way better than my first idea. People were already complimenting it as they walked by while Devo tried to adjust it. The sign guy felt bad about his mistake, so he'd rushed a new sign and had come out to hang it, but it was just a tad askew.

"There," she said with mock attitude. "That okay with you, Mr. Perfectionist?"

"Yeah." I smiled. "It's perfect."

LEADING my sister from the passenger side of my truck to the sidewalk in front of the center, I said, "The new sign was just installed, and I wanted you to be the first to know what it says."

"Doesn't it just say 'community center'?" Ace asked when we stopped in front of the big double doors. We usually only used one, but now they were both polished and open, and I loved how it looked and felt, like we were welcoming the world in.

"No. It's a round sign made out of birch wood. It's five feet in diameter, and it's hanging directly above the front doors. The wood has been stained and coated so there's a little bit of a sheen to it, but the best part is the letters."

"Okay. What does it say?"

"In big, bold, ombré rainbow letters that fade down into black, it says, 'Ace's House.'"

"Ace's—what? You named your community center after me? Why on earth would you do that?"

"Because," I said, holding her hands, "because you are my favorite person in this world. For a long time, you were the only reason I got out of bed every morning. You love me no matter what I do or say or how I act. You always forgive me. You know me better than anyone, better than even Mom and Dad did. You know all of my dark secrets, and still you love and support me. You love unconditionally. There is no better name for a community center than yours."

"Theo. I-I don't even know what to say."

"You don't have to say anything, but I hope you'll visit sometimes to check up on your namesake."

"I will," she said, wiping a tear from under her sunglasses. "All the time. And maybe I could volunteer here somehow. You know, I'm pretty good at running an office."

"Oh, I'm aware. I think I heard somewhere that you're a hard-ass and I should fear your organizational skills."

We laughed, and I hugged my sister the way I'd wanted to months ago when Devo had taken me to the mountains. "I love you, Aislinn, and I will never disappear on you again."

"I love you too. Thank you."

"Come on. I've got *Black Hawk Down* loaded up on my

laptop, or we could watch *Band of Brothers*. There's ten episodes. I bet we could watch them all before midnight."

"Oh my God, Theo. You're kidding, right?"

"Yes…?" She was humoring me. There was no way listening to machine gun fire for ten hours would be fun for her, but she loved me enough to endure it.

"Ugh, fine. One episode, and then we'll make it our weekend ritual till we finish them. But I will be requiring a *big* chai tea latte every time."

Smiling over her shoulder, I hugged her tighter. "It's a good thing then that I live across the street from a coffee shop."

THE FALL FEST fundraiser was a smashing success already. It felt like every resident of Teton County was meandering around downtown Wisper. Sheriff Michaels had approved us blocking off Main Street in front of Ace's House all the way to the library on Franklin Street, and between the two buildings, we had a few carnival rides, food and craft vendors, and all kinds of fun fall activities to get people laughing and spending money. All of it was being donated to the library. I didn't need the funds for Ace's House, but the publicity we were getting was priceless.

"What's shakin', bro?" Finn asked when I passed him and Ace at his arm wrestling booth.

"Hi, guys. How's it going?"

He shouted, "Hey!" across the street and flexed his arm in the direction of three young women standing in front of Coffee Shot, sipping their lattes and batting their eyelashes at him. "Five bucks to watch me decimate this guy!"

Ace tsked. "Are you talking about Theo? Don't you dare! You'll kill him."

"Thanks for that vote of confidence, little sister."

"I'm just stating a fact," she said and shrugged.

But no, I wasn't going anywhere near Finn's biceps. "Sorry, you'll have to decimate someone else. I've got work to do."

"Fine," Finn said, scoffing playfully. "Oh! Hey, Max! Come over here."

A tall blond man wearing a black cowboy hat stepped in front of me, reaching to shake hands with Finn. "S'up, Finnigan?"

"You've got muscles. Wanna arm wrestle? Oh, Max, this is my fianceé, Ace, and her brother, Theo."

"Nice to meet you," I said. We shook. "Please excuse me. I need to get out of here before my future brother-in-law breaks my arm. Have fun."

Max nodded and bent forward, like a bull ready to charge, and then he sat and took his hat off. He plopped it onto the table next to his beer and made a fist. The bulge in his bicep and the twinkle in his eye made me shiver, and I looked over to see Finn gulp. Had he met his match in strength and handsomeness?

The three girls came closer to watch. They paid the five dollars, and Finn puffed up, flexing every muscle he possessed.

"Watch it," I warned him as I backed away, my eyebrows raised in warning. It felt nice to lecture him for once.

He scoffed. "As if I would. I already snagged me the most beautiful woman on the planet." He leaned over to kiss Aislinn, and the girls bristled with disappointment, but they didn't leave. I did before I lost my arm in front of the whole town.

Making my way toward the library, I said hello to Luuk and Oly at the All Animals veterinary booth, where they were doing animal wellness checks for ten dollars each, and then they gave out coupons for half-price spays and neuters at the clinic. There was a line of people with dogs on leashes, cats in carriers, and one goldfish in a bowl, waiting to be seen by the vets.

It was a bit chilly, the early November wind whipping through my jacket, but the sun was out, and it was the perfect day for a fall festival. We had apple bobbing for a dollar and a five-dollar face painting booth that Charlie was manning.

When I stopped to say hi, he introduced me to his grand-daughter, Emmy. She was there for moral support and to bring him new paints when he ran out. Her face had been transformed from a small human to a koala, complete with detailed shading that looked like fur. Charlie really was artis-tically talented. Kids were walking away with faces resem-bling Bengal tigers, bears, and wolves, of course. They almost looked to be art gallery quality.

He tipped his hat to me. "What?" he said. "Yeah, so I'm artsy fartsy. Get over y'self."

The organizers of the farmers market had agreed to host their last market of the season on the same day as our festival, and they had pledged to donate fifty percent of their profits to the library. Some of the booth owners hadn't wanted to because they were already struggling to make ends meet, but the festival was bringing in three times the crowds they were used to, so everybody was winning.

I was looking for Brady as I made my way down Main Street, excited to see him like it was Christmas morning and he was my present, even though I'd seen him at dawn when we met for coffee before all the vendors arrived across the street to set up.

Since we'd decided to break our deal, we were together every chance we got. We knew we needed to take things slowly, so we'd amended our agreement. No sleeping over, no big life changes, and no serious conversations for a year. Next November first was the new deadline, and already, I couldn't wait for it. I wanted him to move in with me, but he was right that we both needed time. I'd just started therapy and my AA steps, and it would take me time to start to wade through everything I'd been holding in.

When I passed Sissy's booth, she waved, giving me a little wink. Her table was almost empty, and that was really saying something since she'd shown up with nearly a truckload of jam, honey, and fresh baked bread.

Finally, I made my way to the library, but I still hadn't seen Brady. Where the hell was he?

"Looking for your man?" Sam said with a smirk.

Was I that obvious? "No," I said. "Just checking on everyone, making sure everybody has what they need. How's it going here?"

"Sure," she said, clearly not buying my white lie. "He's inside." She nodded over her shoulder at the brick building, and my eyes shot to the front door. "But before you dash in there, things are going great. I've had thirty sign-ups for the children's reading hour, and even more people have applied for library cards. Oh, and check out Juneau Moonlight over there."

I looked to her left, at the booth selling romance paperbacks. There was a line of women waiting to buy them and get them signed by the author.

This day couldn't have gone any smoother.

"Hey! Theo."

I heard Billie's voice behind me, and when I turned, I saw

her giving a technology lesson to an older woman. There was a line of people waiting for Billie's expertise.

I walked over to them, and I heard classic, no-filter Billie as she "advised" the woman. "Are you for real? Of course you can't see anything. You haven't turned your phone on yet."

I winced. Okay, so maybe not *everything* was going smoothly.

"Everything okay here?" I asked.

She flashed a grimace. "Good, but I think I might be ready for a break. Where's your sister?"

"She's down in front of Ace's House. Finn set up an impromptu arm wrestling booth."

She snorted. "Of course he did."

"Where's Jay?"

"Oh"—she waved an arm in the direction of the library—"he's out back with his brothers, giving horse rides to people."

"That's right. I forgot they'd signed up to do that. Excuse me. I need to run inside for a minute."

"Sure thing. See ya." She turned back to the woman. "Sorry, but it's my scheduled break time. Give me fifteen minutes, and I'll finish your lesson."

"Okay, but then will you show me how to do the TikTok?"

"TikTok?" Billie complained. "I thought you just wanted to learn how to post on Facebook."

"No. My granddaughters said they like the TikTok ones."

"Okay, but do you just wanna watch the videos or make your own?"

"Which one will my grandkids like better?"

Billie rolled her eyes. "Oh boy." She wasn't known for her patience.

Sam saw the grimace on my face, so she popped over to Billie's booth. "Don't feel bad, Mrs. Dubois. I barely know how to use TikTok."

Mrs. Dubois planted her hands on her hips. "Y'all may be better at these stupid smartphones, but can you sew your own outfit?"

"You can?" Billie asked.

"'Course I can. I could whip out them pants you're wearin' in an hour."

"No shit? Okay, I have a proposal for you. If you teach me how to sew, I'll come to your house once a week and give you lessons. TikTok, Facebook, Insta, whatever you wanna learn. Deal?"

Mrs. Dubois smiled and shook Billie's outstretched hand. "Deal. But you can leave your potty mouth at the door."

Billie laughed, and with the problem averted, I made my escape.

When I was inside the library, the chaotic sounds of the festival died down, and I listened for Brady. I didn't hear anything at first, but then—

"Son of a bitch! Get in there."

I couldn't tell where his voice was coming from, so I called out for him. "Brady?"

"Yeah, I'm in the back room."

When I found him in the library's resource room, he was trying to stuff little blown-up balloons into a huge garbage bag, but they kept popping out.

"This is drivin' me nuts!"

I laughed at the frustrated look on his face as three more balloons popped out and floated down to the floor. "What're they for?"

He rolled his eyes. "Sam wants to have a balloon poppin' competition, but instead of darts, she wants me to tape 'em to this big piece of cardboard so little kids can stomp on 'em." Flicking his middle finger against the offending piece of cardboard set back against the wall, which kept trying to fall on him, he said, "This is damn near impossible, but if I tape the balloons to the board in here, by the time I get the whole thing outside, they'll all fall off. Trust me, I already tried."

"Here," I said. "You hold the bag, and I'll get the balloons in. You need better tape."

"Tell me somethin' I don't know. Thanks." He smiled at me, and my heart thumped inside my chest. His eyebrow pitched as I kneeled in front of him to collect the balloons. "Sorry. I don't mean to be a party pooper, but this is a damn hard job."

"It's not the only thing that's hard," I said, standing and stepping forward to kiss him. I shoved three balloons back into the bag, but I was squashing it between us, and a couple popped.

"Oh no," he groaned.

I laughed. "Shit."

"Ah, fuck it," he said, and he dropped the bag. Balloons scattered everywhere, but he took my face in his hands, and the whole earth could've popped around us. I wouldn't have heard it because his kiss and the soft moan he made when my tongue touched his was the best distraction.

I pressed my body to his and felt him hardening under his jeans as he tilted his head, slipping his tongue in my mouth.

"God, you taste good," he whispered. "Think we could—"

"No," I protested, though I didn't want to. "There are people all over the place. What if someone comes in to use the restroom? And all of the Cades are out back, giving horse rides to kids, although it probably looks more like Thunder

Down Under, Wyoming style, than it does a kiddie pony ride."

"Oh yeah? Wanna peek out the window?" he whispered, and he kissed me deeper.

He reached inside my jeans, squeezing me with his warm hand, and I moaned this time. "Damn, you make it hard to say no."

His lips curled up against mine. "That's always my intention. You know," he said, "we haven't formally discussed it, but I forgot to tell you, you're officially fired."

I pulled back. "*I'm* fired? No. *You're* fired."

He laughed. "We're both fired. I got a new job. But is that okay? I mean, we'll have to find someone else to manage the Cade Ranch trust."

"Yeah, it's fine. I'll be sad to lose your brilliance, but I've already reached out to someone I think will be a good fit."

"Who?"

"Your arch nemesis, Collin Ames."

"Hm." He wrapped his arms around my low back. "Good choice."

"You think?"

He smiled, and I wanted to bite the smirk off of his lips. "Yeah. He's a good guy. Jack and the guys will like him. He grew up on a ranch a lot like Cade Ranch down near Pinedale."

"Good," I said. I was nervous to ask, but I wanted to check in with him. "Are you okay? I saw your mom a while ago. She looks like she's having fun helping at Fran Michaels's bakery booth. I can tell she's sad, but she's trying."

"Yeah," he said. "She's doin' okay. We both are. I mean, it's hard. I think about my dad a million times a day. Sometimes I try *not* to think about him 'cause then I don't have to feel it, you know?"

"I do know. But don't let grief steal your memories. I know that's hard sometimes, but if you push the memories away, somewhere down the line, they won't mean as much. They won't be as bright."

"Thanks." He kissed me quickly. "My dad would've loved today. He would've set up a booth to sell his pieces. He was all about these crafty festival things. I used to travel the state with him during summer breaks, and we'd hit as many as we could. He even let me drive the U-Haul before I got my license."

"That's a great memory."

He chuckled. "It probably wasn't for him. I crashed the damn thing into my mom's car when we got home."

I laughed. "Oh no!"

"Yep. My mom tried to make me pay it off with my allowance, but Dad took the blame."

"Hm." I squeezed my arms around him too. "Sounds like somebody else I know. Someone who puts everyone else's problems before his own."

"You're talkin' about you, right?" He blushed and whispered, "I could fall in love with you, you know?"

My heart stopped. "You could?" I was not expecting to hear that at all.

"Yeah. I could. I mean, I think I am." The smile in his eyes turned gentle and sexy, and it made me want to take him down to the floor. "I know, I know," he said. "No big proclamations. It ain't big though. Or at least, it started out small."

"Me too," I said. "It's kind of overwhelming, and I'm scared, but it feels so fucking good."

He pulled me closer until we were chest to chest. I

couldn't have wiped the smile off my face if I'd tried. "Well, we'll take it one day at a time, right?"

"Right."

"Okay," he said. "Help me get these damn balloons outside before I pop 'em all just to spite Sam."

I smiled and nodded, letting him go and bending to start collecting the balloons again, but he grabbed the back of my jacket and hauled me up. "Just one more kiss."

# EPILOGUE

BRADY – ONE YEAR LATER

MY HAIR WAS HALF-WAY down to my ass now, and sometimes, I'd catch Theo gazing at it. I could imagine what he was thinking about doing with it. I sent him smiling purple devil emojis anytime I noticed him watching me, and it became our thing. Sometimes, it was the only thing we texted to each other. That, or heart-eyes emojis so we'd know when we were on each other's minds.

I'd spent the last year working and working out. Manny Perez had taken me under his wing, and I boxed with him twice a week in his home gym, which was really just his garage, but he had punching and reflex bags, and he made me do so many squats and pushups that I was doing them in my sleep. I supposed that was the way I was dealing with what had happened, with my dad's death and all the anger it caused in me.

"Jeez, Manny," I shouted when his big fist came at me like a shot in the dark. "You coulda broke my nose!"

"Serves you right," the big brute said. "You shoulda ducked quicker. You ain't payin' attention. Where's your mind at?"

Boxing had helped with other things too. Theo and I deciding to only date casually had been good for us in the beginning, but it hadn't lasted very long. There was just too much between us. If I couldn't kiss him at least once a day—and that was the absolute minimum—I was grouchy and unfocused.

But we'd stuck to the "not taking it too far too fast" part. He'd brought up wanting me to move in with him, but I told him not yet. We needed to wait out the year, and reluctantly, he agreed.

I tried not to smile when I thought of Theo, naked in his bed, waiting for me. I hoped that was how he'd be when I showed up there tonight. "Never mind," I said. "I gotta go anyway. I got plans tonight."

"Oh yeah? Goin' trick-or-treatin'?" He punched my arm as I toweled off.

"Ha ha. Nope. I'm movin'."

"Where to?"

"Ace's House."

"You're movin' into the—ohh," he said. "I see. You're shackin' up with your beau, ain't ya?"

"Yep." I smiled so big, my cheeks hurt, and Manny laughed at me. "Get goin' then. See you in a couple days. Seriously, though, no candy tonight. You'll ruin all our hard work."

I rolled my eyes and waved on the way to my car parked at the end of his driveway.

As I drove home, I thought about my family and how much change we'd gone through in the last year. My mom was loving her new job and thriving out at the reservation, and I'd picked up a part-time gig as a mediator for clients like Gene and Cody. It was actually kind of fun, trying to find common ground for people who hadn't been able to agree before. I was good at it.

And when I wasn't working at the courthouse in Jackson, I was working pro bono at Ace's House, helping folks with all kinds of legal issues. Domestic violence protection orders, child custody cases, tenant and renters cases, and yes, occasionally a drunk driving case. I didn't require it, but I tried to encourage those clients to at least try one of the NA or AA meetings offered at the center.

Theo was running them now, and I was so damn proud of him.

Our offices were next door to each other, and I loved that we could eat lunch together or run across the street for coffee, or when we'd pass each other in the hallway, he always found an excuse to touch me in some small way—a brush of his fingers across the back of my hand, a quick hug when no one was watching, or even a kiss if we could sneak away for a minute. It was the best part of my day when we could lock ourselves in one of our offices to make out for five minutes before lunch.

Finally, we'd made it to the one year mark, and I was planning to be at his front door at midnight with my suitcases. I couldn't wait to grab him and pull his mouth to mine in *our* apartment.

I was dreaming of this—the way he'd feel, his tongue in my mouth, the taste of him—when I carried my workout gear into my mom's house, but as soon as I shut the front door, there was a knock on it.

When I opened it, Sam was a little worse for the wear, standing on the front porch, looking exasperated. Living at my mom's place this last year hadn't been the best situation, but at least she and I had been able to check in on each other from time to time. Bonnie was back in Texas with Foss and Gerry, but we got daily pictures in the family group text. The kid was pretty cute, and he was definitely a handful. My dad would've been proud.

"What's up?" I asked Sam when she pushed through the front door. When I reminded her of our adventures, she had remembered me from when we were kids, and now I thought my life would feel empty if she wasn't in it. We talked every day, and when I wasn't working, I'd call her, and we'd go to José's Diner for pie or cake or whatever dessert José had whipped up that day. I had to make him promise he wouldn't tell Manny on me. The guy took my training very seriously.

"Didn't you hear me calling you? I pulled up right behind you."

"Sorry," I said. My head really was in the gutter.

"Oh my God, Brady. I don't know what to do."

"About what?" I tried not to laugh at her Halloween costume. She was dressed like Sherlock Holmes with a hunting cap, an empty smoking pipe, and a magnifying glass around her neck, dangling from a chain, but her hair was pink now, and she was still wearing a long, floral skirt and combat boots.

"Don't you dare laugh at me. I dressed up for the kids at the library Halloween party. And I mean Frank Sims." She popped a hand on a hip. "The guy comes to the library every Tuesday."

"So? Is he harassin' you or somethin'?"

"No, not technically, but still. Every. Tuesday."

"What's he say?"

"He doesn't say anything." She flopped down onto the couch. "Barely a word." She scoffed. "He just picks out a book on his lunch hour, and then he reads. He must be starving by now. He doesn't even eat."

"Isn't there a 'no food in the library' sign by the front door?"

"Yeah, but you and I eat there all the time. I know he's seen me eating. In fact, he *watches* me eat. Besides, I'd make an exception for him. I mean, he's a deputy, and he seems like the kinda guy who'd clean up after himself."

I'd seen Frank chowing down on his lunch in his cruiser when I walked to pick up food for the center crew sometimes, so I knew for sure he wasn't starving. I had a feeling something else was sustaining him these days. *Someone* else, even if glances were all he could get. I was surprised, though, that he hadn't actually spoken to Sam yet.

I sat on my dad's old recliner, and Sam sat halfway up, glaring at me, then she flopped back down, and her hat fell off and tumbled to the floor. "Are you listening to me?"

"I'm listenin'."

I was trying to listen, but I was having a hard time concentrating on anything she was saying 'cause my eyes kept landing on the wall clock, counting down the minutes to midnight.

"Have you tried talkin' to Frank?"

"Of course I have! I've tried talking to him about the books he reads—all history, by the way. Oh, and a few books about home renovations. I've tried talking to him about his job, about town gossip. He made some big arrest last month at a meth lab out in the country. I thought that would be something we could talk about. I mean, not details or anything, but it was a big deal. They wrote about what he did in the Jackson paper, and I told him I'd read it. But no. He didn't say a word. He looks like he wants to—"

"He wants to what?"

"I don't know. Like he wants to kiss me or maybe… spank me? Which, okay, fine, that's hot. But he's twice my age!"

Chuckling, I said, "I don't think he's that old. Maybe forty. You're twenty-nine. That's only an eleven-year difference."

She blushed.

Again, I looked at the clock. Six more hours.

Sam followed my line of sight. "What are you looking— ohh," she said. "Tonight's the night, right?"

"Yeah. I don't think I can wait."

"Brady. Go already. What's a few more hours?"

"No," I said. "I have to wait. I need him to know I respect him, that I respect what we said about takin' this slow. I made it this long. Six more hours won't kill me. At least, I don't think they will."

"All right, well, I'm bitched out. Go get ready. Are you gonna dress up?"

"No," I said, and I smiled. "I'm hopin' to take my clothes *off.*"

Sam laughed. "Well, I, for one, can't wait till tomorrow so we can talk about *my* problems again."

"Sorry, but I don't plan on leavin' my new apartment for weeks."

She sighed dramatically and rolled off the couch. "Fine, but in, like, a month, after you're all sexed out, can we talk about me?"

"Sure thing," I said with a smirk. "And go easy on Frank. I think he's got a crush on you. The poor guy."

"Whatever. I'm out." Snatching her hat from the floor, she plopped it back on her head. "I've gotta hand out candy at the library, but the little stinkers are gonna be pissed when they find out they're only getting a sucker and a book. I ordered a bunch of pocket copies of *The Witches* by Roald Dahl."

"Are you sure that's the right book to—"

"Of course it is. It's a great book." She smiled a little mischievously. "Don't do anything I wouldn't do tonight!" She slammed the door shut when she left, and I ran to take a shower. Now I was worried about what I was going to wear. Even if I was planning to make Theo rip my clothes off, I wanted to look good before he did.

———

## THEO – SIX HOURS AND ONE MINUTE LATER

AT 12:01 A.M., there was a knock on the door downstairs—a loud knock—and I was praying it was Brady. After work this afternoon, he said suggestively, "See you tomorrow," with a wink and a little eyebrow wiggle, but I assumed he meant actual tomorrow, not the middle of the night, though I wasn't planning on complaining if it was him. But over the last year, there'd been many knocks on the door at all hours of the night, so I couldn't be sure it was him.

People showed up at Ace's House for all kinds of reasons. A mom and her two kids came knocking late one night when they'd left their home because her husband was abusive. We had to get the sheriff involved. We had homeless people come looking for a meal or a warm place to sleep in the winter, and we'd had a couple of runaway teenagers come to us after they'd left home but hadn't figured out how they would feed and shelter themselves. Unfortunately, there had been a couple more whose parents had kicked them out without even their toothbrushes.

My dream of being able to help young LGBTQ people was realized many times over, and more and more still as word got out that the center was a sanctuary for *anyone* who needed help. I'd even organized a family group for their parents and siblings when they just weren't able to understand each other. I found a family therapist willing to donate her time, obviously, since I wasn't qualified, but I'd been thinking about going back to school to get my master's in psychology.

Some people were still closed minded in Wisper, but more and more families were signing up for the group, and nothing made me prouder than helping people find common ground. It was something Brady and I had in common.

Sissy Melton stopped in to attend those groups sometimes. She claimed she was moral support, and it was easy to see the pride in her eyes. Everyone adored her fierce and feisty disposition, and they loved the honey and jam she delivered once a month for us to stock in our food bank. We usually ran out within two days.

Who would've thought that I would go back to school to learn how to help underprivileged people? My dad was probably stomping up a fit wherever he was, although once he'd had time to get over the fact that I'd sold his multi-billion-dollar company and had stopped investing in everything under the sun to make *more* money, he'd be proud of me for following my heart. I knew my mom was.

Ace was. She flipped out when I told her I was thinking

about enrolling in online classes at the University of Wyoming.

And I knew Brady would be proud of me, too, just as soon as I told him, hopefully as soon as I opened the door and found him on my stoop.

I pictured him and what it would feel like to wake up to his beautiful face every morning while I pulled a shirt over my head. Good Lord, that man's hair. Dark and shiny and long enough for me to wrap around my fist while he was… If I thought about anything else lately, I couldn't have said what it was.

My hair was longer, too, and when I passed the mirror hanging inside my open closet door, I laughed at how the tight curls stuck out. I'd never let my hair grow. My father didn't like it. He thought, for business, I needed to look as white as I could. Finally, I didn't care at all what anyone else thought, and I pushed my fingers through, making my hair even messier, and went downstairs to answer the door.

My sweatpants were wrinkled and bunching up around one calf, and my shirt was half pulled up my stomach, so I straightened it and then reached for the doorknob. I was yawning when I turned it, so my mouth was already open, and now I couldn't close it. There he was, at 12:02 in the morning with two suitcases at his feet.

Brady Douglas, my now live-in boyfriend.

A thunderstorm was beginning to dump rain all over Wisper, lightning streaking across the sky, and he was standing there like a dream, his hair loose and wet down his back, his white shirt see-through and already unbuttoned. My eyes zeroed in on his hard, smooth chest, and his hands were on his jeans' zipper. When I looked at it, he pushed it down.

"It's been one year. Here I am. If you don't want me to

move in anymore, say so right now. Otherwise, I'm gonna be inside you in about five seconds. You ready?"

I couldn't seem to speak. "I-I…"

"Shake your head if you don't want me."

I blinked but didn't move my head even one centimeter.

He licked his bottom lip, scraping his teeth over it, and he stepped over the threshold. I backed up. It was the only movement I was able to make, and he slammed the door shut. His shirt came all the way off and landed behind him, making a wet slapping noise against the hard wood.

My mouth went dry. Brady's body had changed. *Jesus*. It still made an impact on me every time I saw him. The way his thighs and ass filled out his jeans these days was downright erotic. I thought he was fit before, but now that he'd taken up boxing, his biceps were huge, and the veins stood out, running down the length of his arms to the insides of his wrists. There were veins *everywhere*. One might've thought his body would make me self-conscious since I was skinny and much smaller than him now, but it didn't. I just wanted him, and he wanted me, and we would take each other any way we could.

It wasn't like I never worked out myself. I'd started running in the mornings with Brady's friend, Luuk. The man could pound the pavement, and there wasn't a minute I wasn't struggling to keep up with him, but the workouts always made me feel good. Like, if nothing else, at least I had accomplished my run for the day. It was something to be proud of on the days when the old, dark thoughts would make a comeback.

Somehow, Brady always knew when I was down, and he made lists for me about all the things he was proud of me for.

Thinking about the list he'd made me last week, I

watched his abdomen harden and relax as he kicked off his square-toed boots. He lifted each leg to remove his socks, and then his pants, and then he was standing in front of me, naked except for a pair of black boxer briefs, which made his naturally tanned skin look even sexier.

Finally, I found the nerve to move, and I reached for his hair. He pressed his hand over mine, gathering the wet strands between them, and he lifted our hands to his cheek.

I closed my eyes, breathing deeply, feeling him. I could smell his light, woodsy aftershave, and the scent did something to me. It made me hungrier than I'd ever been before, like I'd been starving for a year. I hadn't been. We had sex every damn time we could, but we'd never stayed the night together, had never woken up in each other's arms. That would change tomorrow morning.

I was nervous. This was different for me. *I* was different. CEO Theo was a distant memory. Tortured Theo was, too, thankfully. Now, the guy inside me was Theo the man. A man who wanted and lived, who laughed and got angry. He forgave and he was hopeful. And I was a man in every *other* way.

A man in love.

"You okay?" he whispered, and I opened my eyes.

His were open, watching me expectantly, waiting for me. He seemed nervous too; a hesitant twitch of one eyebrow gave him away. Did he not know how much I wanted him? How many nights I'd dreamt of waking up next to him?

"I'm ready. I've been waiting for you." Moving my hand deeper through his hair, I pulled him closer. "You're so fucking beautiful, and I'm still scared I'll mess this up, that I'm not good enough for you. But the part of me who knows that I *am* good enough is here. He's right here, Brady, and he wants you badly. It might take a long time for me to be that guy every day. Living together might be harder than we think. I'm not perfect. I never was."

"I don't want you to be perfect. I like this man, this uncertain guy who maybe doesn't know where to go or what to do. I like him—no, I *love* him—'cause he might be lost, but he's clawin' his way back, and nothin's gonna stop him from bein' the guy he wants to be." He dipped his chin, looking at me through heavy lidded eyes. "And that guy is sexy as hell."

"Really? Sexier than a CEO down on his knees?"

"So much fuckin' sexier." He reached for my hips, wrapping his hands around them and pushing me backward, toward his office. There was an old couch in there, and when the backs of my knees felt the rough tweed fabric, he pushed harder, and I landed on my ass with him between my knees.

"How sexy is a small-town lawyer down on *his* knees for *you*?"

"Oh God, you have no idea," I said, moaning when his fingers gripped my pajamas and, with a rough tug, he pulled them under my ass and down to the middle of my thighs.

"Wait," he said. "My mom says we have to go over for dinner at least once a week. If we don't, we're gonna be in big trouble."

I laughed. That was fine with me. His mom was badass, and I loved talking to her. She'd been accepting of me from the get-go.

"Sorry," he said. "I dunno why I'm bringin' my mom up right now." He shook his head, and his hair fell over is shoulders. "Shouldn't we go upstairs?" he asked, dragging his lips back and forth softly over mine. They felt like velvet.

"I won't make it upstairs. Fuck me here, and then we'll go up."

He looked down between my legs. "Have I ever told you how much it turns me on that you don't wear underwear?" Licking his lips, his tongue left a shiny wet trace there, and I couldn't look away from it.

"You might've mentioned it. Usually, I sleep naked, but I was cold, all alone, thinking about y—"

He pushed my thighs apart while he lowered his head, and then—

"Oh, fuck, Brady."

His mouth was warm, his tongue lapping a slow, soft path from the base of my shaft to the tip, and then he gorged on me. Lightning crackled outside, but it was close, and I thought I could feel the static in the air while he took my cock to the back of his throat and swallowed, and my eyes rolled shut while my hips fought with his strong hands. He didn't want me to move, but staying still was impossible with his mouth on me, his hands finding their way to every sensitive area of my body. He pinched my nipple between his fingers, but then he was pushing my shirt above my chest and pulling my pants lower, trying to slide them further down my legs.

And then he gave up, all of his concentration now focused on sucking me off, his body moving in rhythm with his mouth, like a dance, a very erotic one where he was on his knees and my hands were tangled in his long hair, gripping fistfuls while I clenched my ass to pump my body into his face.

I watched his shoulders flex and move with every push of his hands on the couch beside my thighs, that sexy hair a nearly black, straight waterfall, the ends whispering across my legs as he sucked.

He was beautiful and so eager, and the knowledge that he hadn't stopped wanting me all this time and that he believed in me was driving me crazy. I was moaning and begging him, saying his name over and over and over because he was making me feel so good. I'd never felt this good. I'd never been with anyone who knew and wanted the real me. Rich or not, powerful or not, disaster or not.

Brady wanted *me*, and that was the biggest turn-on.

"More," I begged him. "Give me more."

He moaned, and when he gripped my hips again, he sucked with everything he had, digging his fingernails into my ass.

Focusing on the head of my cock, he teased me while he used his shoulders to open my legs as far as possible, and before he could go any further, I was breathing hard, slowing my body, trying to hold back, not wanting this to be over.

He hadn't been kidding when he said he was good at sucking dick. The man had skills. He'd made me come from the slightest of touches from his tongue, and oppositely, from gorging on my cock, cum and saliva flowing everywhere, attacking it like he was a wild animal and my dick was his meal.

I panted through it now, but he gripped the base of my dick, pumping fast and hard. He knew I was close, and he wasn't giving me the option to slow down. I wanted to make this last, but he swallowed again, and my whole body arched off the couch and into him.

He sucked until I softened, and goosebumps rose while I drowned in the intensity of this thing between us. My pants were still pulled down, almost to my knees now, and when he grabbed my waist with both hands, flipping me and sliding me down on my knees, my legs were tangled with his, but he kneed them apart.

I heard the slide of a desk drawer, paper ripped, and a plastic lid snapped open, and Brady moaned when he palmed lube onto himself. His voice was shaking. "I *need* you. I want you so much, I can barely wait."

"Yes," was all I said. It encompassed everything I was feeling. Yes, I wanted him, and yes, I was ready to spend my life with him.

And yes, I wanted him inside me.

I wanted him hard inside me, pounding into me because it would burn, and the burn would convince me that this was real. I wasn't dreaming anymore.

The urge to ask him to pinch me was there. How could it be real that I had everything I'd ever wanted, that my dreams were coming true? How could it be real that I could have him? That I deserved him? That we could be together every day, building a life and relying on each other?

It was reality because we'd made it so. We'd both worked hard this last year for what we wanted, and we deserved this.

We deserved love.

"This won't last long," he said, breathless, his hands shaking as he spread me open, pushing into me as slowly as he could. My back muscles tensed when I gripped the couch cushions. He moaned and licked those muscles, and with his mouth still on me, he punched inside with one swift thrust of his hips, whispering in the lowest, most seductive voice, "But I promise you days of this. Just me and you. Lovin' each other. Pleasin' each other. Do you want that?"

Breath rushed out of my mouth when he began to move, and I lost my hold on the couch and fell forward. It was the furthest thing from sexy, but it seemed to urge him on.

He was fucking me now as rain fell in sheets outside his office window. He was thrusting fast and hard, and all I could hear was his rapid breath. It cooled the wet skin where he'd licked, and then his hand was in my hair, pulling it a little. "I love your hair like this. It gives me somethin' to hold onto. I like holdin' onto you." He fucked faster, sharp exhales exploding out of him, rainwater dripping from his hair and sweat fusing us together. "Can I hold onto you?"

"Yes."

Lightning cracked again, the wind pummeling the building and shaking the windows, but a perfect, beautiful wail was the only thing I heard when he came, and I hoped I'd never forget the sound of it.

---

IF YOU LIKED *Storms Inside Us* (or loved it, I hope), please leave a review—even just a few words would help—on your favorite bookseller, Goodreads, or Bookbub. Self-published indie authors rely heavily upon reviews to get our stories out to the masses. And thank you. I know it takes time to do this. I appreciate the time out of your day and the effort.

---

DEAR READER,

Here we are again at the end of another Wisper love story.

I've thanked you before, but I'm so grateful that you're willing to follow me down this road, so I wanted to say it again. I'm quite aware that there are plenty of people out there who don't appreciate LGBTQ love stories. I even received feedback from a reader, ranting that she was angry with me because she'd fallen in love with the Cade brothers, but then I went and "made [her] favorite character gay." (Kevin)

You know, receiving a good review can make your world shine bright. On the other hand, getting a bad review isn't fun, and sometimes, if you let it, it can knock you down on your butt, steal your confidence, and ruin your day, but *that* review? Man, did it fuel my fire! Whoever they are, that reader fell in love with Kevin *because* he's gay. They loved him—the way he acted, the things he said, and the manner he held himself in—but NEWS FLASH: All of those things were a result of him hiding his true self. So why would reading about him finding open, honest love be a bad thing?

People always say that being an author takes a thick skin, and girl, they ain't kiddin'. This one had the opposite effect, but if one of these reviews ever get me down, all I have to do is think about all the emails readers have sent me, telling me that Kevin's book changed them or that they'd never read an MM romance before but they just had to because they love the Cades so much. The emails and encouragement you send me help me to know that telling these stories is the right thing to do, and that, sure, there are some who will quit the Cade Ranch series after book 2, but there are plenty of readers (YOU!) who are willing to give love a chance, no matter who that love leads to. Brady and Theo's story is no different. They're both as much a part of Wisper as Kevin is a part of the Cade family. Without these men, the books wouldn't be the same, and they wouldn't be as rich and full and fun. And most of my books probably wouldn't exist, because Brady, Theo, Luuk, and Kevin Cade are some of my favorite characters, and they've pushed me to go further than I ever thought I could. I've learned so much and connected with so many people, including myself, in my pursuit of trying to get their stories right.

So thanks again for reading them.

Here's to more stories that make our hearts (and other body parts) tingle, and to more complex characters that make us yearn for Wisper, Wyoming to be a real place. Deputy Frank Sims is up next, and don't be surprised if Deputy Abey

Lee's book is headed your way soon too. Hint: She's not straight. And she's a woman. So I guess we'll be ticking off more people.

Can't win 'em all. ;)


LOVE YOU,
greta

FRANK

When I picked Samantha up at the library, she was wearing a different dress.

"You changed," I said.

She looked down and fidgeted with the hem of the sexy black dress that fell to an inch above her knees. "I did. You don't like it?" She looked up, her eyes uncertain.

"I didn't say that."

Twisting her lips to one side, she said, "You didn't really say anything."

*Shit*. I was already blowing this.

"You look beautiful no matter what you wear."

That made her smile, and she stood a little taller then. So, Samantha Russo liked to be praised. I made a mental note of that.

"You ready?" I asked. "It's kinda cold. I'll drive."

"No," she said. "Let's walk. It's not that cold."

"It's February."

"So, the sunset is nice, and I've been sitting all day."

"Okay then." It was below freezing, and driving would be much more comfortable, but I wasn't about to argue with her on our first date.

She clomped down the library's front steps in her black combat boots, and I tried not to let my smile show. I'd been a keen observer of all things Samantha Russo for over a year, and the one thing I knew about her was that she was a kind and gentle soul, so the boots she wore, the colorfully dyed hair, and the flashes of silver from all the rings on her fingers and the one in her nose was all just a part of an armor she tried to project around herself. She wasn't tough. She wouldn't even hurt a spider. I'd seen her rescue them and carefully remove them from the library in a cup. She placed them in the grass outside and then watched as they crept away.

No, Samantha was nothing if not sweet.

I fell in step beside her, and we walked slowly and silently down Franklin to the corner. When we got there, before we crossed, she pushed her arm through mine.

She looked up at me, and I nearly tripped and fell on my face. Her eyes this close up were the prettiest hazel-brown color. I'd always thought they were just plain ol' brown, but there were flecks of amber and green in them, and they twinkled at me.

"Where are we going?"

"Paulo's."

"What's that?"

"New restaurant downtown."

"Okay. That sounds nice."

She pulled her arm out from under mine, and the slide against my side was warm, but she was shivering a little. It was barely noticeable, but I took my jacket off and draped it over her shoulders, then reached for her hand and placed it under my arm again.

"It's weird that you're so forward," she said.

"Weird?" I wasn't forward. I just didn't want her to stop touching me.

"Yeah, because you don't really talk. I thought you were shy, but—"

"I ain't shy."

"I'm getting that."

She squeezed my forearm and faced forward as we walked past Henly's Gift Shop on the north end of Main Street. Henly was a long-time Wisper resident, but we'd had a few new businesses move into town since Theo Burroughs had opened up the community center, like Paulo's. The Italian restaurant really was too fancy for our small town, but I'd heard the food was good.

"So," she said, "did you grow up here?"

"No."

"Oh, I guess I assumed 'cause of your accent."

"I grew up in Texas."

"Where in Texas?"

"Little town called Rusk. East Texas."

"I've never been there."

"Not many people have."

We crossed Washington Street and Samantha's grip on my arm got a little tighter. Not that there was any traffic for me to protect her from, but I liked that she knew I would.

She stopped in the middle of the road, pulling ever so gently. "Frank?"

I turned and we were face to face. Seeing her in my

leather jacket was some kind of turn-on. The jacket dwarfed her, but she'd settled into it like it was her own. I didn't think she'd noticed me watching out of the corner of my eye when she'd sniffed the collar and sighed.

"If you've changed your mind, it's okay. We don't have to go to dinner."

Pulling the sides of the jacket together to keep the warmth in when she shivered again, I looked in her eyes and said, "I haven't changed my mind."

"Okay, it's just… You're barely talking to me. You give one-word answers, but even that feels like pulling teeth."

Barely talking? I'd just said more to her than I had to anyone in the last year. Dammit. I needed to salvage this or she'd change *her* mind.

Checking behind me for traffic that wasn't there, I turned back to her and lifted my hands to her face. I held it, feeling her warm cheeks heat my skin. "I haven't changed my mind, Samantha. I'm not a social guy, but I promise you, there's nowhere on earth I'd rather be."

MOUNTAINS DIVIDE US
AVAILABLE SPRING 2023

# WANT MORE?

## Become a Wisperite!

Join my newsletter for exclusive stories, Wisper news, and The Cade Ranch Sexcapades—naughty little interludes for my subscribers ONLY!
Jack and Evvie's wedding scenes are there!
Sign up for your first FREE short story,
*Wild Heart: Welcome to Wisper*
on my website!
gretarosewest.com

I would love to hear from you, email me at
greta@gretarosewest.com.
I'll reply.
You can find me on the usual social sites, but I mostly hang out on Instagram, Facebook, and Goodreads.

## Join my Team!

Receive an advanced review copy of my next book. Join my ARC Team, a wonderful group of people who help get the word out when I release a new book!
Sign up on my website
gretarosewest.com

# ABOUT THE AUTHOR

Greta Rose West was a floundering artsy flake until cowboy Jack Cade showed up, knocking on the door of her brain, pounding on it, and then he just plain kicked it down. She's a boy mom to a grown freakin' man, and she lives in NW Indiana with her husband and her two precocious kitties, Geoff Trouble and Sally Mae Midnight. When she's not writing, she's reading and devouring music. She enjoys indie films no one else likes, and her favorite food is Aver's Veggie Revival pizza.

You can find her on Instagram @gretarosewest, in her Facebook group, Wisperites Unite!, or on her website.

gretarosewest.com